LOOK
AWAY

THE BOOK FOR THE MORBIDLY CURIOUS

BY JULIAN FONT

TRIGGER WARNING
This novel contains depictions of or mentions the following:
Suicidal ideation
Self-inflicted harm
Drug use
P.T.S.D.
Schizophrenia depiction
Infidelity
Cancer diagnosis & treatment
Mentions of sexual violence & assault
Violence

If you find any of the above potentially triggering, please exercise caution and consider whether this book is suitable for you to read at this time.

Forever dedicated to the ones who sometimes question
whether or not life is worth living.
You were born to live.

WARNING!

This novel is *not* for the faint of heart.
I, Julian Font, want to make it painfully clear that while this fictional world glorifies self-inflicted harm, that is by no means the intent behind this novel.

The sole intent behind this novel is to prove to you that, despite the darkness in this world and the hardships you've been through, you were, nevertheless, born to *live*.

This book is nothing like the others I have written. There will be characters you love and characters you despise. They will make decisions you support and decisions you won't. Ultimately, they will shed light on a darkness that looms over their existence.

With this in mind, read on…

CHAPTER ONE

JOSEPH

"PUT THE MONEY IN THE FUCKING BAG!"

The robber points his gun at the cashier's wrinkled face and slaps an empty backpack on the countertop. The cashier, a defenseless old man, doesn't know how to respond. The poor guy is in shock. Makes sense. *It's a robbery after all.*

"ARE YOU DEAF?!" the robber shouts at the cashier. "PUT THE MONEY IN THE BAG!"

Call me unlucky because I'm the only other person in the gas station store, hands raised. In one of my hands, I hold a Kit Kat bar. It's not my weapon of choice, so I choose not to use it. The cashier trembles, slowly making his way to the register.

I can't help but notice the gun shaking in the robber's hand. He's easily twice my size with tree trunks for arms, but he's trembling like he hasn't done this before. "First time?" I ask coolly, my hands still raised.

The robber looks down at me. "The fuck are you talkin' for?!" his voice cracks, a vein throbbing along the side of his neck under his black ski mask.

His eyes are a light brown with hints of panic swirling about in his iris. I don't know much about this guy, but it's obvious he doesn't rob gas stations very often. I shrug, saying, "It's smack in the middle of a Tuesday, and you didn't even check the gas station for witnesses before pulling the gun out."

The robber cocks his head back, finally scanning the gas station. "Fuck off, old man," he mutters before turning back to the cashier. *Old? I'm not that old. Is 37 old?*

I check my watch. I'm due in court in less than an hour. The judge won't be too happy if I'm late again. However, the judge *would* be happy to hear I was shot dead in a gas station before my hearing. The judge doesn't like me all that much. You get the gist.

"HURRY... THE FUCK... UP!" the robber shouts at the stunned cashier.

"He's not gonna respond well to your shouts, bud," I explain. "He knows you want the money. You should ease the tone a bit. It'll help your case."

The robber's eyes narrow at me. "Why the hell should I listen to a 'Joe-Schmoe-schmuck' like you?!"

"It's Joseph," I correct him. "My name isn't Joe. It's Joseph."

He grips the gun tighter, wanting to pull the trigger. "Are you serious?! I'm holding a fucking gun right now, and you're correcting me?!"

I click my tongue to the roof of my mouth. "I just thought it was ironic. You called me '*Joe Schmoe*,' and my name is Joseph. They're pretty close, you know? It's ironic."

You can suddenly cut the tension in the room with a knife. This robber wants to shoot me, and frankly, I don't care if he does. I consider putting a bullet in my own head at least once a day as it is. But that's not why I'm so relaxed right now. I represent guys like him in court every damn day... when business isn't as slow as it's been lately. Despite his wanting to put a bullet in my skull, he turns back to the cashier, who is finally filling the backpack with cash.

"I'm a lawyer," I blurt out.

He waves me off. "Good for you, pal."

"I'm a *criminal* lawyer," I add. "I can give you my card. You'll probably need it someday soon if you keep robbing places the way you are right now."

The robber releases a shallow breath–kind of like a laugh. When the cashier puts the remaining cash in the backpack, the robber turns back to me one last time. "Give me the card," he reluctantly mutters.

I grin. In one swift motion, I reach behind his head and reveal a half-crinkled business card with my name on it: JOSEPH VERITA. His eyes widen as a response to my subtle magic trick. "Hopefully, I won't see you soon," I tease with a wink.

The robber curses at me under his breath, then sprints out the door. I look up at the old cashier standing near the register. His sweat seeps through his polo, his watery eyes fixated on the countertop between us. I casually fondle the Kit Kat bar, set it on the counter, and check my pockets for loose cash.

"You can have it, Joseph," the cashier says. "I think you just saved my life."

I force a smile. *This guy thinks I'm some kind of hero.* I wonder if he would think the same if he knew about the skeletons I hide in my closet. "Cheers…" My eyes drop to his name tag. "Cheers… Anthony."

I make my way out the door to catch the bus I'm sure I already missed.

◆ ◆ ◆

I shove the courthouse lobby doors open and make a beeline toward security. Nothing is heard but my beat-up dress shoes clicking against the stained tile floor. I was already running late before the robbery, so I can only imagine how late I am now.

"Late again, Joseph?" the security guard scoffs.

"Better than never," I mutter as I start stripping.

I fill the tray with my phone, keys, wallet, briefcase, and my gold coin–*the usual*. Once I'm through the body scanner, I gather my belongings and sprint through the grand hall. People turn at my echoing footsteps but instantly look away when they recognize me or when they don't.

I realize I'm only six minutes late when I approach the courtroom for my hearing. *Not bad, Joseph.* Just as I approach the towering wooden doors, I stop at the sight of my client sitting on a nearby bench. His tie hangs loosely from his neck as he sits slouching forward.

"What're you doing out here?" I ask. "Let's go! We have a case to win."

The old wooden bench creaks under his cheap suit. "You're late." He gives me a half-glance as if I'm not worthy of his full attention.

I check my watch, still catching my breath. "I'm not that late. It's only six minutes past four."

"The hearing was at three-thirty." My client stands. "It's thirty-six minutes past three-thirty. Lucky for me, the judge rescheduled my hearing because she knows I have a shitty lawyer."

"Shit, I'm sorry," I sigh, lowering my head. "When was the hearing rescheduled to?"

He laughs. "Like *you* need to know. Your sorry-ass is fired."

I try to find comfort by twiddling my gold coin in my pocket. Gas station robbery or not, I would've missed this hearing. *Full disclosure, I have a tendency to fuck things up.* With the very little dignity I have left, I gather the decency to apologize. Before the words leave my lips, I catch a glimpse of the judge leaving the courtroom.

I peek around my client. "Bailey!" I clench my briefcase to my chest and sprint up the hall after the judge. "Bailey, wait!" The security guard next to her serves as a barricade. All he has to do is cross his arms, and I bounce right off him. "Bailey, I only need a moment of your time!"

"*Judge* Bailey," Bailey corrects me. *I mean... Judge Bailey.*

"I know this looks bad. I swear, I was stuck in the middle of a gas station robbery. That's why I'm late for the hearing."

She sighs, her lazy gaze studying me. Even her thick prescription glasses can't hide the fact that I'm a joke in her eyes. After years of barely getting by representing criminals in her court, my juvenile behavior is now expected. "I judge criminals for a living, Joseph. Your sob story holds no power in my courthouse." Bailey–*Judge* Bailey waves me off and continues up the hall.

"My client is going to fire me for this, Judge Bailey!" I shout over her officer's shoulder.

"Long overdue! Have a good night, Joseph." She disappears into another room, leaving me alone in the now-empty hall.

I slam my briefcase against the floor. "But I need the money," I whisper under my breath. The weight of my thoughts suppresses me, one thought outweighing the rest: *You're pathetic, Joseph.*

The thought sinks in as my eyes pan around the hall. A thick white hue of light stretches from the window over the green and white tiles, chilling the atmosphere. The air is still, and I grow anxious when I realize I'm standing alone in silence. *No, no... anything but the silence.* I break into a cold sweat because it's in the silence that I hear the whisper.

I clench my briefcase against my chest, and something crunches in my breast pocket. My anxiety lessens when I remember that I still have the Kit Kat bar. I pull it out, smiling at the glistening red wrapper. *Joseph, maybe you're not so pathetic after all.*

◆ ◆ ◆

It takes two attempts before I successfully shove my front door open with my full body weight. I've been meaning to get the door fixed, but that requires cash I don't have right now. I shut the door, and Ava flashes me a smile from the kitchen at the end of the narrow hall. I usually love coming home to her smile, but right now I hate it because it means she doesn't know that neither of us is getting paid this week.

I hang my coat on a hook near the front door. Even under the dimmed lights, the horrendous orange-plaid wallpaper pops. I swear, the moment I can afford to, I'm fixing up this old dump. I weave my gold coin between my fingers, anxiously approaching the kitchen.

"I made your favorite," Ava says. Her voice is smoother than silk as she whispers, "Bucatini al Limone."

The dimples on her cheeks introduce themselves as she beams over the stovetop. She flicks her wrist over a series of sizzling pans, the aroma so alluring that I crave it as if I haven't eaten in days. Her dark, lustrous hair is pulled back into a loose bun, and her bangs dance over her big brown eyes as she glides from one side of the kitchen to the other.

Ava has always moved with passion and grace. I like to think that's how you move when you love what you do. Ava loves what she does, which is caring for the people who need her care the most.

"Stevie!" she chirps. "Hope you're ready to eat!"

A defeated sigh escapes me before I step into the kitchen. As Ava lifts the pot from the stovetop to the kitchen counter, her eyes meet mine, and I can tell she already knows. *And yet, she keeps caring for us anyway.*

"How was work today?" she asks, somehow still smiling while scooping pasta into 3 bowls set on the kitchen table.

I roll up my sleeves, slip my hands into my pockets, and stand near the table. "Ava, I–"

"Don't." She sets the pot of remaining pasta in the middle of the table. Her eyes overflow with sincerity as she says, "It's okay."

My head weighs a trillion pounds when I nod. She said the same thing last week.

"It smells amazing, Ava." Stevie's voice is soft over his squeaky wheelchair rolling over the wood floor. He approaches his side of the table, leans over his bowl, and inhales the aroma. He smiles, a thin layer of fog coating his glasses.

Ava sits across from Stevie, her eyes flicking between mine and his. "Well, I hope it tastes as good as it smells."

The two begin eating, and once my remaining pride dissolves, I do the same. I don't deserve to be eating my favorite food. I don't deserve to be with the only two people in my life who actually give a shit about me. I don't deserve to laugh, love, or even live. If you knew the memories that threaten my will to live each and every day… if you heard what I hear in the silence… you would agree. I don't deserve to live, but I somehow continue living anyway.

When we're finished eating, Stevie thanks Ava, then smirks at me. "You better have a good one ready, Dad."

"When do I not have a good one?" I tease, eyes narrowed. He beams up at me when I toss the Kit Kat bar onto his lap. "Give me 10 minutes."

Ava and I clear the table and it's not until we're doing the dishes that I finally muster up the courage to tell her what happened today. "I'm not gonna be able to pay you again." My forearms tense as I force the dish towel against a bowl like it wronged me. I'm frustrated with myself, and I imagine Ava is, too.

I feel Ava's eyes studying the side of my face. "This is the third time," she exhales.

"I know. I–"

"Let me finish," she snaps. Her wet palm is warm against my bare forearm. "This is the third time you haven't paid me, and I'm still here. It's because I want to be."

My hand loosens on the dish towel, and our eyes meet.

Ava's gaze is one of understanding—one of empathy. She sees that I'm frustrated, but she also feels my frustration. She feels my pain. One of her many beautiful qualities is her inherent ability to recognize when I fail without holding it against me. Ava knows I'm a fuck-up who keeps somehow getting by in life, and she sticks around anyway. *My wife's the same way.*

"I'm going to pay you," I state. "I'll find another client. I won't fuck this next one up. I promise."

Ava's hand finds mine, and warmth ripples up my arm like a pebble meets water. No splash, just enough to make an impact. She's soft at the touch, but only for a moment. She quickly pulls her hand away, realizing the invisible boundary we almost broke.

"I'll be here at the same time, tomorrow morning!" she says, reaching for her jacket and bag.

"Same time, tomorrow morning," I reply, watching her walk away. After two failed attempts at opening the front door, she finally manages. I dry my hands, making my way up the hall. "Ava…" As much as I want to open up about my feelings for her, the words refuse to be spoken. *My wife would kill me.*

A few beats pass before she smiles. She already knows. "Goodnight, Joseph."

I lower my head. "Goodnight."

She leaves me alone in the entryway. Habitually, I take a few small steps to Stevie's room before I'm overcome by the silence Ava left behind.

KNOCK! KNOCK!

"Come in." Stevie's voice is faint from behind the bedroom door.

I slowly open the door to see Stevie reading a book. His wheelchair is positioned by his nightstand, where he's able to read under the dull lamp light. "Why are you so awkward with Ava?"

I exhale a laugh, forcing my hands into the pockets of my slacks. "Why are you such a smart-ass?"

Stevie lifts his tiny chin and adjusts his glasses. "My dad is a lawyer. Smart-ass runs in my veins."

It blows my mind to see how quick Stevie is growing. I hear the growth in his voice. I see it in his face. He's 11 years old now, and not a day goes by when I don't picture that tiny bald baby my wife handed me in that delivery room 11 years ago. "*Steven*," she whispered, her chest rising and falling with every tired breath. "*Steven Verita.*"

Becoming a father is my fondest memory. It's the memory I cling to when the unwanted memories creep back into my mind with the help of the whisper. Even in the presence of my son, I grow uneasy.

"You said you have a good one tonight." Stevie's voice pulls me from my tainted mind.

"I do!" I reply, clapping my hands. I lift Stevie, lie him on the bed, and sit in his chair. "Alright, alright," I sigh, running my hand over my slicked curly hair. "Give me a hero."

"Stevie," he responds without hesitation.

"Of course." I let out a laugh. "Okay, give me a villain."

"Let's do a witch."

"A witch, huh?" I purse my lips, eyes trailing up to the corner of the bedroom as I ponder the bedtime story soon to be told. Stevie closes his eyes, and I begin. "Once upon a time, there was a boy named Stevie… *Super* Stevie. And he could fly…"

"How high?" Stevie asks.

"Higher than Superman."

He smirks, eyes still closed. "Can I be buff in the story?"

"Stevie, you can be whatever you want."

"Then I want to be buff," he states. "I want big muscles and I want to fly through the sky faster than a rocket ship."

"Listen, if *you* want to tell the story, I'm all ears."

Stevie's hands tighten around his blanket. "No! Sorry. Okay, go! Go!"

"One night, Super Stevie was flying over Manhattan, making sure all was well in the city. But he noticed something. A massive crowd of people were gathered in Times Square. They were watching a lady dressed in black. Her eyes were big and green, her skin white as snow. She held her hands high, hypnotizing the crowd…"

"Hypnotizing the crowd to do what?" Stevie asks in a sleepy tone.

I ponder his question for a moment. "It wasn't so much the crowd being hypnotized to do something. No, it was more like… the witch was hypnotizing the crowd *not* to do something. Yeah, the witch was distracting the crowd from being able to have superpowers like Super Stevie."

Stevie moans, and I'm not convinced he heard me answer his question. I continue anyway. "But you see, here is the thing about Super Stevie. He wants to make other people super, just like him. Because Super Stevie knows that the more people with superpowers like Stevie, the better the world will be. He flew closer to the witch and snuck into the crowd from behind. He knew that if he looked the witch in the eyes, he would lose his powers. So, he looked away, even while getting closer. He knew he was risking losing his powers, but the reward of helping others see what he saw when he looked away… that was worth the risk for Super Stevie."

I pause, silently waiting for Stevie to prove he's still awake. *Nothing.* I lift myself from the chair and tiptoe out of the room without waking him. It takes less than a minute for me to turn the living room couch into my bed. Sleeping on a couch in a one-bedroom townhome wasn't my original plan when I bought this place five years ago. I just didn't consider Stevie would grow as quickly as he has. The kid is simply too big for me to share a bed with now, so I figured, *what the hell.* He can have the only bedroom.

I stare at the black screen of the vintage television across the room. The T.V. is unplugged, a jumbled wire hanging from the base just inches from the orange-plaid wall. I haven't watched a single episode of anything since we moved out here to the Bronx, and I have no desire to. I prefer to be in control of my mind. I do my own thinking; God forbid I ever let the T.V. try to convince me otherwise.

But music, on the other hand…

The record player in the corner of the room screeches when I place the needle on the record. Smooth Jazz fills the room, playing quietly enough to keep from waking Stevie and loud enough to protect me from the silence. I gently nod, flicking my gold coin and snatching it out of the air while returning to the couch.

This is my life, all day and night. Barely getting by, avoiding the silence.

Because it's in the silence that I hear the whisper.

It wallows in the shadows of my mind.

It lurks in the hole of my heart.

It reminds me of its existence and the inevitability of one day coming back for me.

The whisper belongs to *Death*.

And it's in the silence that I'm reminded…

Death is near.

CHAPTER TWO

NORA

"We need another human plague," I state, because it's fucking true. "There are too many people in this world."

The front of my car is inches from the piece-of-shit station wagon in front of me. I want to slam into the back of it for making me late to work. But doing that would mean I have to put down my cigarette, and if I don't smoke this cigarette, I will lose my shit in this traffic.

"Nora, you have to stop saying stuff like that. You're gonna get canceled before you even get famous," Ryan whispers through my phone speaker.

I slam the back of my head against my headrest. The leather wrapping my steering wheel pleads for me to stop digging my nails into it, but I can't help it. I've never been late to work a day in my life, and I refuse to let that streak end today.

"Tell me it's not true," I whine into my phone. "There are too many people in this world. Too many nobodies." The palm of my hand meets the horn, adding to the orchestra of honks on this busy city street. "I swear, every person in this entire world is in a car on this fucking street and they're keeping me from getting to work on time and I'm not happy about it and I'm–"

"You're freaking out over nothing," Ryan's tone is soft but stern. "You've never been late, and you're the best showrunner at Mendax. You'll survive."

I let out a quick breath, then take a calming drag of my cigarette. Ryan has been my assistant for most of my five years at Mendax Productions. Since we first met, he's known exactly how to put my cluttered mind at ease. I check my reflection in the rearview mirror as if my appearance might have changed since I last looked a minute ago. "Okay, okay," I sigh.

"How far are you from the studio?" he asks.

"20 minutes."

I anxiously lower the air conditioner, raise it, then lower it again. With Mendax being the highest-ranked television network in the country, being late could cost me my career. Since day one of being an intern doing coffee runs for middle-aged perverts, I've had a perfect track record. I worked my way up to being a showrunner, and I do a damn good job for a woman who hasn't fucked a studio executive like most of the other women who work in entertainment. My time in the limelight will come, and I would rather it come without me having to spread my legs.

Regardless of my shows being among the best Mendax runs, our overall television ratings have plummeted. With streaming apps and podcasts taking over the entertainment industry, hardly anybody watches cable networks anymore. Money follows eyes, and the world's eyes are on random internet bullshit instead of the shows we're producing. Simply put, I'm slipping when I should be at the height of my career.

I exhale a cloud of smoke through my half-open window. Buildings border the jam-packed street, reaching for the sky, which has turned to the lightest shade of gray. In a mere second, the world around me is stripped of every color but yellow and dark red when I finally see what's causing cars to stop. To the right of the road, a mangled body has molded itself to the sidewalk pavement. The human corpse is nearly flattened to a thin layer of flesh and bone, streams of blood flowing through the cracks and divots in the pavement like overlapping rivers on a map. Bright yellow caution tape borders the morbid scene, extending to the sidewalk's edge.

No matter how hard I try, it becomes impossible for me to look away from the body. Fascination envelops my mind, butterflies manifesting themselves in my core. To think that at one point today, the remains of this body held life, and now it's mere flesh and bone.

This is real. This is… art.

"Fuck," I mutter under my breath.

"Nora?" I hear Ryan's voice through my speaker.

The world has slowed to a stop. It's not until I see a nearby crowd fighting for a chance to see what happened that I realize traffic has finally loosened. I apply more pressure to the pedal, looking forward again, not knowing how much time has passed since I stopped.

"Nora." Ryan's voice reaches me this time. "Nora, why'd you say, '*Fuck?*'"

I flick my cigarette out the window as I pick up speed. "All this traffic was because people wanted to get a better look at a dead body."

"You just saw a dead body?!"

"Just saw it right now," I reply, returning from my trance. "That was pretty fucked up."

"Seeing a dead body does sound pretty fucked up."

"No, not that," I retort coolly. "It's fucked up that I'm late for work because people can't mind their own damn business. Put time on my calendar for a 'human plague brainstorm' meeting."

"Fuck, Nora. You can be cold sometimes." Ryan laughs. "Just get over here."

"Be there soon."

I hang up the phone and ruffle through the pile of trash in the passenger's seat for another cigarette. I turn up the music, roll down the windows, and sing to the song with newfound energy.

I've been fascinated by Death since I was young, the way it looms over us humans, shrouded in myth, legend, and fear. It's the greatest unknown. It's beyond comprehension. The smartest cannot outsmart it. The fastest cannot outrun it. The strongest cannot defeat it.

Death transcends all boundaries and refrains from showing mercy to a single soul. It has an agenda, a responsibility to uphold. Death decides when a life has been lived, regardless of whether or not it's been lived to the fullest.

This might sound crazy, but I actually owe Death for my success, considering the way I portray death is what my viewers love the most about my shows. I've found ways to weave my fascination with Death into my productions, and I want to be known for depicting Death in its truest form on television because *death is art*. I want to highlight it, romanticize it, give it the respect it deserves.

When I arrive, I quietly slip through the lobby doors. Within seconds, the elevator is lifting me to the 66th floor. I feel my anxiety seeping from my pores the moment I see the illuminated sign that reads, "MENDAX," above the 66 white buttons.

The elevator rises… *2, 3, 4.*

The inside of the elevator reflects the interior of the entire building–glossy black walls reflecting the dimmed fluorescent lights shining from above. I catch my reflection in the mirror to my right, admiring my straight black hair cut sharply just above my exposed collarbones. My black blazer is low cut, tailored to accentuate my body frame down to the bottom of my black slacks and heels. There's no denying that I look fucking amazing–I always do–I just can't stand the thought of looking this good only to be recognized as late.

The elevator continues to rise… *35, 36, 37.*

Eyes, chin, shoulders, I remind myself. I fixate my gaze on the steel elevator doors, lift my chin, and move my shoulders back, exposing my chest. Confidence manifests within as I remind myself that today is a new day… a new day presenting new ways to build my legacy.

I started at the bottom of Mendax, and after years of alphabetizing folders, planning meetings, and stroking the egos of men who offer roles to women they're either related to or sleeping with, I managed to work my way up to where I am now. It's only a matter of time before I make it on the big screen.

The elevator slows… *64, 65, 66.*

PING!

The doors separate, and I cautiously make my way up the hall. A pit forms in my stomach at the thought of running into a studio executive, so I mute my footsteps the best I can. In entertainment, people who aren't already at the top are easily disposable. One slip-up is all it takes to be thrown back out on the streets, where I would be offering up my soul for the next opportunity the way I offered mine for this one.

When I reach the black marble desk at the end of the hall, the secretary doesn't notice me, per usual. Normally, not being noticed drives me mad, but given the circumstances, not being noticed is all I can hope for this morning.

My phone suddenly vibrates in my hand, and I look down to see a text from Ryan.

RYAN: Conference Room C

I peek down one of the long halls, then continue upon seeing it empty. I keep my head down. *If I can manage to slip into this conference room unnoticed, I'm golden.* My eyes fixate on the flooring I step over, tracing the white veins in contrast with the black marble as I tiptoe past the conference rooms, one after another.

Room A…

Room B…

Room C.

I silently open the door, step in, and shut it. I let out a sigh of relief, then find it hard to breathe when I turn to see a man sitting at the head of the table who isn't Ryan. The man is accompanied by a chilling aura that sends shivers down my spine. His eyes are the darkest shade of brown, so dark they could be black against his pale skin. His face is wrinkled and long, drooping into his saggy neck and narrow body. *Time has not been kind to his complexion.*

"You must be Nora," the man says.

I must be in the wrong room.

"Y-yes. I'm sorry, I think I'm in the wrong room."

"Nope," the man replies calmly. He crosses one leg over another, and his yellow-toothed grin spreads across his wrinkled face. "Please, sit." His black eyes follow me as I reluctantly lower myself into one of the many empty seats. "I'm Samuel Roth."

My heart plummets from my chest into my stomach at the sound of his name. This man is more than just a man.

He's the "King Behind the Screen…"

The "Pay-Per-View Prophet…"

The owner and founder of Mendax…

Samuel fucking Roth.

As the man who owns the most powerful T.V. network in the country, Samuel has managed to go unnoticed for the entirety of his career. Not a single picture of his face on the internet, not a single word spoken to the press. An entire career, and a successful one at that, gone undetected and unnoticed. The people around the studio have shared myths about Samuel. Still, none of their unsettling descriptions of him compare to seeing him in the flesh.

As much as I want to ask why he's gone his entire career

lurking in the shadows of the entertainment industry, Samuel's presence begs a more important question: *Why has he chosen to reveal himself now?*

"You're my showrunner," Samuel states, dragging his eyes up and down my body. His voice is omnipresent. It fills the room, replacing air. I no longer breathe oxygen. I breathe Samuel's influence.

"Yes, I'm one of them," I murmur.

"You're my showrunner," Samuel states again. "I meant what I said." He lifts a wiry finger in my direction. "You're my *only* showrunner."

"I'm confused," I reply. "I'm not your only showrunner. I'm one of quite a few, actually."

The corner of his thin lips curls up. "As of this morning, you're my only showrunner."

I pinch my eyebrows together, confused at his remark. Was it me who fell off that building earlier? Did I die on the way to work and end up in Heaven? If being late gets me promoted the way it seems to have, then I'll be late more often. "Is this some sort of promotion?" I ask.

"Consider it a lifeline that can turn into a promotion if you use it right." Samuel laughs under his breath. "It's no secret that Mendax's overall viewership has nearly collapsed. The competing networks remind the world of that every damn day. But the viewership of your shows… they have somehow remained stable, and I think I know why." He slowly leans forward, his movements similar to a snake preparing to strike. "The characters and stories you create have a common thread. You explore a darker side of human nature in every show you've run, and with your viewership remaining steady while the other shows dropped, I think what you explore can be tapped into even more." He releases me from his gaze, checking his phone. "So, I got rid of the other showrunners and kept you."

A part of me is relieved, while another part is frightened to discover what all of this means. *With the other Mendax show-runners being let go, will I need to run their shows on top of my own?*

Samuel sets his phone down, waiting for my response. He appears fascinated by the fact that I'm more concerned than I am excited. "Mendax has always topped the charts of every television genre," he explains. "We've been the best across the board, but we're hurting, and I think it's because we're not focused." I find myself nodding, absorbing his words as if I need them to live. "I've spoken with the network investors, and we agree it's time to trim the fat. It's time for Mendax to cancel all running shows and pour our efforts into one. We need one brand-new T.V. series that will capture the eyes of millions and keep them."

"Mr. Roth, I'm…" My legs force me up to my feet before I even decide to stand. "I'm honored." I offer him my hand. "I won't let you down."

"Call me Samuel." Samuel stands. His shadow casts itself over me as he stands well over six feet. When his large hand envelops mine, his frozen grip causes my blood to run cold. There's such a lack of warmth in his skin that I question whether or not this man is actually living. "I know you won't let me down. Regardless, I plan to be around a bit more. I'll remain behind the scenes, but you and I will work closely on weaving our narrative through the show you create."

"Our narrative…?" I ask as he releases my hand.

Samuel ignores my question, silently gliding out of the room. The moment he leaves, I feel the warmth return to my body. I fall back into a chair, letting out a deep breath. I rub my palms over my eyes, feeling the weight of this morning lift itself from my shoulders.

"Nora, I'm so sorry," a familiar voice says from the doorway. I open my eyes to see Ryan walking in with his hands raised. "I had no idea Roth was coming in. He came looking for you and made me text you to meet. What happened?"

"It's fine," I exhale. "We're fine."

He runs his fingers back through his dirty-blonde hair while taking the seat next to me. He subtly leans forward and places a hand on the table just inches away from mine. His hazel eyes are gentle, sympathetic. "Do you want to talk about earlier?"

"The meeting?"

"I meant what happened on your way here–seeing that dead body, the one on the side of the road."

After meeting with Samuel, it takes me a moment to remember why I was even late in the first place. My mind is pulled back to what was left of the person who jumped off that building. The flattened skull, the blood-soaked hair forming a web over the pavement. I hadn't put much thought into the spectacle since seeing it.

"Oh, that?" I shrug, forcing back my grin. "That was nothing."

I spend the entire day in my office, burning through one ridiculous show idea after another. By 8p.m., my trash can is overflowing with decent show concepts, but none are good enough. I've always gone morbid with my scripts, some too dark to ever see the light of day. But it seems like Samuel is looking for something so morbid that it will change the way people see the world–the way they live life. He didn't give me much direction besides wanting to focus on one single show based on the darker side of human nature. Frustrated and craving a cigarette, I pry myself from my desk and decide to head home.

It's about an hour's drive to the Bronx around this time. I add five minutes to the trip when I realize I need to pick up another pack of cigarettes. As I finish my last, I pull into a gas station. It's not the nicest part of town, so I lock my car before getting out, wrapping myself in my coat to hide the shape of my body as I walk into the gas station store. I work hard for this body. The last thing I want is for a man to think he has a right to it without my consent.

The night sky is replaced by blinding fluorescent lights as I step through the sliding doors. I stand in line behind a curly-headed man speaking to the cashier. His trench coat is weathered, his briefcase beaten and worn. He says goodbye to the cashier, and when he turns, we collide.

"Jeez!" I hiss, watching him drop the Kit Kat bar he just bought. "Watch it."

"Sorry about that," he says while bending down to pick up the bar.

Our eyes meet as the man stands straight, and I wince at the scar along the left side of his face. It runs from his left eyebrow halfway down his cheek, the rest hidden by the stubble on his face. He notices me staring. After a respectful nod, he walks out the sliding doors.

I shiver at the thought of having to live with a scarred face like that. Growing up in sole pursuit of fame, my life is devoted to my image. *My image is my everything.*

Before I know it, I'm out the door with a lit cigarette between my lips. "Dammit!" I shout when I see my car keys sitting on the driver's seat. "Nora, you fucking idiot!"

I yank at my door handle. It doesn't budge.

First I was late this morning. Now, I'm locked out of my own car. What next?

"Locked yourself out, huh?"

The cigarette nearly falls out of my mouth when I see the man with the scar in my window's reflection. My eyes refocus, and I see my pepper spray in the passenger's seat. *Of course.* "I have a gun," I lie without turning to face him. I remove the cig from my lips, prepared to burn him with it if he gets close.

The scarred man nods. "Is the gun locked in the car with your keys?"

I let out a defeated sigh, finally facing him. "What do you

want? My money?" I offer him my purse. "Take it. The cops will be on your ass in no time."

He takes a step toward me. I leap out of the way, but he just continues to my car door. Without saying a word, he rummages through his briefcase until he pulls out two lock picks. "What's your name?" he asks calmly.

I narrow my eyes, watching him break into my car right in front of me. "Nora."

"I'm Joseph," Joseph replies before kneeling in front of the door. He continues picking the lock. "What do you do, Nora?"

"I'm a showrunner."

"Hmm," he replies, unimpressed.

"For Mendax Productions," I boast between cigarette puffs.

Joseph keeps his eyes on the lock. "Never heard of it."

"Then you must not watch T.V.," I snap.

"You're right about that."

I pause a moment, then blow smoke over my shoulder. "What do *you* do? Besides pick locks. Are you some kind of criminal?"

Joseph stops picking the lock, sighs, then continues picking. "I'm not a criminal, but I represent them. I'm a lawyer."

"Ah, is that how you learned how to pick locks?"

He laughs. "If I'm gonna represent criminals, I need to know how they commit their crimes, right?"

"Good point." I lift my chin, taking in my surroundings. A neon hue casts itself across the empty parking lot. The night sky is starless, leaving my mind with nowhere else to go but Joe.

"Do people call you Joe?"

"Nope. Joseph," he says.

"Even your wife calls you Joseph?"

"She used to."

"Before she divorced you?" The words leave my mouth

before I realize how rude I'm being.

Joseph shoots me a half-glance. "Before she died," he corrects me.

I exhale a deep breath, feeling a sliver of sympathy for this guy. Before I can say another word, he undoes the lock and opens my car door. He stands and faces me. "You can shoot me with your gun now."

I hate how nice this guy is.

"I'm sorry for being a bitch. I'm under a lot of pressure at work."

Joseph raises his palms. "We all got problems." He steps around me and heads for the bus stop. "Have a nice night, Nora."

I suck in a deep breath, then exhale. "You too, Joseph."

My drive home is a silent mixture of thoughts revolving around my meeting with Samuel.

I see his black eyes.

I see his crooked grin.

I see Mendax.

I see the opportunity of a lifetime, to reach an unfathomable level of fame, to build a legacy that will continue to live long after my own life. This is my chance to make my mark on the world, but I can't come up with a show idea for the life of me.

Samuel's words echo throughout my mind… *"Pour all of our efforts into one brand-new T.V. series that will capture the eyes of millions and keep them."*

How am I supposed to capture millions of eyes and keep them? It's one thing to get people to watch and it's another to keep them engaged, yearning for the next episode. This show needs to be cutting-edge. It needs to disrupt the industry. It needs to entertain the crowd and keep them entertained–keep them from looking away.

As I drive past the exact spot I witnessed the dead body this morning, I'm overcome by the urge to pull over. I park beside the curb, and the second I'm immersed in silence, a whisper slips through the crack of my window. My eyes lock on the dried droplets of blood that have stained the pavement.

I step out onto the sidewalk where the body once lay, and I curiously open myself up to hear the whisper. It's ever so faint, the message delivered in an ethereal form. All of those cars slowing to a halt this morning just to see the dead body along the side of this road. The whisper floods my mind with its influence, encouraging me to replay the scene over and over again as I stand over Death's most recent masterpiece.

I smile when the whisper finally plants the show idea in my mind.

It's morbid.

It's dark.

And it's hard to look away.

CHAPTER THREE

JOSEPH

I met Death five years ago, its presence suffocating and ominous. Our encounter was brief but long enough to leave an eternal impression. Death didn't say much–actually, Death didn't say anything at all. Death merely slipped into my car, cloaked in darkness, embraced my beloved wife in the passenger's seat, and–

"Joseph?"

I shake my head, now present in the church basement. The lights shine from above, one of them flickering in the back corner of the small room. My chair is unsteady beneath me as I prepare to address the group. The group members sit in a circle, their faces etched with sadness and pain. Some stare blankly into the distance, lost in their thoughts like me a moment ago. Others wipe tears from their eyes.

I clear my throat. *Alright, Joseph. Now is the time to finally tell them why you're here.*

As I prepare to open up, the walls of the church basement start to close in, making it tough to breathe. I try to speak, but forming words takes more energy than I can manage. The words don't want to come out, so like every time before, I don't force them to.

"Take all the time you need, Joseph," Pastor Ben speaks softly from directly ahead.

A comforting smile spreads across his bearded face. It's a genuine smile that almost makes you feel like everything is fine, even when your world is falling apart. I fill my chest with air, twiddling my gold coin in my pocket. Upon exhaling, I come to the harsh conclusion that I'm not ready to open up. *Next time*, I think to myself the same way I did last week.

"Joseph, we support you and we're here for you. Whenever you're ready, just let us know." With his attentive gaze, Pastor Ben picks up on the war waging within me. Thankfully, he gestures to the man sitting to my left. "I thought I noticed a new face. Would you like to introduce yourself to the group?"

The man to my left fidgets in his chair, nervously wringing his sweaty hands together. "I'm… I'm Rodrick."

"Hi, Rodrick," the group greets in unison.

"Welcome to Positive Pathways," Pastor Ben adds in a soothing tone. "I want to start by congratulating you on making the effort to attend our support group tonight. It takes a lot of courage to not only show support but to also seek support."

A dimple reveals itself in one of Rodrick's plump cheeks as he rocks back and forth. He's sweating through his striped rugby shirt that he's carefully tucked into baggy cargo shorts. His ankle socks are just centimeters above clunky white running shoes that tap against the floor as he whispers, "Th-thanks."

"What brings you to Positive Pathways?" Pastor Ben asks delicately.

I've been coming to Positive Pathways for a year now. I've just about heard this question a million times, and it's a new answer every time. But it's always something along the lines of…

"I'm here to feel less lonely."

"I need emotional support."

"I'm an addict."

Judging by the innocent looks of Rodrick, I'll bet all my money on him being some kind of lonely mama's boy looking for the courage to move out.

Rodrick looks at the floor as he confesses, "I'm addicted to pornography."

Don't ever let me bet again.

Pastor Ben does what every decent support group leader does best... *he listens.* He locks eyes with Rodrick and gently nods, communicating that judgment has no place here.

"It started off as regular porn." Rodrick's eyebrows draw apart. "I was 12 when I started watching pretty regular types of porn, I guess? It became an everyday habit. And when I was in my late teens, I wasn't getting 'aroused' by regular porn anymore. I began watching more aggressive types of porn. One thing led to another, and now I'm hooked on..."

His voice fades out as his leaky eyes scan the group for some kind of response, but nobody reacts. Some continue staring blankly in the distance, others still wiping tears from their eyes over their own struggles. What Rodrick doesn't realize yet is nobody cares about what he's going through. The sad truth is that we're not here to make others feel better. We're here to feel better about ourselves.

"I'm a sicko," Rodrick mutters.

Pastor Ben leans forward, breaking the silence. "Rodrick, that's not true. It takes serious courage to share what you've shared. The first step in recovering is acknowledging the problem, which you've done wonderfully." Rodrick purses his lips, listening intently as Pastor Ben continues. "The next step is committing yourself to make the change. Now, this is a scary and difficult step, but it's an important step toward growth and healing."

My phone suddenly vibrates, and I pull it out of my pocket to see an incoming call from Ava. My fatherly instincts force the thought of Stevie into my mind. When you're a dad like me, you never miss a call from your kid or the person looking after your kid. I quickly stand to my feet and tiptoe out of the room.

"What's up?" I whisper into the phone as I enter the hall. "Everything alright?"

"Everything is fine," Ava instantly assures me. "But Stevie hasn't talked much since I picked him up from school. I don't mean to bother; I can just tell something is wrong."

"You're not bothering at all." I check my watch to see it's a few minutes past when our meetings usually end. "I'm on my way."

"From the courthouse?" Ava asks innocently.

I pause a moment before lying. "Yep!" The door opens behind me and group members begin funneling out. "I gotta go. I'll be there soon."

A gentle hand caresses my shoulder the second I hang up the phone. I flinch, pulling away until I realize it's Pastor Ben. *Shit.*

"Hey, Joseph." He removes his glasses and wipes the lenses with the bottom of his plaid shirt. His salt-and-pepper hair is unkempt, his beard untamed. "Do you want to grab a cup of coffee down the street? There's this old diner that serves a great roast."

He asks the question as if he doesn't ask me every time we finish class. I usually bolt the second class ends to avoid these awkward encounters with him. But, on rare occasions like this, Pastor Ben manages to subtly chip away at the wall I spent five years building up. What he doesn't realize is that I come here to be reminded that people have it worse than me. One of these days, I hope to meet the sorry individual who does.

"I'm uh… busy," I reply with a hollow smile. "See you next week, Pastor Ben." My shoes squeak against the tile floor as I make my way to the exit.

"Call me Ben!" I hear him shout. "I'll see you next Thursday!"

Within minutes, I'm on the bus, fondling a Kit Kat bar. With every tap against my thigh, I run through a potential reason Stevie is in a sad mood, already pondering ways to get him out of it. Stevie has been my son for 11 years, and I still find it amazing how our moods are connected. When Stevie is on top of the world, I'm on top of the world. When Stevie is down in the dumps, I'm right there with him. What makes this connection so fascinating is that nobody sits you down and tells you that this is how it works. As a parent, it just is. And you learn to question the connection less as life goes on.

After two failed attempts at shoving my front door open, the third attempt is a success. Ava greets me on the other side. "He's in his room," she whispers. Our fingers brush against each other as she takes my coat and hangs it on the hook. "Another late night at the courthouse?"

"Huh? Yeah," I lie with half my mind on her and the other half on Stevie.

I prefer Ava doesn't know that I go to a support group once a week just outside of the neighborhood. With almost every part of my life teetering on the edge of destruction since the accident five years ago, the last thing I need is pity.

I knock, then slowly push the bedroom door open. Stevie is sitting in the corner of the dark room, his back to me as he sits slumped in his wheelchair. "Hey, buddy," I greet softly, turning on the lamp. I sit on the edge of the bed and reveal my open palms. With a single clap, I make the Kit Kat appear in my right hand. "Brought you dessert."

He ignores my magic trick. "I don't want it," he mutters between sniffles.

"That's a first." I lie sideways, trying to get a look at Stevie's face. He pushes his fogged-up lenses closer to his eyes before they slip down the bridge of his nose, then turns away. "I know I'm ugly, but too ugly for you to look at me?" I tease.

He doesn't respond, just sniffles. "What happened at school today?"

"Nothing."

I delicately run my hand through his curls and catch sight of his left wheel. *It's flat.* "Not again," I exhale. "Tell me it was an accident."

A tear falls under Stevie's glasses, a response more powerful than one I could've asked for. "It was an accident," he whispers.

Bullshit.

I run my thumb along the tire, feeling the plugs I used to fill every hole poked in the past. It's the third time in two weeks that those fucking kids have poked holes in one of his tires. "Stevie, who did this?"

"It was an accident!" he shouts, his voice high with a rageful undertone.

I sigh. "How do you expect me to do something about this if you don't give me a name?"

Stevie shrugs.

"At least tell me—"

"I'm not gonna tell you anything because there's nothing you can do! It's not like you can afford to get me a new chair. You can't even afford to fix the front door!"

I flex my jaw to keep from letting my own tears fall. *He's right. Business has been so slow I can't even afford to defend my own kid from middle school bullies.*

After a few silent beats, Stevie wipes at one of his tiny cheeks. "I'm sorry."

"Don't be. You're right." I place a hand on his arm. "But, I'm gonna fix this. I'm gonna fix all of this, I promise."

With his head still hanging low, Stevie lifts his arms for me to lift him into bed. Sure, he's growing heavier by the day, but my son will never be too heavy for me to lift. Be it his growth, a bully, or the weight of this broken world, I will always be there to lift my son when he's down. It's moments like these that remind me why I can never act on the thought of ending my own life, no matter how enticing Death makes the thought seem. *My son needs me.*

I tuck Stevie in, then sit in his wheelchair with my feet now resting on the bed. "You know the drill," I blurt out, lacing my fingers behind my head. "Give me a hero."

"Stevie."

"Give me a villain."

"A dragon."

I tilt my head, pondering where to begin the story. "Once upon a time, there was a knight named Stevie–*Sir Stevie*. And he rode a valiant steed…"

"How fast?" Stevie asks, pushing through his pain.

"Faster than Prince Charming's horse, that's for sure." I notice Stevie's lips curl up. "Sir Stevie is far more handsome than Prince Charming, too. Because Sir Stevie has his dad's good looks."

Stevie giggles. "Shut up."

"Sorry. Anyway…" I lean forward, using my hands to help tell the story. "Sir Stevie rode west, looking for something more precious and more rewarding than all of the gold in the entire kingdom."

"What's more precious than gold?"

"Well, it's…" I pause a moment. "I'll tell you what's more precious than gold." I pan around the room until I fixate on the bookshelf in the corner. The authors' names are etched into the worn spines of the old novels, some written decades ago and others centuries ago. Each novel is left behind to be read years after the authors' lifetimes. "Leaving a legacy," I state. "Sir Stevie was in pursuit of leaving a legacy."

"A legacy?" Stevie scrunches his face. "What's a legacy?"

I stand and raise my hands for dramatic effect. "A legacy is the story of a life well-lived. It's the story about the main character that lives on, long after the main character dies."

Stevie props himself up on his elbow. Even in the dim

light, I catch the gleam in his eye. "How will Sir Stevie leave a legacy?"

I lower myself, the two of us now eye to eye. "Sir Stevie will have to slay the dragon threatening the western lands. Then, the people will remember his name for years to come. The people will tell the story of his bravery for generations."

"Can we name the dragon Mikey?" Stevie's eyebrows raise with excitement.

I cock my head back. "You want to name the dragon Mikey? That's a weird name for a dragon. Why Mikey?"

Stevie's face softens. "Mikey is the kid who pokes holes in my tires at school."

◆ ◆ ◆

I wake up the same way I do every morning, with excruciating back pains. Believe it or not, my 50-year-old couch doesn't make for the best bed. I stand with my hands on my hips, and jerk my upper body to hear a series of cracks. My spine re-aligns itself, relief trickling from my shoulders to my waist. Jazz fills the room as it's played from the record player. I pull the needle from the record and rub my eyes. Horizontal streams of golden light seep through the narrow slats of the window blinds. I pull them up, and the morning light floods the cramped living room.

When my eyes adjust, I fixate on the guest house on the opposite side of my backyard. I had it built shortly after moving into the neighborhood so that I could rent it out. It sure as hell helps with the bills.

My house isn't the prettiest, but it's still prettier than my guest house. The roof is weathered and slopes in all the places it shouldn't. The inside has a kitchenette, bed, and table packed into a single room, plus a bathroom.

Somehow, just a few days after putting out a "For Lease" sign, I found a guy willing to rent it out. We didn't talk much when we met. Still don't. I remember the guy telling me he'd pay me more than I asked and *in cash* if I agreed to leave him alone. You're not supposed to ask a lot of questions when people offer to pay you twice the asking price in cash, so I made it real simple for him. I said, *"No drugs. No hookers. No guns."* He nodded. We shook on it.

So, all our relationship consists of is an envelope filled with cash on the backyard patio. I don't need to know where the money comes from. As long as it's on my doorstep at the first of every month, I can afford to pay the mortgage. It really helps when business is slow like it's been. As much as I hate to admit it, I need to cross paths with a criminal.

I'm in Stevie's room helping him get ready for school when…

BAM!

There's a loud thump against the front door.

"Ava's here," Stevie says casually.

BAM!

Another loud thump, then Ava swings the door open. She smiles cheek to cheek, still catching her breath. "Good morning!" She blows brown strands of hair out of her face. "Who's ready for school?!"

Stevie forces a cough while rolling into the hall. "I should skip school today. I think I'm getting sick."

"Not sick enough," I add from behind. "What happened to slaying dragons and leaving a legacy?"

"Dragons, huh?" Ava takes Stevie's backpack from my hands. She pulls a strap over her shoulder, and her eyes flick between Stevie and me. "Am I missing something?"

"Sir Stevie is battling a dragon at school," I say from the doorway. When her eyes meet mine, I mouth, "Bully."

"Ahh, a dragon?" She crouches in front of Stevie, lifting his chin. "You can't slay dragons if you're too busy hiding from them."

Stevie sighs. "Fine."

We watch him roll out the front door with his head hanging low. Ava stands to her feet. Her beauty is striking, even when dressed to run her everyday errands. Her bright-blue denim jacket hangs over her red flannel, black yoga pants wrapping her legs down to her black boots. Her bangs cover her forehead but not enough to cover her straight brows. *Is it inappropriate to be attracted to your son's nanny?*

"Joseph?" Ava asks. "Did you hear what I just said?"

"Huh?"

She giggles, having caught me staring. "I asked if you have any dragons to slay today."

Shit, I missed that.

"Dragons… right." I try to play it cool. "Yeah, no–tons of dragons."

"Best of luck with that." She flashes me a cheeky grin and then turns out the door.

I mosey my way back into the living room with nowhere to be. No court hearings to be late to, no calls to miss. When business slows like this, I usually flood the streets with my business cards. But business has been so slow I can't even afford to buy business cards. I sink into the couch and weave my gold coin between my fingertips, brainstorming ways to make extra cash. I have an extensive network; the only thing is that it's an extensive network of criminals.

Throughout my career, I've been offered jobs in both organized and underground crime. It's the only way my clients can express gratitude for proving their innocence. From laundering money to being a middleman in drug deals, I could do it all, and here I am with none, nada, zip, zero. I'm stuck with nothing but empty pockets and my looming desperation.

I'm stuck in my head for most of the morning until my ringtone sends me into a panic. I dive onto the kitchen table and take a deep breath before I pick up. "This is Joseph."

There's silence on the other end, then a long exhale. "I need help." The deep voice belongs to a man.

Don't fuck this up, Joseph. I lean forward, gripping the phone closer to my ear. "You're looking for representation?"

The man sighs. "Yup."

"Okay, well, I would be more than happy to help. How soon can you meet to talk over the details?"

"Now," he snaps.

I pinch my lips together. I've been on hundreds of introduction calls with a wide range of conflicted people, but not a single one has said so little. "Now. Right, okay. Where would you like to meet?"

"I'm at city jail, bro," the man replies as if I'm supposed to already know.

"Not a problem at all!" I make my way up the hall, my phone sandwiched between my cheek and shoulder. "Which jail?"

"Metro Central."

I slip my coat on. "I'm on my way. Have you said anything to the police yet?"

"Hell no. I ain't dumb."

"Good man. What's your name?"

"Nicky."

"Did your parents give you a last name, Nicky?"

"Williams."

After two pulls, I swing the front door open. "I'm on my way, Mr. Williams."

I rehearse my introduction while on the bus ride to the city jail. With an empty briefcase for looks and a handful of gel forcing my curls out of my face, I confidently shove the front doors open. The jail's reception area is sparsely furnished with metal benches and plastic chairs. The walls are depressingly painted in shades of gray, while a wall of steel black bars separates police officers from alleged criminals.

"Unbelievable!" I shout, raising my arms. "You've got my client behind bars without even taking him out to dinner first?!"

The two officers at the front desk—one with a bushy mustache and the other with her head buzzed—glance at each other, then at me. "Been a while, Joseph," Officer Buzzcut says, her voice much deeper than mine. "You been on vacation or somethin'?"

Officer Mustache smirks at her dig.

I shrug, then lie. "Been so busy, I had to take a break. I'm looking for my client, Nicky Williams."

Officer Mustache's smirk dissolves. "Of course, you're the one representing that punk."

"*That punk?*" I pinch my brows together. "Best be careful letting your opinions keep you from being professional, officer. Would hate to see your name-calling result in suspension or termination of employment."

Both officers roll their eyes. Officer Mustache stands and makes his way to the wall of bars, dangling a dense set of keys. "Williams! Come meet the mistake you made."

I ignore his insult, eager to impress my new client. As I make my way around the officers' desk, I notice a phone propped up, streaming some T.V. show they were watching before I arrived. My eyes pan from the desk to one of the holding cells where a cyclops of a man is now standing. The man, who I assume is Nicky, places his hand on a bar which the officer quickly swats away.

"Give me six feet!" Officer Mustache commands.

Nicky flexes his jaw, obeying his command. He's in a black T-shirt three sizes too big. It hangs over a pair of dark blue jeans that are also three sizes too big. His shoes are brand-spankin' new, leading me to believe that whatever crimes he's been committing, he gets away with.

The officer gestures for me to enter the cell, and I extend

my hand for Nicky to shake. "Joseph," I greet, looking up at him. He doesn't shake my hand. With his eyes on mine, he sits back on the bench lining the wall. I clear my throat. "You're right. No need for introductions. Let's just get right to it."

Officer Mustache lets out a laugh before shutting the cell door. "Knock 'em dead, you two."

I wipe off the space next to Nicky before I sit. "First thing's first. What're you in for?" His eyes flick to mine, and my heart drops when I recognize the familiar panic swirling about in his iris. I struggle to keep my voice a whisper. "Holy shit, I know you. You're the guy who robbed the gas station."

Nicky itches at his coarse goatee before crossing his massive arms. He looks at the ground, and I can already tell that this guy is the epitome of stubborn.

I lean closer. "Is that why you're here? Because of what happened the other day at the gas station?"

He nods. I turn back to see the officers entranced by their T.V. show. My gaze meets Nicky's again. "Listen, you'll need to talk if you want me to help you."

"Yeah, that's why I'm here," Nicky mutters, his ego shot because we both remember me telling him he would eventually use my business card.

I suck in a quick breath, contemplating whether or not Nicky is worth representing. An armed robbery in broad daylight? *No chance we win this case.*

"It wasn't a real gun and they know it, too," Nicky mutters.

"Come again?"

"It was a fake gun," he continues, avoiding eye contact. "I wasn't gonna hurt nobody. The cops arrested me right after. They know it was fake."

Maybe Nicky isn't fucked after all.

I break down the facts the way I always do…

Nicky robs a gas station with a fake gun. Not 'armed' robbery.

Casualties? No one was hurt.

Witnesses? Me and Anthony, the gas station cashier.

We actually have a fighting chance here, which means I'll get paid, which means I can pay Ava. "I think I can get you out of this," I whisper. "But before I do, I need to know if you can afford my rate."

Nicky looks up at me. "If you can keep me out of jail, I'll double your rate in cash."

I salivate at the mouth. "You got yourself a fucking deal, pal," I say, offering my hand. He shakes it this time, his grip so firm it cracks my knuckles. "I'm sure I've got enough information to get you out on bail. Where do you live?"

I turn and wave the officers over.

"The Bronx," Nicky replies.

"Small world," I chuckle. "I do, too. What street?"

"Fordham Road."

I blink at him. *That's my street.*

"Fordham R-... what address?"

Nicky folds his lips between his teeth. Reluctantly, he mutters, "4711."

Impossible.

My heart drops and a cold sweat comes over me.

4711 Fordham Road is my *address.*

CHAPTER FOUR

NORA

"Roth is in again," Ryan warns from my office doorway. His muscular frame tugs at my gaze from under his dress shirt and cropped slacks. "You got your pitch ready?"

I tap one of my matte-black acrylics against my temple. "I have it all up here."

"You always do." He smirks, his palms raised in surrender. His compliment nearly makes me blush, and I'm reminded of this undeniable light he carries. I catch glimpses of it in the words he speaks and sometimes in the way he simply carries himself.

Ryan's light suddenly dissolves as unease sweeps the entire building floor. Through the wall of windows separating my office from the network nobodies, I see Samuel Roth. His energy permeates the room, forcing heads to turn. People stand from their seats just to catch a glimpse of his alluring presence.

To word it bluntly, Samuel is one ugly son of a bitch, but he's also a brilliant son of a bitch. I've picked up on the fact that he knows T.V. screens are for the beautiful and the charismatic, not the ugly. So, he rules from behind the screens, dominating the entire industry.

Eyes, chin, shoulders. I adjust my posture, preparing to pitch Samuel the T.V. show idea I've worked through non-stop the past two days. "It's showtime," I whisper, now standing next to Ryan at the doorway.

Since Samuel promoted me, I've sought out silence, working on a show idea that will disrupt television in the best possible way. I remember driving home the other night, hearing the faint whisper at the sight of that morbid display. The whisper hung the idea in my mind like a delicate, ethereal mistletoe waiting for me to step into its embrace. It called, and I answered. I'm sure Samuel will do the same.

As Samuel approaches my office, the distance between us dissolves. He looks down at me, and his elongated face leans forward, his long and wiry fingers finding mine. "Hello, Nora." His touch is devoid of human warmth, the same way it was the first time we met. I welcome the chill, making it known in the way I shake his hand.

Ryan and I greet Samuel in unison before Samuel's slender body slips between us into the office. With his hands locked behind his lower back, he observes the small room. My office is more of a glorified cubicle than it is an actual office. It's hardly spacious enough for Samuel, Ryan, and myself.

Samuel's black eyes flick to mine. "It's a shame we have a woman of your caliber working in such a confined space. You can't keep creatives in a cage like this."

I struggle to hide my smile. *It feels good to finally be recognized.*

"I think you'll be happy to see what I've created, regardless of where it was created," I reply.

Samuel grins. "Let's begin."

He glances at Ryan, the look in his eyes serving as a silent act of dismissal. Ryan turns to me, disheartened. As much as I want him to stay, my career takes precedence over our relationship. To me, it's nothing personal. To Ryan, it's only personal, which is why he's my assistant and I'm not his. Ryan won't fight for the chance to play with the big shots like Samuel. Instead, he walks out of the office. Samuel's eyes follow Ryan, his disappointment lingering until the door closes.

"You have a new show for me, and it's good," Samuel declares as he claims the chair in the corner of the room. "I can feel it in the way you carry yourself. Something is different about you since we last met, and I like it."

I beam in his direction as I sink into the chair behind my desk. Usually, I'd be nervous pitching a concept to the owner of the biggest network in the country. He's going all in on me and I have no choice but to succeed, but that's not what keeps me from being nervous. What keeps me from being nervous is the fact that there's some kind of force pushing my idea. Samuel was right when he said something was different about me. Ever since the moment I opened myself to that faint whisper, I've felt different. There's a greater good at play here; I just don't know what it is yet.

Before a word leaves my lips, Samuel raises a finger toward the blank T.V. screen on the wall. "No presentation?"

"There's no need for one," I say confidently.

There's no need for one because I've run through this pitch non-stop the past 48 hours.

I've sat with it, slept with it, fallen for it.

Samuel's yellow teeth reveal themselves in a crooked fashion. "I love it already."

I take one last deep breath before becoming the voice for the whisper that gave me this idea. "The morning I met you, I was late to work. Bumper-to-bumper traffic, but not for the reason you would expect. Someone had committed suicide– jumped off the building, landing on the sidewalk pavement. The scene itself had no physical impact on the cars driving past it, yet the cars slowed to a halt before continuing on their way. The traffic was a result of something called '*morbid curiosity*.'

"Based on my research, morbid curiosity is the intense desire humans have to learn more about disturbing topics like death, violence, and tragedy. This form of curiosity lives in the shadows of our minds, waiting to be fed. It fuels the urge to look at car accidents when we drive by. It's why my shows have done so well. Our brains use morbid curiosity as an instinct for survival, forcing us to analyze a morbid situation until we consider it safe or dangerous. It's why it's nearly impossible to look away, no matter how hard we try. Our brains are already programmed to react in that way. All Mendax needs to do is take advantage of that evolutionary programming."

Samuel leans forward, placing his elbows on his knees. He covers his wicked smile, his excitement fueling the whisper now working through me.

I continue. "You said you want to go all in on one show, a show that will capture the eyes of millions and keep them. We capture their eyes by creating a show for the morbidly curious. We put Death on center-stage. We give the crowd violence. We give them tragedy but deliver it with a positive spin and an opportunity for the crowd to engage.

"So, with that in mind, here is the idea. Imagine a game show, each episode featuring three contestants. The contestants will be cast based on a simple criteria–they're already suicidal, and now they're willing to commit suicide on *live television*. Each of the three contestants will share their story, every detail that led to them wanting to take their own life. We will broadcast all three of the contestants' emotional stories edited in mini-segments, and viewers will vote for whichever contestant they feel the most sorry for. Once the voting window closes, the contestant with the most votes will win the cash prize, which is made up of every donation tied to a vote… in the condition that they commit suicide on stage at the end of the episode."

Samuel's eyes narrow. Even in the darkness of his gaze, I see his giddiness. I feel his excitement brewing, and it manifests between us. "How will the winning contestant receive the cash prize if they commit suicide at the end of the episode?" he asks, crossing one leg over the other.

"The winning contestant won't receive the money," I reply casually. "Their estate will."

Samuel's eyebrows rise. *Right on cue.*

I lean forward. "The winning contestant commits suicide at the end of the episode, and the next day, the cash prize is hand-delivered to their estate or to a charity by a Mendax representative we'll call a '*Prize Handler.*' What we're doing is capitalizing on the crowd's morbid curiosity. What the crowd thinks we're doing is giving suicidal people the chance to die for a greater good–their families, their friends, charities–anybody the winner chooses to donate the cash prize to."

Samuel stands, locks his hands behind his back, and lifts his chin. His face is straight, difficult to read. "Greater good," he whispers, repeating part of what I had said. "We call the show '*Greater Good.*'"

"The show for the morbidly curious," I add with a smirk.

The room goes still. Chills cover my arms when I realize I'm standing. *When did I stand?* I just spoke with more passion than I ever could have fathomed, and while I want to take credit for this idea, I can't. It belongs to the whisper, the spirit that slipped this idea into my mind.

"How did you come up with this?" Samuel asks, his skeptical tone suggesting he knows the answer.

I fold my lips between my teeth, putting careful consideration into my answer. Samuel might think I'm crazy if I tell him the idea came to me through a whisper–a faint voice growing within the confines of my mind. If I'm not careful with this gift I've been given, I could find myself locked up in a psych ward before I make it up on stage. A devious grin crosses Samuel's face, and I suddenly become aware that Samuel knows. *Has he heard the whisper, too?*

"I think airing a show like Greater Good is how we can win back the crowd," I conclude. "My only concern is how a show this morbid can be on live television. Getting people to literally off themselves on stage? It sounds nearly impossible."

Samuel laughs under his breath. "If you haven't learned this yet, the media runs the world. And Mendax *is* the media. If you can put together a test pilot episode as early as next week, I will get the approvals of every individual who can get Greater Good on television."

He offers me his hand, and I shake it before I even decide to. I no longer feel his frozen grip. I hardly feel the chill at all, and I'm led to believe it's because whatever lives in Samuel now also lives in me.

It takes me an hour to get home from work, but the adrenaline makes the drive feel like the blink of an eye. I can't stop thinking about the look in Samuel's eyes when I won him over with my pitch. I won his approval and didn't realize how much I wanted that approval until I finally had it. But now I want more. More appreciation, more praise.

My lobby doors slide open, and the dark pavement turns to freshly glossed wood floors under my heels. Even with the loud clicks of my heels, the few men scattered around the lobby somehow resist looking my way. It's not until the elevator doors close that I find silence for the first time today. My adrenaline has settled since meeting with Samuel, giving me a second to call upon the whisper. I close my eyes, filling my chest with air. "Come on, tell me something," I exhale. "He loved the idea. Now what?"

The elevator is silent, no sounds but the machinery pulling the box of air to the 18th floor. No whisper. *How the hell am I supposed to build on an idea that wasn't even mine in the first place?*

I push my apartment door open. It's dusk now, the city lights popping in contrast to a sky that has yet to turn black. The second I toss my purse onto the kitchen counter, I realize the lights are on. I never leave the lights on. A ruffling sound comes from my bedroom down the hall. *Someone is in my apartment.*

I lower my stance, creeping around the kitchen island. With my eyes glued to the light cast across the hallway, I fish through a drawer for the longest knife I can find. My grip tightens on the knife when I see the shadow of a man stretch across the hallway wall. The shadow glides across the wall, but only for a split second before disappearing. He's in my room.

I take a long, silent step, my back pressed against the wall leading to the hallway. I hold the knife, attempting to calm my nerves with shallow breaths. I peek around the corner, and the shadow glides across the wall again.

I could call the police, I could cry for help, I could run. But, then I'd miss the chance to see Death at work. Warmth flows under my skin at the thought of Death introducing itself to me or this man in a matter of moments. I hear him sifting through my dresser. *Now is my chance.*

I reach the bedroom door and point my knife toward the man's naked back. My eyes trace down his sculpted torso, each ripple and contour telling a story of discipline and hard work. His muscles bulge and flex with even the slightest movements as he rummages through my lingerie.

With the subtle clearing of my throat, he turns back to me, his hazel eyes meeting mine. He looks down at the knife in my hand as I raise it toward him. "You like what you see?" I ask with a cheeky grin.

The corner of Ryan's lips curls up. "You just love pulling that knife on me, don't you?"

I shrug. "I'm in show business. I take my role-playing seriously."

Ryan laughs. I don't think he realizes his muscles tighten when he laughs. *I like when Ryan laughs.*

"Why am I always the bad guy in these scenarios?" He takes a few steps closer. I gently slip the knife's tip through one of his belt loops. "Nora, don't–"

I twist the knife, ripping through the belt loop.

"Now you owe me a new pair of pants."

"I sign your paychecks. Haven't I bought you enough pants?"

I toss the knife across the room seconds before Ryan's lips meet mine. His chest forces my back into the wall, and I'm overwhelmed by his desire. I let him explore every inch of my mouth, though he already knows it so well.

"How long has it been?" I exhale as his lips work their way down my neck.

"Almost a week," he whispers against my collarbone. *Almost a week too long.*

Yes, Ryan is my assistant. No, I probably shouldn't be sleeping with him. In my defense, we set boundaries: No talks of a future between us, no dating. Just rough, passionate, stress-relieving, sensational sex.

Ryan's hand trails down my chest, orchestrating the warmth that settles between my legs. A high-pitched squeak escapes me when he lifts me with ease. "You made me wait a damn week," I whine, wrapping his obliques with my legs.

He smirks. "You could've asked me to come over."

"Asking you to come over defeats the purpose of the spare key." *Not to mention, it's hard to feel desired when I have to ask you to come over.*

Our kisses deepen as I feel him grow hard between my thighs. I tighten my legs around him so he knows that *I know* how bad he wants me. He throws me onto the bed. His hair hangs along the sides of his head as he shakes his pants off. I raise my skirt and slip my panties off while I admire his physique. A light shines from above, casting shadows over his cheekbones, pecs, and the V-lines just below his abdomen. His lips dance along my calf, then my thigh, all the way up to my neck. My body responds by making it easier to receive half the length of him, then *full* after he lifts one of my legs onto his shoulder, then lays over me.

I let him have his way with me the way I always do. With every thrust, I'm forced deeper into my own bed. Eventually, I hear him say the word that always seems to get me off–*my name.*

"Nora," Ryan moans as I straddle him. "Fuck, Nora!"

I pleasure him the way I want to be pleasured. I praise him the way I want to be praised. Since I can't take, I will continue to give so that I can get. Though I yearn for his praise, I will never force it from him because true praise is never forced. True praise is from those who choose to praise. Ryan is one of the few who chooses to praise me. *If only his praise were enough.*

The two of us lay still in bed, our eyes fixated on the ceiling. The lights are off now, a cool breeze sweeping in from the open door separating us from my balcony. The warmth of our bodies radiates as we lie between the sheets.

It's the most bittersweet part of these nights we share. It's bitter for me because it leads to the potential crossing of the boundaries we set and it's sweet for Ryan because he likes to push those boundaries. I should call it a night. I want to call it a night. But I've noticed that the more nights I spend with Ryan, the more I open myself up to the light he carries.

"How'd it go with Samuel today?" Ryan asks, his voice raspy.

I gently graze my thumb over his chest hair. "It went well. He loved the show I pitched and wants to shoot the pilot episode next week."

"Next week?! He really must have loved it if he's pushing to have it air that soon."

I smile, the side of my cheek nestled against his shoulder. "He still needs to get some approvals, but as long as I line everything up on my end, we're all set."

"When do I get to hear the idea?"

My smile fades. With Ryan taking everything at work personally, there is no way he would support Greater Good. I suppose there is also a chance this show doesn't get the approvals it needs, so I might as well wait to tell him. "You get to see it live with everyone else." I prop myself up on my elbow, tracing his lips with my finger. "No spoilers."

Ryan rolls his eyes. "Spoken like a true entertainer, Nora Fictus." He dips his head to mine, stealing a soft kiss. "Or should I say, 'Nora *Bennett*.'"

I playfully slap his chest as he laughs. He knows I hate when he assumes that we would end up married, or worse… that I would change my name. I've always made it apparent that my last name will never change, regardless of who I marry and when. "Don't even joke!" I groan.

Ryan continues laughing as he pulls me over him. "You say you don't like it, but you can't deny that it has a nice ring to it."

"Let's get this straight once again." I grab his jaw, forcing him to look me in the eyes. "It's Nora Fictus, forever and always," I whisper before nipping his bottom lip.

The conversation dissolves as we embrace each other again. With every second that passes, I force myself to hate the idea of taking Ryan's last name. I've always believed I'm meant for more than marrying a man or having kids. It would mean giving up on myself–giving up on my name, which is what the world will soon remember me by.

◆ ◆ ◆

"Left!" I shout to the two crew members hoisting up the L.E.D. screen. They move it right. "Are you deaf or are you dumb?! I said left!" The crew members look at each other, mumble something, then move the screen left. I hold down the button on my earpiece and ask, "Can you confirm the audience prompter on stage-left is visible from the back row?"

"Confirmed," Ryan's voice responds through the earpiece.

"Let's turn the prompters on!" I shout over the bustling crew members.

People rush around the set, making final arrangements. The L.E.D. screens are mounted high on both sides of center-stage. My heart drops when they flash white a couple times before going black again.

"That's not on!" I hiss, and within seconds, technicians are climbing ladders to fix the screens.

There's only one place in this world I want to be and it's on set for my T.V. shows, the cameras and lights creating the illusion of reality. The air is thick with the hum of energy and activity as my crew members move with passion and determination–a determination to tell a story–to put on a show. And it's my duty to make sure that the viewer is captivated by every second of it.

Being on set is like being in on a secret. I'm one of the few who see what happens behind the scenes. I see the imperfections and flaws that viewers are blind to. There's an alluring sense of power that comes with knowing what others don't know. It puts me above the masses. It separates me from the crowd.

As I stand in the middle of the set, I take in my surroundings. Center-stage is made up of wide-paneled wood flooring, elevated a mere two steps. It's high enough to earn the audience's respect but low enough to make them feel like whoever is on stage is their equal. Three orange chairs are evenly spaced on the stage, each facing the stadium seats rising behind me. The back wall behind the stage is one massive screen, reading, "GREATER GOOD," in vibrant, retro-style orange letters.

It's happening.

In only three days, Samuel and I were able to turn one of Mendax's studios into a captivating, 70s-inspired set. Samuel insisted that I focus on running the show from behind the scenes, so I reluctantly spent late nights skipping through T.V.

host audition tapes until I found Dorothy Meadows, the most beautiful and charismatic woman I have ever laid eyes on.

It was the middle of the night and I was just about ready to give up on finding the perfect host. The weight of giving my creation a face that isn't mine was unbearable from the start. Within a few seconds of each tape, I knew these nobodies weren't fit for Greater Good. I remember skipping through one after another, thinking, *Too skinny, too fat, too tall, too short, tits too big, tits too small.* Casting is often harder than it looks, and the professionals aren't kidding when they say, "*When you know, you know.*"

The moment Dorothy's doe-eyed face filled the screen, I knew she was the one. With Greater Good's set being the paradox it is, the more innocent and attractive our host is, the more morbid the show can be. On top of Dorothy's alluring charisma, the cherry on top is that Dorothy is a woman of color, and women of color are in. Every showrunner and casting agent in the industry knows it.

While I spent the nights looking for Dorothy, I spent the days looking for the perfect contestants, Manhattan's saddest and most hopeless individuals with nothing to live for. That was the easy part, considering nowadays they flood the city streets like vermin.

"Dim the main lights," I command into my earpiece. The studio lights dim, lending more power to the three lights shining over each chair on the main stage. "Wonderful!" I spread my arms, inhaling the sweet aroma of a perfect set prepped for a perfect show. The surrounding crew members share my enthusiasm through smiles and looks of admiration.

I make my way up the staircase that separates the audience section down the middle. Ryan opens the door at the top of the stairs. Without moving his head, he flicks his eyes toward Samuel.

Eyes, chin, shoulders, I remind myself as my posture follows.

I smile, prepared to introduce Samuel to my impending masterpiece. I turn into the dark room to see him admiring the 22 screens stacked and aligned orderly along the back wall of the control room. The orange and blue lights emitted from the various camera feeds decorate his face as he stands over the three crew members toggling between control panels.

"I didn't think you would be able to pull it off in three days," he says, his black eyes meeting mine.

I didn't think it was possible either, but I still can't relax until this pilot episode is a wrap. "You underestimate me." I step up to his side, the two of us observing the camera feeds. From views of center-stage to views of the stadium seating where the crowd will soon sit, the control room is where we can see every angle of the show and studio. "Thoughts?"

"Why the 70s theme?" Samuel asks.

"The 70s aesthetic is one of boldness and vibrancy. It's respectfully invasive. It's a captivating eyesore…"

"It's a paradox," Samuel interrupts.

I can't help but blush. *He gets it.*

"Exactly. The warmer the set, the colder the display can be without us scaring our audience away."

Samuel nods. "And the contestants?"

I turn my back to the screens and face the window overlooking the entire television set. It's the perfect view, positioned over the back row of the audience. The backs of the seats cascade down to the cameras propped up in front of the stage. It's one thing to witness a spectacle through a screen; it's another to witness it live.

I feel Samuel's chilling presence glide to my side. I keep my voice hushed, whispering, "I've cast three pretty well-spoken homeless people. One is a junkie, one is a handicapped veteran, and one is a blind beggar. I was able to get each of them to share their stories with Dorothy in front of the camera, and my team worked all night on creating the edits, interview-style."

"And the winning contestant? Do they know what they need to do to win the cash prize?"

I chew on my bottom lip. "Sort of."

"Sort of?"

"To the contestants' knowledge, the pills the winner will overdose on are 'fake.'"

Samuel pinches his eyebrows together. "But they aren't fake."

"They aren't fake. They're real, and the winner *will* overdose." I take a deep breath, then exhale. "But Mendax is in the clear. I worked with the legal team on the contract agreement. We flooded the contestants with paperwork and enough legal jargon to get the contestants to sign without understanding–"

"That they are literally signing their lives away."

I nod, eyes locked on center-stage, where Dorothy is testing her microphone. "That's right. The contestants saw the cash amount they can win, and they didn't read much after that. They just got right to signing."

Samuel laughs under his breath. "You were made for this business, Nora."

My heart nearly skips a beat. *Oh, Samuel. You just wait and see...*

GREATER GOOD

TEST PILOT EPISODE

3 SPOTLIGHTS ILLUMINATE 3 PLUSH ORANGE CHAIRS ON STAGE. AN UNSETTLING PRESENCE MAKES ITSELF KNOWN AS THE L.E.D. SCREEN BEHIND THE CHAIRS READS, 'GREATER GOOD,' IN BRIGHT ORANGE LETTERS.

DOROTHY (voice-over): On tonight's episode of Greater Good, three contestants will share their stories—the hardships they have faced and what has led them to their breaking points. We've hand-selected these contestants based on their generosity and willingness to take their own lives on live television tonight, giving the winner's cash prize to their family estate or charity of their choice!

70S MUSIC PLAYS, AND THE AUDIENCE APPLAUDS AS DOROTHY MEADOWS [HOST] ENTERS FROM STAGE-LEFT. DOROTHY MEADOWS RAISES HER HANDS, WAVING ENTHUSIASTICALLY TO THE LIVE STUDIO AUDIENCE. HER HAIR HAS BEEN SLICKED BACK, FALLING STRAIGHT DOWN THE ARCH OF HER BACK. THE DIAMOND CHOKER ON HER NECK GLISTENS, HER BLACK DRESS TRACING HER CURVES AS SHEER SLEEVES FLOW GRACEFULLY TOWARD THE DIAMONDS ON HER WRISTS.

DOROTHY (now standing center-stage): Good evening, and welcome to Greater Good, the show for the morbidly curious!

AUDIENCE APPLAUSE EVENTUALLY FADES.

DOROTHY: Death is in the building! And it's prepared to take the life of tonight's winner in exchange for bettering the lives of others. Each contestant you will meet tonight has already decided where their cash prize will be donated, and it's up to *you* to determine how much that prize will be and which contestant will receive it. Now, let's meet our first contestant!

DOROTHY MEADOWS TURNS BACK TO THE L.E.D. SCREEN. ON THE SCREEN, A VIDEO PLAYS OF CONTESTANT #1 IN AN INTIMATE, DIMLY-LIT STUDIO ROOM.

DOROTHY (on-screen): Can you start by telling us a bit about yourself?

CONTESTANT #1: Sure. Name's Alex. I'm 29. I've been struggling with a… drug addiction… for a while now. It's been rough.

DOROTHY: If it's not too much to ask, can you tell us about the first time you started using?

CONTESTANT #1: High school. I had a friend or two who smoked pot. I decided to try it, and I remember thinking it was the best thing ever. I was relaxed. I was happy. I didn't wanna feel no different.

DOROTHY: When did you realize drugs had become a problem?

CONTESTANT #1: It wasn't a problem at first. I did it every now and then, but I don't know. It got dull. It took using more for me to feel the high. That's when me and my buddies at the time—we started messin' around with the more serious shit—acid, coke, eventually heroin. It all spiraled after that. The past 10 years of my life feel like one jumbled-up blurry dream. I lost my job, my place, my girl. I lost everything just to keep from coming down from that high.

DOROTHY: Tragic. What was your lowest point?

CONTESTANT #1: I hit rock bottom a few years ago. I was homeless, sleeping on the streets. I was beggin' for cash just to get the next fix. Worst part was that I knew before I even got the cash that it was going toward more drugs. I really needed help.

DOROTHY: How did you find help?

TEARS WELL IN CONTESTANT #1'S EYES.

DOROTHY: *Did* you find help?

CONTESTANT #1 SHAKES HIS HEAD, THEN PRESSES HIS FIST TO HIS LIPS.

CONTESTANT #1: I'm stuck in this never-ending cycle. I can't get out.

DOROTHY: And that's why you're here today?

CONTESTANT #1 NODS.

DOROTHY: What do you plan to do with the winnings?

CONTESTANT #1: Give it to addicts to help them break the cycle. I ain't ever gonna break mine.

L.E.D. SCREEN FADES TO BLACK. CONTESTANT #1 ENTERS STAGE-LEFT TO AN APPLAUSE FROM THE LIVE STUDIO AUDIENCE. CONTESTANT #1 TAKES A SEAT IN THE ORANGE CHAIR ON STAGE-LEFT. THE SCREEN BEHIND CONTESTANT #1 DISPLAYS A PICTURE OF CONTESTANT #1.

DOROTHY (standing behind CONTESTANT #1 with hand on his back): We feel for you, Alex. We commend you for your bravery and willingness to take your own life for a good greater than yourself.

DOROTHY (to camera): And now, let's meet our

second contestant.

A VIDEO PLAYS ON THE L.E.D. SCREEN, REVEALING CONTESTANT #2.

DOROTHY: Can you start by telling us a bit about yourself?

CONTESTANT #2: My name is Jonathan Bailey. I served for three tours, wounded in combat.

DOROTHY: Wow. Thank you for your service, Jonathan. Can you tell us about your experience in combat?

CONTESTANT #2: It was intense. Wish I could say it was rewarding. I saw things that no human should ever have to see. I was injured during combat and had to be medically discharged. I didn't come home the same.

DOROTHY: What has life been like for you since your discharge?

CONTESTANT #2: I struggled to adjust to civilian life. I couldn't work a job while dealing with my P.T.S.D. I can't shake the noise, the cries of my brothers-in-arms who lost their lives right next to me. I remember the looks on innocent people's faces just seconds before their lives were taken. Everywhere I go, I hear the noise. Everywhere I go, I see their faces. Kids and their mothers and fathers screaming and crying. I watched the world burn and fed the fire at the same time.

DOROTHY: What would you like for people to know about veterans struggling with P.T.S.D.?

CONTESTANT #2: We're trying to get better. We're not all drug addicts, lazy bums, or damaged people. We have witnessed hell on Earth. We're dealing with physical and mental health issues. We need your help, not your judgment.

DOROTHY: I understand. What do you plan to do with your winnings?

CONTESTANT #2: I want it donated to my twin daughters, Maggie and May.

CONTESTANT #2 LOOKS DIRECTLY AT THE CAMERA AND REMOVES HIS HAT.

CONTESTANT #2: Maggie? May? Wherever y'all are. Your daddy risked his life for his country. And now, he's gonna take his life for you.

SCREEN FADES TO BLACK. CONTESTANT #2 LIMPS ONTO STAGE-LEFT TO AN APPLAUSE FROM THE LIVE STUDIO AUDIENCE. CONTESTANT #2 TAKES A SEAT IN THE ORANGE CHAIR ON CENTER-STAGE. THE SCREEN BEHIND CONTESTANT #2 DISPLAYS A PICTURE OF

CONTESTANT #2.

DOROTHY (standing behind CONTESTANT #2 with hand on his back): We feel for you, Jonathan. We commend you for your bravery and willingness to take your own life for a good greater than yourself. I'm sure Maggie and May admire you for your willingness to sacrifice your life for them.

DOROTHY (to camera): And now, let's meet our third and final contestant.

VIDEO PLAYS ON L.E.D. SCREEN, REVEALING CONTESTANT #3.

DOROTHY: Can you start by telling us a bit about yourself?

CONTESTANT #3: M-my name is Maria.

DOROTHY: What's your story, Maria?

CONTESTANT #3: I was a high school teacher up until a few years ago. I'm blind. I… I live on the streets and have been for a while now. I lost everything—my sight, my home.

DOROTHY: Have you always been blind?

CONTESTANT #3: I lost my sight to a rare disease. I get worse by the day and can't afford to pay for any sort of treatment. I have no family to take me in, no friends. It's not like it matters. I'm sick, and being this kind of sick? It's just going to kill me eventually. It'll be the death of me.

DOROTHY: I'm sorry to hear that, Maria. What's it been like living on the streets as a blind woman?

CONTESTANT #3 (voice cracking): I've… I've just about experienced it all. The worst of the world is on the streets, you know. I've been…

CONTESTANT #3 PAUSES, ATTEMPTING TO CONTAIN HER EMOTIONS. SHE PLACES HER SHAKING HAND OVER HER LIPS BEFORE CONTINUING.

CONTESTANT #3: I've been robbed, beaten, r-...

CONTESTANT #3 LOWERS HER HEAD IN SILENCE.

CONTESTANT #3 (with head lowered): I've been sexually abused out there. Time and time again. I can't see the men myself, but I know that some of these men aren't even homeless like me. Sometimes, I hear them walking by, and they whisper to each other, fighting over who should get to have their way with me while I sit there on the sidewalk. They fight over me like it matters, but it doesn't. They all end up having their way with me anyway. I have no strength to fight back. Simply living has become a form of suffering.

DOROTHY: There are such terrible, terrible people out there.

CONTESTANT #3: They make me feel like I'd rather be dead.

DOROTHY: Is that why you're here today?

CONTESTANT #3 (nodding): I'm here because I can't go back out there.

DOROTHY: Then the two of us can only hope that our viewers pick you as our first-ever winner. If you win, what do you plan to do with your winnings?

CONTESTANT #3: I want it donated to my former students' college funds. I believe in them, and I only want the best for them. It's always been about the kids. It's not their fault I ended up where I am today.

SCREEN FADES TO BLACK. CONTESTANT #3 ENTERS STAGE-LEFT, ESCORTED BY A CREW MEMBER TO AN APPLAUSE FROM THE LIVE STUDIO AUDIENCE. CONTESTANT #3 SITS IN THE ORANGE CHAIR ON STAGE-RIGHT. THE SCREEN BEHIND CONTESTANT #3 DIS-

PLAYS A PICTURE OF CONTESTANT #3.

A CLOSE-UP SHOT SHOWS DOROTHY MEADOWS STANDING
IN FRONT OF THE THREE SEATED CONTESTANTS. A
DIRECT SPOTLIGHT HIGHLIGHTS HER STRIKING FEA-
TURES.

DOROTHY (directly to camera): Well, folks. You
have heard the testimonies of tonight's contestants. They have entrusted you with their
vulnerability, and in turn, they offer themselves as martyrs for a greater good. So,
now it's up to our live studio audience. Attached to your seats, you will find a clicker
with buttons labeled *1*, *2*, and *3*. This is your
chance to select which contestant will earn
tonight's cash prize!

CAMERA FEED CUTS TO CLOSE-UP SHOTS OF EACH
CONTESTANT FROM THE COMFORT OF THEIR CHAIRS ON
STAGE. THE L.E.D. SCREEN FLASHES "$3,000,000"
IN NEON ORANGE TEXT.

DOROTHY (voice-over heard over videos of each
contestant): Will it be Alex who wishes to donate his winnings to the support groups fighting addiction? Will it be Jonathan who wishes
to donate his winnings to his beloved daughters? Or will it be Maria who wishes to donate
her winnings to her former students' college
funds?

CAMERA FEED CUTS TO PANNING VIEW OF AUDIENCE
MEMBERS OBSERVING THE BUTTONS ON THEIR CLICK-

ERS. SOME ARE RELUCTANT WHILE OTHERS MAKE UP
THEIR MINDS ON THE SPOT.

CAMERA FEED CUTS TO THE LARGE L.E.D. SCREEN
DISPLAY BEHIND THE CONTESTANTS. AN ORANGE BAR
PRESENTS ITSELF ON THE BOTTOM LEFT OF EACH
CONTESTANT'S PICTURE. THE NUMBER "0" IS DIS-
PLAYED ABOVE THE BAR IN YELLOW.

DOROTHY (directly to camera): Once all the
votes are in, the orange bar will rise, showing us who received the most votes, making
them the first-ever winner of Greater Good!

MOMENTARY SILENCE AS THE CAMERA CONTINUES PAN-
NING OVER AUDIENCE MEMBERS. THEY DISCUSS WITH
ONE ANOTHER AND MAKE THEIR FINAL DECISIONS.

DOROTHY (directly to camera): I've just received word that the votes are in. We have our
winner!

THE AUDIENCE APPLAUDS.

DOROTHY: After careful consideration, you have
made your votes. You've graciously chosen who
will take their life to better someone else's,
and collectively, you have made the world a
better place. So, the winner… of tonight's episode… is…

THE STUDIO IS SILENT AS THE ORANGE BARS RISE

AND THE YELLOW NUMBERS CLIMB HIGHER, COUNTING THE VOTES. THE BARS EVENTUALLY COME TO A HALT, CONTESTANT #3'S BEING THE HIGHEST.

DOROTHY (clapping): Maria!

THE AUDIENCE AND THE OTHER CONTESTANTS APPLAUD AS A CREW MEMBER ASSISTS CONTESTANT #3 IN STANDING AT CENTER-STAGE.

DOROTHY (to CONTESTANT #3): Maria, how do you feel being Greater Good's first-ever winner?

CONTESTANT #3'S HANDS SHAKE NERVOUSLY AS HER CLOUDED EYES STARE INTO THE DISTANCE.

CONTESTANT #3 (reluctantly): I… I don't know what to say… or feel… I'm starting to think maybe this is—

DOROTHY (with great enthusiasm): It's okay to be so excited that you're lost for words! Is there anything you'd like to say to your former students who will receive a generous three million dollars thanks to you?

CONTESTANT #3: I… hope that they live very happy lives. And… I hope they find their place in this world.

DOROTHY (patting CONTESTANT #3 on back): Well

said, Maria. Mendax thanks you for giving up your life to better the lives of others.

A CREW MEMBER ENTERS FROM STAGE-LEFT WITH A GOLDEN TRAY. PLACED IN THE CENTER OF THE GOLDEN TRAY ARE 3 BLACK PILLS AND A GLASS OF WATER. THE CREW MEMBER STANDS PATIENTLY BETWEEN DOROTHY MEADOWS AND CONTESTANT #3.

DOROTHY (directly to camera): Now, Maria will commit this act out of sheer bravery, courage, and generosity.

DOROTHY (turning to CONTESTANT #3): Maria, please extend your open palms to receive your three pills and water glass.

CONTESTANT #3 EXTENDS HER OPEN PALMS. THE CREW MEMBER PLACES THE 3 BLACK PILLS IN THE CENTER OF HER QUIVERING LEFT PALM, THEN THE GLASS IN HER RIGHT. THE CREW MEMBER EXITS STAGE-LEFT.

DOROTHY (respectfully): When you're ready, Maria.

CONTESTANT #3 LIFTS THE PILLS TO HER LIPS, POURS THEM INTO THE BACK OF HER THROAT, THEN CHASES THE PILLS WITH WATER.

CONTESTANT #3'S FOGGY EYES HOVER OVER THE AUDIENCE. THEY SUDDENLY PAUSE, FIXATING ON SOMETHING DIRECTLY IN FRONT OF HER. ONCE BLIND,

SHE NOW SEEMS TO SEE SOMETHING NOBODY ELSE CAN SEE. THE WATER GLASS LEAVES HER HAND, SHATTERING AGAINST THE FLOOR BETWEEN HER FEET AS SHE STRUGGLES TO BREATHE. HER BODY STIFFENS SECONDS BEFORE SHE COLLAPSES ONTO THE BROKEN GLASS. SHE CONVULSES ON THE FLOOR, THE SHARDS OF GLASS SLICING HER ARMS AND BACK OPEN AS SHE FOAMS AT THE MOUTH.

DOROTHY MEADOWS'S JAW DROPS AT THE SIGHT OF CONTESTANT #3. SHE STUTTER-STEPS BACK, COVERING HER MOUTH. CONTESTANT #3'S BODY FINALLY STILLS. SHE NOW LIES MOTIONLESS ON THE FLOOR. SHE REMAINS NOTHING BUT A CORPSE, HER EYES STILL FIXATED ON THE AUDIENCE BEFORE HER. FOAM TRICKLES DOWN HER RIGHT CHEEK, FORMING A PUDDLE ON THE FLOOR. DOROTHY MEADOWS GLANCES AT THE CAMERA, SPEECHLESS.

AFTER SEVERAL SILENT BEATS, THE CROWD SUDDENLY ERUPTS IN APPLAUSE. THEY CHEER THE LOUDEST THEY HAVE CHEERED TONIGHT. THEY STAND TO THEIR FEET—A STANDING OVATION—THEIR CLAPS SHAKING THE STUDIO.

DOROTHY (shaking off her confusion): Th-thank you for… thank you for tuning in to Greater Good. And we'll… we'll see you next week!

70S MUSIC STARTS TO PLAY AS THE AUDIENCE CONTINUES TO APPLAUD. THE CAMERA PANS OVER THE APPLAUDING CROWD.

THE SCREEN FADES TO BLACK.

"That's a wrap," one of the crew members exhales, removing his headset.

"Fucking hell," the crew member next to him mutters. "That was intense."

The control room is silent, the wall of screens still capturing the different angles of the studio and set. Movement is picked up on every screen but one, the screen showing a close-up of Contestant #3's face. It brings me joy, realizing I can't take my eyes off the screen, no matter how hard I try. It means the audience most likely had the same reaction.

I feel a comforting hand on my shoulder. "That was art," Samuel whispers smoothly.

Without turning from the screens, I ask, "Do you think the audience actually liked it?"

"You heard them clapping," Samuel replies.

I let out an exhale. "Because the prompters told them to."

I remove my earpiece and catch Ryan staring at me from the back corner of the room. A line shows between his eyebrows, his jaw clenched. For some reason, the light he once carried has no effect on me. He also doesn't need to voice that none of this sits right with him because it's written on his sheer look of disapproval. Maybe one day he'll understand that this is just show business.

KNOCK! KNOCK! KNOCK!

Ryan opens the door to a crew member struggling to catch her breath. "Nora, we've been trying to reach you."

"What is it?" I ask.

"The audience prompters," she blurts out between heavy breaths. "Remember when we ran the test earlier, and they cut out? Well, they cut out again mid-show, and we never got them to work again. The audience's response… was completely organic. The standing ovation was their natural, real response."

My eyes widen as I drop my earpiece to the floor. It echoes in the silence.

And it's in the silence that I hear the whisper again, this

time clear as day.

It makes its way into the shadows of my mind.
It fills the hole in my heart.
It introduces me to the inevitability of its existence.
It calls upon me to do its bidding… and I willingly accept.
The whisper belongs to *Death*.
And it's in the silence that I finally hear…
Death is here.

GREATER GOOD
THE SHOW FOR THE MORBIDLY CURIOUS

Wednesday, July 17th, 2019

Introducing GREATER GOOD, the show for the morbidly curious! Countless game shows on television focus on entertainment and prizes. But what if there was a game show that not only entertains but also positively impacts society?

Greater Good is a new live television game show that features three contestants who come from different walks of life but have one thing in common—they no longer want to live. Sad, right?! From struggling with mental illness to fighting off physical disabilities, each contestant has a heart-wrenching story to tell. The stories are raw and emotional, portraying the injustices some humans face daily. Lucky for them, Mendax Productions found a way to create beauty out of pain.

At the end of each episode, viewers are invited to vote for the contestant whose story resonated with them the most. But this isn't just any ordinary vote. Attached to each vote is an amount of money that the voter pays. The more money a voter donates, the stronger their vote. This means that viewers have the power to not only vote for their favorite contestant but also make a difference.

The contestant with the most votes at the end of the episode wins. But, unlike other game shows, the prize money isn't awarded to the winner. Instead, the money is donated to the winner's estate or charity of their choice under *one* condition. The winner's estate or charity will receive the cash prize under the condition that the winner takes their own life on live television.

That's right, the contestants who no longer wish to live not only found a way out but are heading out, granting the wishes of their loved ones and those in need! Talk about a life of suffering paid off and paid in full!

Download the MENDAX+ app to vote from home and tune in to MENDAX, Channel 6, on Monday nights at 8/7c to witness all-time lows become all-time highs.

NEW GAME SHOW REINVENTS TELEVISION

Last night, Mendax Productions unveiled its first official episode of Greater Good, and America has been buzzing since the closing credits. The show's unique concept of combining entertainment with philanthropy was a breath of fresh air, and it quickly gained attention from viewers and industry professionals alike.

The episode's impact was immediate; if you tuned in, you'd know exactly why. #GreaterGoodShow is trending across social media platforms as influencers post their positive reactions and boast about their voter donations.

The show's positive impact on society and its contestants has caught the eyes of advertisers and sponsors, who are beginning to align their brands with the socially responsible program.

The success of the first episode paved the way for Greater Good to become a hit show with its record-breaking viewership and long waitlist of fans willing to line up at the studio to witness the spectacle live.

Greater Good's success proves that entertainment and philanthropy go hand in hand, and it set a new standard for what viewers expect from their T.V. shows.

MEDIAFLOW

mendax

Liked by **1,247,331 others**

mendax It's the phrase we can't seem to get enough of!

Greater Good host, Dorothy Meadows, opens up with the game show's chilling tagline, "Death is in the building!" The phrase has officially left the Mendax building in the form of apparel, accessories, posters, and even bumper stickers!

With some of the country's largest store chains picking up Mendax's latest Greater Good merchandise, you can spot Death anywhere any time! #GreaterGoodShow

MEDIAFLOW

 mendax · · ·

NOW CASTING

Are you someone who's been feeling down more often than not? Feeling like you're far past the breaking point? Is suicide officially no longer a matter of "if" but "when?" Then **GREATER GOOD** is the show for you.

Liked by **604,991 others**

mendax Greater Good, the new game show America is raving about, is opening its doors to cast contestants for future episodes. This is the chance of a lifetime for the hopeless to end their lives in order to better the lives of others.

To apply, simply visit the Mendax website or download the app and fill out the online application form. You'll be asked to provide basic information about yourself and your story, as well as a short video explaining why you should be selected as a contestant.

With the show making an impact on the television industry, here's your chance to take part. Give your life meaning by taking it for a good greater than yourself.

Apply today for the game show that is officially to die for!
#GreaterGoodShow

CHAPTER FIVE

JOSEPH

I have a criminal living in my guest house. It's funny–no, it's fucked up. You know what? It's both. Over the past two weeks, time has ticked slower than usual and it's for good reason. I've been knee-deep in this case with Nicky, the man who held me at gunpoint, who I now know is *also* the man I've been letting live in my guest house. God, the universe, or whatever controls fate has to be messing with me.

It's never been easy working with criminals. Most of the time, they're illiterate, uneducated assholes. And still, I would prefer to work with them over stubborn Nicky Williams.

"Sooner or later, you're gonna have to tell me more about you," I whisper to Nicky from across the kitchen table. "There's got to be more to your story than robbing a gas station for 'extra cash.'"

I cock my head back, look down the hall to the front door, then check my watch to see it's almost noon. Stevie is at school and Ava is running errands, so I only have a couple more hours to pry any information I can out of my tenant and now-client.

Nicky's stubborn face holds no emotion, his thick arms crossed over his wide chest. We've met a handful of times in my kitchen since the first time we met in county jail, and still, I know nothing about the guy besides the one fact he shared with me: *The gun he robbed the gas station with was fake.* Seeing the fake gun in the Property and Evidence Unit last week lent me some peace of mind, but the more information I can get from Nicky, the stronger our case.

"It was a fake gun," Nicky mutters. "What more do you want me to tell you?"

I roll my eyes. "You got to tell me more about you! I'm on your damn side, you know. You're treating me like a judge. I'm not going to use anything against you. I'm trying to help your case."

Nicky folds his lips between his teeth, looking out the kitchen window toward his house. I tap my fingertips over my notepad, which has been blank for two weeks now.

"I ain't a criminal," he mutters.

"You sure about that? Because I'm not sure, and I can't be sure until you tell me who you are." I can't help but feel stupid for not knowing more about the guy living in my own backyard.

Nicky sighs, reaches into his pocket, and pulls out a tightly wound wad of cash. My mouth salivates the moment he slaps it on the table top. He gestures to the cash with his eyes. "For you to stop asking questions."

My chest fills with air. Only a small portion of what's on the table will fix the front door. Half would settle my debt with Ava. The full amount could be used to fix up the house. "I don't want your filthy money." *I need your filthy money.*

Nicky's eyes narrow. "You take my filthy money once a month to pay your mortgage. Why is it any different now?"

"Good point. It's different because I know it's filthy now."

"So, clean it."

I stab the cash with my pen and push it toward Nicky. "Is this what you stole from the gas station?"

"If you knew how much I ended up stealing from the gas

station, my case would be a joke," Nicky laughs, itching his goatee. "Didn't even make a hundred bucks from that trip."

He frowns when he sees me take my first note: *Stole less than a hundred dollars.*

"See? This is progress." I smile up at him. "Now I have two facts. The gun was fake and you didn't steal more than a hundred bucks." Nicky bites his lip, fighting the fact that I just cracked him a bit. "Look, Nicky. We don't have to be friends. Frankly, I don't want to be your friend. Not because you're a criminal, but because having you around wouldn't make me the best example for my kid."

Nicky's face softens. I tap the cash with my pen as I continue. "I'm gonna be real honest with you. I need this money, so I'm going to accept it *and more* for representing you. Now, I know you don't want to go to prison, so you're going to tell me who you are and why you robbed a gas station in broad daylight. Help me help you. Talk to me."

Nicky's face flattens as he stands and makes his way to the back door. Upon swinging it open, he turns back to me. "I ain't gonna tell you why. I'll show you why."

He continues out the door and it takes me a second to realize that that's my cue to follow him. I drop my pen on the notepad and run after him. The bottoms of his brand-new sneakers echo against the cracked concrete steps leading down to my backyard. I haven't landscaped since, well… I've never landscaped, so weeds are growing through the cracks in the asphalt, the grass forming bumps between mounds of dirt taking up most of the yard. I'm only a few steps behind Nicky when he knocks on the guest house door.

He lives alone. Why is he knocking on…?

The door slowly opens, a narrow sliver of light illuminating the eyes behind it. Nicky whispers something through the crack between the wall and door. The almond-shaped eyes flick to me as I now stand a few feet behind Nicky. Her brows are arched, framing her innocent eyes. She looks back up at Nicky, nods, then opens the door.

My jaw drops at the sight of the curve in her abdomen bulging from under her shirt. She is timid, awaiting my response. Judging from the fear in her expression, she assumes I'll be upset that Nicky's been hiding her in a house that's already too small for one person alone.

I try to hide that I'm upset, not because Nicky is a criminal hiding out in my guest house and not because the deal is supposed to be one tenant, not two. I'm upset because now I have more than Stevie and Ava to provide for. Even though it's the last thing I should do, I inherently make these two my responsibility. *Dammit, Joseph.*

"When is she due?" I mutter, my eyes fixated on her stomach.

"Few months," Nicky replies.

The woman places a gentle palm over her belly. "Are you gonna kick us out?"

Nicky flashes me a look. For once, it's not one of the stubborn looks he's been dishing me the past few weeks. It's a look of genuine concern. He knows I have the right to kick them out. I should kick them out and find a new tenant who actually follows my rules.

I chew on my bottom lip. "I'm not gonna kick you out." My answer is what they want to hear, or at least, I think it is. It doesn't faze them. It's as if they think I'm lying to their faces. I tap Nicky's shoulder with the back of my hand. "I'm not gonna kick you out, *but* I need you to pay me for this entire case upfront. I also need you to talk to me, or this…" I wiggle my finger between the two of them and the house. "Or this isn't going to work."

To my surprise, Nicky cracks what might actually be a smile. I know very little about the guy besides the fact that he's so large he could crush me with his pinky. I also know he doesn't smile often, so I'll count whatever he just did with his face as progress.

"I'll talk," Nicky says.

"He'll talk!" I shout, throwing my hands up in the air. "Thank the heavens." My eyes meet the woman, a pretty smile decorating her face. "You got a name?"

"Tanya."

"Well, Tanya, don't you worry. I'm gonna clear Nicky's name, pay my nanny, then renovate my house and yours." I grab a small portion of Nicky's massive shoulder. "Is that alright with you?"

Nicky lets out a laugh. "Yeah."

"Yeah, what?!"

"Yeah, that's alright with me."

"You should talk more. You got a nice voice." I give his shoulder a squeeze. "Now, let's get to work before my kid gets home from school."

When Nicky and I sit at the kitchen table again, the mood has shifted. Nicky's posture is relaxed, his lower body and back overpowering his seat. "Before we get into it, you got any beer?" he asks.

"Wish I could tell you I do," I say to my notepad as I scribble down another note: *Nicky drinks during the day.*

He scrunches his face. "What're you writing?! I haven't said nothin' yet."

"It's not a big deal."

"Big enough for you to write it down."

I lift the notepad and shrug. "I just wrote that you drink during the day, that's all."

"You judging me?!" he scoffs, slapping his palms on the table that nearly cracks down the middle.

I exhale, suppressing the wave of frustration consuming my head. "I'm not judging you, but the judge will. As your lawyer, I'm taking notes on you. The notes are going to include your everyday habits, your motives, anything I think will help your case. Now, will you let me do my damn job?"

Nicky closes his eyes and nods. "Sorry," he sighs. "When I'm asked questions, it's usually because people are trying to prove I'm guilty."

"Ah, you see, that's where I'm different." We lock eyes, and I lightly pound my fist against the table with each word that follows. "I'm proving you're innocent."

Nicky nods. "Alright, alright. Ask a question."

I itch the scruff on my chin with my pen. "I noticed you have a lengthy criminal record made up of smaller crimes. This is your first robbery?"

Nicky glares at me. "The fuck you wanna know that for?" he barks.

"For Pete's sake," I exhale, burying my face in my palms.

I'm about to give up when I hear a snort. I spread my fingers to see Nicky chuckling. "I'm just playin' with you!" he playfully slaps my arm. "It's my first robbery. I did time a while ago for dealing, and I've had my hand slapped a few times," he adds casually. "Hey, what do you say we both ask questions? That way, this doesn't feel like some kind of interrogation."

I'm starting to wish I didn't need his money as badly as I do.

"Go for it," I mutter as I continue taking notes.

"Why don't you have beer in your house?"

"I'm sober."

"How long have you been sober?"

In one swift motion, I pull out the gold coin from my pocket and flick it across the table. Nicky is caught by surprise but still snatches it out of mid-air. He studies the coin, its gold finish reflecting the afternoon sunlight. The coin's surface is smooth and polished, the number "*5*" slightly raised over the phrase, "*One Day at a Time.*"

"Damn," he whispers, dragging his thumb over the intricate design. "Five years sober, huh?"

"And counting."

"You got a drinking problem?" He gently slides the coin to the center of the table.

"I don't have a drinking problem." I place my palm over the coin, and pull it into my grasp. "I have a problem because of drinking."

Nicky watches me weave the coin effortlessly between my fingers. In the blink of an eye, I clap my hands together, then reveal my empty palms. I wiggle my fingers, my eyes wide open.

Nicky squints. "How did you just–"

"Magic."

I reach across the table and pull the coin out from behind his ear. Nicky sticks out his bottom lip and gives me a nod of approval. Little magic tricks are the best way to steer people away from asking about parts of my life I keep to myself. Call it an illusion or a distraction; I can pull someone's attention in any direction I want.

I slip the coin back into my pocket and pick up my pen. "How old are you?"

"26. Who gave you that scar on your face?"

My pen pauses on the paper. I look up, taken by surprise. It's the first time anyone has ever asked about my scar. It could also be the first time I tell anybody why the scar is there. I point my pen at him. "Your questions are more personal than my questions."

Nicky shrugs. "A question is a question."

"I'll remember that." I cross my arms. "I got into a car accident a while back."

It's the truth, just not all of it.

"When?"

"You asked your question. It's my turn."

Nicky smirks. "Fair."

"What do you do for work?"

"I'm an entrepreneur," he lies through his teeth.

"Is that right?" My eyes trail down to the wad of cash on the table between us, the amount suggesting that the only things Nicky sells are sold illegally. "How long have you been an 'entrepreneur' for?"

"My whole life," Nicky answers. He lowers his chin, his body language suggesting that we change the subject.

Before I can ask a follow-up question, the sound of fumbling keys comes from the front door. My head jerks left. "They're here!" I whisper.

The chair screeches under Nicky as he stands to his feet. "Back door?"

"Back door," I snap, gathering my notes. "Take the cash."

"It's yours," Nicky states, tossing the fistful of cash at my chest.

I slip the cash into my pocket. Despite his size, Nicky slips out undetected as Ava shoves the front door open on her third try. "You would think that after all this time, it'd get easier to open!" Ava jokes to Stevie as she rolls him into the entryway. "Joseph?"

I slip my notepad into a nearby drawer. "There they are!" I greet softly, taking a couple of grocery bags from Ava's hands.

"You're home early," Stevie says skeptically. "I hope that's a good thing."

Ava glances at me as we organize the groceries on the kitchen counter. It's usually not good when I'm home during the day. Being home means I have no reason to be at the courthouse or meeting with clients.

I flash her a reassuring smile when I feel the cash in my pocket. "Today was actually a good day, so we're celebrating tonight!"

Stevie's eyes twinkle with excitement. "Can we order pizza?"

"You got it," I reply with a wink.

Stevie claps his hands. "Sweet! Can Ava stay for dinner?"

I raise a brow at Ava. "I don't know, *can* she?"

"I…" Ava blushes. "Yes. I would love to stay for dinner."

When the pizza arrives, we gather around the kitchen table. The air is filled with the comforting aroma of melting cheese as smooth jazz echoes throughout the room. For the first time in a while, I find peace in the present. Since I slipped Nicky's cash into my pocket, hope has manifested within me. A few weeks ago, I promised Stevie that I would fix everything, and at this rate, I'll be able to follow through on my promise.

"How was school today?" I ask between bites. "I haven't heard any mention of Mikey, the dragon, for a couple weeks now."

Stevie holds up a finger as he takes a bite bigger than he can swallow. I feel like I've been a shitty father for not asking this question sooner, but I couldn't help it. My nose has been buried in my laptop, going through Nicky's criminal record and trying to form a case. I suppose a part of me assumed that no news about Stevie's bully is good news.

"School is school." Stevie shrugs upon swallowing his food. "Everyone has been talking about some new T.V. show called, 'Greater Good.'"

"Greater Good? What's it about?" Ava asks.

"I don't really know," he says, lifting a string of cheese from the slice on his plate. "All I know is that it's not for kids. But, some kids' parents let them watch, and those kids get all the attention now."

I let out a laugh. I remember being in middle school and the struggle that came from doing whatever it took to fit in. All these kids navigating the world, seeking attention from peers they will most likely never see again when they get older. Not much has changed since I was Stevie's age. Back then, which-ever kids had the most laid-back parents were destined to be the coolest.

Stevie looks toward the unplugged T.V. on the opposite side of the living room. "Can we watch it? Just one episode."

I bite my lip, considering it for a moment. Letting Stevie

watch the show these kids are raving about may get him the attention he needs right now. I imagine Mikey and all the other kids swarming around Stevie, praising him for something as silly as watching a show they're too young to watch. I imagine them asking to come over, wanting to spend time with Stevie. I imagine them seeing how amazing of a kid Stevie is, and I realize all I've ever wanted is for Stevie to be appreciated by others the way I appreciate him.

My gaze hovers over to the television on its stand, the plug hanging just off the back of the screen. I suddenly remember the headlines, seeing our names and photos light up the screen.

The flashing images…

The crash…

The headlines…

The hurt…

The pain…

The whisper.

"No." The word leaves my lips the second I escape my trance. "No T.V."

Stevie's face hardens as he and Ava stare at me from across the table. "Why not?" he asks, his voice sharp. "Why do you even have one if it's always unplugged?"

He doesn't remember why, and I thank God he doesn't.

"Don't you raise your voice at me," I state. "No means no."

Stevie purses his lips, then shouts, "This is the one chance I have to actually fit in for once!"

"You don't need the damn T.V. to fit in, Stevie. You're an amazing kid who–"

"Who what?!" he snaps, his voice cracking. "Who can't walk, Dad! I can't do anything any of the other kids do! Nobody talks to me! Nobody looks at me! I can't even stand up for myself when kids push me around!" He wipes at the tears under his eyes. "All I'm good for is being in front of a screen and you won't even let me do *that*!"

"You don't understand…"

"No!" Stevie pushes his plate across the table. "You don't understand and you never will."

Stevie's words are knives through the heart, pinning me to my chair. He turns and rolls down the hall before disappearing into the bedroom. I'm left wondering whether it's difficult for me to breathe or if I've simply lost the will to breathe.

WAM!

I wince at the sound of the door slamming behind him. Jazz continues to play as I'm left treading water in a river of Stevie's pain and my own. It kills me to see him hurt, and it kills me to know that I'm the reason for it all. It's moments like these that serve as a reminder that I don't deserve to live because…

Ava places her hand on mine, pulling me from my thoughts. A wave of warmth flutters up my arm, a feeling that has become so foreign. Before I can pull away, she lifts my hand from the table. We stand, and as she slowly guides me to the middle of the living room, I feel as though she's guiding me from the river of pain to a distant shore, now in reach. I'm looking down at the top of her head as she gently wraps her arms around me. Almost habitually, my arms make their way around her shoulders until my hands rest firmly on the small of her back. We sway side to side, the music still playing in the background. We sway left, then right, then left. Her heart beats sympathy from her chest into mine, and though I feel I shouldn't, I allow myself to receive it anyway.

"I have a lot of respect for you," she says softly.

"You have respect… for me?"

She nods. "I don't know what you've been through, but I know it's more than I could ever imagine. I see it in the way you are with Stevie. You want the world for that boy, which is why you hide it from him."

We continue to sway left, then right, then left.

"Was I overreacting about not letting him watch that show?" I ask.

"I'm sure you have a good reason for keeping that T.V. unplugged. So, I don't see a point in going against what you believe is best for him."

I gently dip my forehead to Ava's, and we take each other in with our eyes closed. We sway, becoming one with the moment. I open my eyes to the depth of her gaze and feel her presence pulling at me like gravity. I need more of this woman. I need it now.

Our lips are nearly touching when she releases me. "I should probably get going," she blurts out. "I'm sorry, it's not my place. This isn't... I shouldn't feel like this."

"Ava..."

She turns, grabs her purse, and makes her way to the front door.

"Ava!" I shout.

I'm only a few steps behind as she yanks the front door once. *It doesn't budge.*

I'm a step away when she yanks a second time. *It doesn't budge.*

She pulls a third, and I catch the edge of the door before she fully opens it. She reluctantly looks up at me as I lift a handful of hundred dollar bills, her share of the money Nicky paid me today.

"This belongs to you," I say.

Ava's face softens. With both of my hands, I force it into her palms. "Drive safe," I whisper. "And we'll see you tomorrow."

"Same time, tomorrow morning," she says the way she always does.

I smirk. "Same time, tomorrow morning."

Ava smiles, then takes a few silent steps out the door. With one palm against the plaid wallpaper and the other on the door, I let out a sigh of relief. Though Ava and I came close to kissing, I wasn't ready. Not yet.

After cleaning the kitchen table, I pull the needle from the record and do something I never thought I would do. I plug in the T.V., then sink into the couch and kick my feet up onto the coffee table. The screen cuts to a broadcast.

There's an eerie shift in the room, and chills trickle down my spine as I begin flipping through channels. I haven't watched in years, and now here I am, indirectly peer-pressured by my 11-year-old son's friends. I stop flipping through channels the second I see the news headline: 'GREATER GOOD' WINNER RECAP.

I set the remote on the cushion and watch, remembering Stevie talking about how kids at his school are too young to watch this show. The anchorman's smile is painted superficially above his chiseled jawline. His hair is perfectly quaffed to the side, his eyes connecting with me as he talks about the show. "As Greater Good's viewership continues to soar since the premiere of its first episode, we're left recapping the highlight of the night! Let's take a look at the winner of this week's episode as he becomes a martyr for a good greater than himself."

The screen cuts to what looks like a 70s-style game show. The set is made up of a slightly elevated wooden stage with three orange chairs evenly spaced, facing the live studio audience. Two women sit in each of the chairs bordering an empty middle chair, as a man stands in the middle of the stage next to the host.

I mute the T.V. and look right, feeling an unsettling presence make itself known on the couch beside me. *I'm not watching alone.*

I unmute the T.V. and crank up the volume to rid myself of the eerie presence. On the screen, the host takes a few steps away from the man standing on stage. A crew member dressed in black steps onto the stage as a white noose lowers itself from the ceiling.

What... the... hell?

The man allows the crew member to tighten the noose around his neck. As the crew member steps out of the frame, the platform under the man slowly rises. The audience stands, fighting to get a view of what happens next. With everything in me, I try to look away, but I can't. Chills seep into my bones as the presence next to me becomes undeniable. Its invisible weight cloaks me, reminding me that not only is it here, but it hasn't left since we first met. The presence belongs to Death, and Death is in my living room.

The crowd cheers as the rising platform slows to a halt, the man now elevated at least 10 feet above the stage. *This man is going to hang himself on live fucking television.* With all my strength, I reach for the remote but can't look away. I feel for it with my hand, grazing its edge with my fingertip.

Death's grip on me gets tighter, its weight keeping me from standing. Death forces me to watch, its whisper becoming more audible by the second. I fear that what I hear will lead to the end of me. So, I try to drown out Death's voice with my own. "It's not my time," I whisper, grinding my teeth. "Not... yet..."

"Dad?" Stevie's voice gives me the strength to lunge for the remote and turn off the T.V. I look right to see Stevie half-awake in his chair. "I can't sleep without a story."

I subtly wipe the sweat from my forehead, forcing a smile. "You got it, buddy. I'll be right there."

Stevie smiles, then turns out of the room. The second he's out of sight, I make my way across the room and unplug the T.V. In the silence and safety of my own home, I'm forced to consider the worst.

What I just watched is real.

And I fear this is only the beginning.

CHAPTER SIX

NORA

It's taken me decades to get famous and only a few weeks to learn that fame is a dangerous game. It's a double-edged sword with the power to shape and corrupt the mind. It also promises success and glimmering cups overflowing with adoration. Even with the knowledge of its intoxicating and alluring nature, I lift the cup to my lips. But I don't just sip. I gulp like I've thirsted since before I can remember.

"Celebrating *before* your performance?" Samuel teases from the seat across from me.

My finger traces the rim of my martini glass. "In just two weeks, Mendax is back on top with record numbers. I think that calls for drinks no matter the time of day."

Samuel's black eyes study me. "I just want to make sure you're sharp tonight. These talk show hosts can be your best friends or worst enemies." He leans forward, resting his elbows on his knees. His pinstriped suit is perfectly tailored to his body, hardly wrinkling as he adjusts his posture. "You've impressed me a lot in the time I've known you. Young, ambitious, a career woman above all."

I hide my smile behind my martini glass. When you're

dealing with men of Samuel's stature, it's crucial to never let them know what you're thinking, not for a second. Men can tailor their responses to emotion, but I thrive on emotion. Being aware of this is one of the strongest cards I've been dealt. Therefore, I keep it closest to my chest.

Samuel leans back, the flickering city lights casting shadows across his face as our car makes its way to Times Square. "Do you plan to have kids someday?"

His question makes me cringe. "Never," I answer, suppressing the thought of having children with all my strength.

"Why not?"

I set my empty glass in one of the cupholders lining the side of the Escalade. "Bringing a child into this broken world just seems cruel and selfish. Plus, this planet already has far too many people living on it." I glance out the window at the passing traffic, then back at Samuel. "Why do you ask?"

Samuel lightly pulls at the loose skin on his neck, inspiring me to take my skincare regimen more seriously. I find it sad to see a successful man like Samuel losing his battle against age. I can't help but wonder if he's always been this ugly. Maybe he was so ugly growing up, he had to make up for it with wealth and power. If that's the case, he must have been one ugly kid. I respect him for that because I can't imagine what I would do without my looks.

"I ask the people I work closely with if they want kids someday because if they say yes, it suggests they aren't willing to put their calling first." He leans forward, and I smell prescription pills on his breath, the same pills probably keeping him alive. "I'll let you in on a secret, Nora. When you reach a certain level of power in this world, you receive a calling. It's crucial you understand that once you accept your calling, there is no turning back. The world's favor will bend in *your* favor. You'll be forced to put yourself above all else, including a family. Believe me when I say that you've been called. You are what Mendax needs right now."

No matter how hard I try, I can't force back my smile. Since I was a child, I seeked recognition. At one point, I would have sacrificed my tongue for a taste of fame, and now here I am, finally being called to it. From hearing Death's whisper for the first time to agreeing to do its bidding after Greater Good's pilot episode, I've grown fond of my calling. It's nice to know Samuel is aware of it and can guide me every step of the way.

"And it's funny that you mentioned the status of the world. You're right."

"I'm right about it being broken?" I ask.

"You're right about there being too many people in it," Samuel says casually as the Escalade comes to a stop. "If we can't get rid of them, we'll control them. And if we can't control them, we'll distract them with our narrative… all for our own gain."

That's the second time he's mentioned a "narrative" since we first met. Before I can ask him to elaborate, the door to my right opens, and I'm consumed by a wave of cheers and shouts. Flashing lights from cameras and phones blind me as I'm guided from the car onto a narrow walkway. Both sides of the walkway are bordered by hands reaching toward me. Two security guards pave the way, serving as barriers to keep me from being swarmed by my admirers.

It's not news that Greater Good has grown exponentially popular over the past few weeks. I've been featured in magazines and recognized on the street a handful of times, but this is a level of fame I never thought I could achieve. Not too long ago, the secretaries wouldn't bat an eye when I entered the room. I was a nobody, and now they don't just know my name. They shout my name…

Nora.

Nora!

NORA!

Fame makes the air easier to breathe. The colors around me become more vibrant. Now, this I can get used to. This isn't just the praise I've been looking for. It's the praise I deserve. I look back for Samuel, but he's nowhere to be found. Back on the street, a security guard shuts the car door. Within seconds, it leaves with Samuel still inside. A heavy hand forces me toward the entrance of the T.V. studio. It takes craning my neck back just to see the neon letters illuminating the sign I walk under…

THE NIGHT SHOW WITH DANNY DAVIS
Featuring Nora Fictus, the Creator of Greater Good!

The second I'm inside the building, the crowd is muted by the heavy doors shutting behind me. Crew members and producers overlap one another, making final arrangements before the talk show airs. Screens are sporadically displayed, each portraying a still image of Danny Davis, the show's host.

Danny Davis has one of the hottest talk shows on television. The man is charisma in human form, with cheekbones sharper than glass and a hairline so thick it might as well be drawn above his wrinkleless forehead. Not to mention, he knows how to work the crowd and dominate a T.V. set.

I don't watch talk shows often, at least not until Samuel told me it would benefit the network if I spoke on its behalf. Since the moment he told me this had to happen, I've studied talk show hosts and their guests alike. I studied their mannerisms and how they used or didn't use their hands when speaking. I took note of how often they made the audience want to laugh or cry. I adopted their charisma while preparing myself for the host's scrutiny.

Despite my underlying jealousy toward Dorothy for hosting Greater Good, I even asked for her help to prepare for tonight. She was more than willing to give me advice, which I found surprising. We're supposed to be competitors, given we're both charismatic and beautiful women seeking the limelight in the same industry. Women like us are a dime a dozen, so I found it best to keep to myself up until this point.

Lucky for me, The Night Show with Danny Davis is a production put on by a network Mendax owns. These people–Danny included–are on my side, and if they aren't, Samuel will pour his wrath upon them. *"The media runs the world. And Mendax is the media,"* I remember Samuel saying. With Mendax's name at my disposal and Death's divine intervention working in my favor, I'm invincible.

A showrunner gestures for me to follow him down a narrow hall. I obey, taking note of the celebrity portraits lining the walls as we walk. From famous movie stars to billionaire entrepreneurs, Danny Davis has interviewed them all, making or breaking them on the same stage I'll soon take for my own.

The showrunner faces me and lifts his arm toward an open door. "Right this way, Ms. Fictus."

Before entering the room, I smirk at the man the same way I've rehearsed repeatedly in front of my bathroom mirror. I struggle to keep from marveling at the golden plaque on the door that reads: *NORA FICTUS.*

"Welcome to your own personal green room. The bar lining the left wall is for you, so help yourself. Feel free to relax on any of the couches in the meantime. The hair-and-makeup team will be here shortly," the showrunner says. He points to the digital clock mounted on the wall behind me. "I'll be back at 6:50p.m. to escort you to the stage."

I subtly flip my hair while turning back to him–something Dorothy suggested I do. I remember her reason being spoken as though she's a master in seduction. *"When you flip your hair, you're bringing attention to your neck, which is one of the most stimulating parts of the body,"* Dorothy explained. *"Men subconsciously know this, and while most aren't aware of it, drawing their attention to your neck will increase their attraction toward you."*

With my eyes locked on the crew member, I smile, exuding an abundance of charm as I say, "Thank you," my voice a river of silk.

He blushes, then trips over his words. "Th-thank you. I mean... I'm... y-you're welcome." He shakes his head in dismay while shutting the door.

I laugh under my breath while tucking a few strands of hair behind my ear. My confidence has grown in accordance with our viewership. I'm learning to leverage my looks, finding it easier to connect with others and mold them into whatever I want them to be, which is beneath me.

My eyes pan around the green room. I instinctively compare it to the one we use to prepare our contestants for Greater Good. This room is smaller, but it does the job. It's still spacious, adorned with muted color tones. The soothing ambiance is complemented by the dimmed lights shining upon plush couches and armchairs.

My phone vibrates, and I look down to see a text from Ryan.

Ryan: Can we talk later? Things have been a bit off since the first episode aired

I shake my head, forcing myself to focus on tonight's show. Without reading too much into Ryan's text, I set my phone face-down on the coffee table. I sit at the couch's edge, placing my hands on my knees. With my eyes closed, I lower my chin and lend my ear to the whisper that grows louder by the day. As if on my command, the eerie stillness hangs heavy in the room. It enters the room, not in physical form, but as an omnipresent spirit. Death's spectral fingers, long and twisted, comfort me with their embrace. With each breath, I draw upon Death's essence, tapping into its profound wisdom. While I don't know why Death has chosen me to do its bidding, I continue to seek clarity.

"The fame, the success," I whisper, eyes still closed. "Why me? Why Greater Good?"

The weight of Death lingers, warming my neck and shoulders. I find its embrace comforting, yet I can't help but want answers. *Why has Death chosen me to do its bidding*? While I don't hear words, Death makes it clear in thought that soon I'll know why I've been called. For now, I must stay the course.

Eyes, chin, shoulders. My posture follows the demand of my thoughts. I feel the comfort of Death's hand on my shoulder, instilling an unfathomable amount of confidence within, a sort of confidence that's not of this world. It transcends my mortal existence, pulling me closer to the vast unknown that lies beyond.

"Hi, Nora!" a woman's voice greets from the doorway. "We're here to prep you for the show."

"I've been expecting you," I reply smoothly, standing to my feet.

The hair-and-makeup team funnel in one after another, each referring to my physical appearance as if I'm not in the room.

"My goodness, her skin is so pale. When is the last time she's seen the sun?" one says.

The other pinches at my blouse. "Keep her away from dark tones. What about orange? It'll make the green in her eyes pop."

They sit me in the back corner of the room where a vanity station has been built into the wall. At first, I'm insulted by their remarks, but when they lift a pastel-orange dress behind me, and my eyes somehow become even greener through my reflection, everything they have said is justified. They're professionals, experts in their craft. A sense of comfort washes over me, and I feel Death's calming presence, reassuring me that I'm on the right path.

While I've never been considered "talent" before, sitting in this chair feels right. It's as if this is where I'm destined to be. Maybe not in the past, maybe not in the future, but here and now. I'm being used for something greater than myself, and I welcome my fate with open arms.

The mirror before me stretches tall and wide, portraying a version of me that grows more alluring by the second. My bright green eyes are sharpened by a thick layer of mascara that complements my freshly-plucked brows. I purse my lips as a thin layer of highlighter is applied to the tops of my cheekbones.

"Your complexion could cut glass, Nora," one of the team members whispers against my ear. I straighten my posture as a response, feeding on their admiration.

"Bullshit," I reply playfully, though he's right.

When I step out of the fitting room, everyone gawks in my direction. Their jaws hang low, eyes fixated on my face, then down the curve of my waist and to my heels. They clap, and it's not until I see myself in a hallway mirror that I realize what I'm capable of, which is *surprising myself.* I recognize the woman in the mirror, but she possesses something that surpasses human attraction. I know it, and soon, the world will know it, too.

Once I'm escorted from the green room to backstage, I feel a warm hand caress my shoulder. I turn to see the show host, Danny Davis. I can smell booze on his breath as he whispers, "Are you ready to go deep?"

Danny's skin is glowing, his freshly trimmed beard accentuating his defined jawline. His physical appearance suggests that he was made in a lab, sculpted by the gods. But I knew the second he opened his mouth that this man is a victim of his vices.

"I *live* in the deep," I whisper back, giving Danny just a bit of what he wants—some attention before it's all on me.

"We're live in five!" a voice shouts from nearby.

Danny turns away from me to do a small bump of cocaine. He wipes at his nose, then subtly offers me his coke vial with a smirk on his pretty face. "It helps bring the energy."

"I have more energy than you can handle," I say sadistically. "I don't need a drug. I *am* a drug."

He straightens his posture, shaking his shoulders loose. "I know you're a big shot behind the camera, Nora," he whispers to me while looking across the stage. "It's my job to make you a big shot in front of the camera."

His words make me wet.

Danny continues. "Just know, if you make me look good out there tonight, I'll see to it that you're adored both behind and in front of the camera." He lifts his chin, eyeing me with a cheeky grin. I'm so fixated on his cunning expression, it takes me a second to realize his hand is palming my ass. He gives it a light slap. "Break a leg," he adds before running out on stage.

Ryan is the only man I have ever let touch me the way Danny just did, yet I don't seem to mind Danny doing it without my permission after hearing what he just said.

I can't see the audience, but their applause shakes the building as Danny takes the stage. I close my eyes, and without having to ask this time, Death wraps me in its embrace, preparing me to do its bidding.

I need to sell the world on Greater Good.

And in order to sell the world on Greater Good, I'll need to sell myself.

THE NIGHT SHOW WITH DANNY DAVIS

FEATURING NORA FICTUS

NORA FICTUS WALKS OUT ON STAGE TO A ROARING APPLAUSE. HER ORANGE DRESS POPS AGAINST DANNY DAVIS'S BLACK SUIT AS THEY EMBRACE EACH OTHER. NORA FICTUS LIFTS HER HAND, HER CHARISMA RADIATING THROUGHOUT THE STUDIO. SHE SITS GRACEFULLY ON A DEEP-RED VELVET COUCH. DANNY DAVIS SITS IN THE VELVET CHAIR POSITIONED NEAR THE COUCH, THE TWO ANGLED TOWARD THE LIVE STUDIO AUDIENCE. DANNY DAVIS EXTENDS AN OPEN PALM TOWARD NORA FICTUS, URGING THE CROWD TO ADMIRE HER BEAUTY.

DANNY (with great enthusiasm): Look at her! Wow! Wow! Wow! Alright, let's settle down! What a pleasure it is for you to come see me, Nora. What a pleasure it is.

NORA (crossing one leg over the other): Oh, please, Danny. The pleasure is all mine.

THE CROWD'S APPLAUSE FADES AS DANNY DAVIS AND NORA FICTUS GET SETTLED IN THEIR SEATS.

DANNY: Okay, before we begin, I have to hear you say the infamous opening line. I know Dorothy usually says it, but I want to hear the creator of the show say it out loud and in the flesh! Will you say Greater Good's opening line for us?

NORA (lets out a laugh): Oh, I don't know…

DANNY (to crowd): Who wants to hear Nora say the line?!

THE CROWD ROARS IN SUPPORT OF NORA FICTUS.

NORA (to crowd): Okay, how about this? How about we all say it together?!

THE CROWD CHEERS, THEN GOES SILENT AS NORA FICTUS RAISES HER HAND, HOLDING UP THREE FIN-GERS.

NORA (to crowd): Ready?! Three… two… one…

EVERYONE: Death is in the building!

DANNY (clapping, then calming crowd): Alright, *now* we can dive into it! Nora, talk to us. What inspired you to create one of the most impactful T.V. shows of our generation?

NORA: You won't believe it, but it was actual-ly inspired by Death itself.

DANNY (narrowing eyes while adjusting his black tie): Please! Tell us more.

NORA: Well, I feel like Death is misunderstood. It's pushed away rather than embraced. It's neglected rather than celebrated. The idea behind Greater Good came to me as a sudden thought, like a voice in my head—a whisper. I knew in that moment the hurt people of this world needed a reward in return for all their hurt, which is why I created Greater Good. We're giving everything to those with nothing to live for.

DANNY DAVIS AND THE AUDIENCE CLAP FOR NORA FICTUS.

DANNY: Incredible. What a powerful message working through such a powerful woman. So, Greater Good is known for being the "show for the morbidly curious." Have you always considered yourself to be morbidly curious?

NORA: Oh, absolutely. I'll tell you all a little bit about myself. I grew up a mountain girl, always hunting game with Dad. We set out in the early mornings before the sun would rise. It was out in the woods where I learned all about the cycles of life and death and how to embrace the responsibility of participating in the dance between the two. Every hunt was a chance to witness the relentless pursuit of survival, where I saw Death at work. It was in those moments that my morbid curiosity began. Then, I got into the entertainment business, where my thriller shows took off because of how I portrayed death, and now here we are!

DANNY: Wow, given your beauty and charm, I never would have thought—

NORA (flirtatiously): That a woman like me could get her hands dirty? Oh, Danny, I could teach you a thing or two about getting your hands dirty.

DANNY: Getting dirty with you? You don't have to ask me twice!

CROWD BUZZES WITH EXCITEMENT AND AMUSEMENT, PICKING UP ON DANNY DAVIS AND NORA FICTUS'S FLIRTATIOUS BANTER.

DANNY: I'm sure the crowd is dying to know. Do you have a special someone behind the scenes?

NORA (blushing): You expect me to give myself away without making you work for it?!

DANNY (laughs, then winks at the crowd): I need to know if I stand a chance.

NORA: Nora Fictus is single, and she always will be. But you can flirt all you want. I find it cute. No, but on a serious note, people in my position put their calling first. I'm an entertainer, forever and always.

CROWD CLAPS FOR NORA FICTUS.

NORA (playfully): So, don't get any ideas, Danny!

DANNY: Man, I feel bad for the man who thinks he can pull you away from your calling. However, I will say that I'm still willing to take my chances.

NORA: I'm flattered, but no man will ever pull me away from Greater Good. My show is more than just any show. It's my destiny, my answer to the call. I would give my life for Greater Good.

CROWD ERUPTS, GIVING NORA FICTUS A STANDING OVATION.

I slam my front door behind me, feeling on top of the world. From the moment I stepped on stage with Danny tonight, I was perfect. I carried myself with poise, confidence, charm, and just the right amount of mystery. Whether prompted to or not, the audience's applause validated my beliefs in myself. They strengthened my worth. Tonight marks the beginning of a new dynasty that consists of me becoming more than just the mastermind behind the screen. I've officially proven that I'm worthy of becoming the face of my own show.

My phone vibrates, and I look down to see a text from Dorothy.

DOROTHY: Killed it! Proud of you xx

A bad taste lingers on my tongue when I read the text. It would be a lot easier to hate Dorothy if she wasn't so damn nice. I reluctantly thank her for her help.

I lift my chin, waiting for Ryan to praise me from my living room couch. He's in a black t-shirt that stretches over his muscular arms. The only lights in the room are the ones emitted from the T.V. screen. He slowly raises the remote, pausing the T.V. "Did you mean what you said?" he asks.

"During which part?"

I set my purse on the kitchen counter and slowly enter the living room. Ryan raises the remote again, rewinding tonight's episode to a specific moment. He presses *Play*, and I watch myself speak on Danny's show. "*Nora Fictus is single, and she always will be. But you can flirt all you want. I find it cute. No, but on a serious note, people in my position put their calling first. I'm an entertainer, and I always will be.*"

Ryan says something, but I don't hear him. I'm too fixated on the sight of myself on the screen. The world around me becomes null as I'm entranced by my own beauty. The way the camera captures my striking features–my aura. The way Danny and the crowd absorb each and every word I speak. I think I'm in love.

"Nora?" Ryan's voice pulls me from my trance. It suddenly dawns on me that I'm sitting beside him on the couch. "Did you hear what I said?"

No, because it doesn't fucking matter. I'm on T.V.

I lightly drag my nail down his chest. "Oh, I'm just playing the part," I assure him smoothly. "The crowd wants to see a hardworking woman win. I'm giving them what they want."

Ryan's thumb grazes my naked shoulder, his eyes on my lips. "Right. But what do *you* want?"

I want more...

More fame, more power.

It's only been a few weeks, and I'm already more famous and more powerful than I could have fathomed. And yet, I want more.

"I want you," I lie, merely saying what he wants to hear. The two of us stare at each other's lips. "We don't need to get too deep into what I said on the show tonight."

"It's not just what you said, Nora. It's the way you said it. It's the way you carry yourself now," Ryan says softly. "Ever since you started Greater Good, something has been different about you."

"Don't worry about me." I gently trace his full lips with my thumb, then whisper, "I said I want you... all of you."

I flip my hair, exposing my neck. Ryan caves on cue, his lips molding to mine, our tongues sweeping each other's lips and sounds escaping us without our control. His pecs tighten around me as he reaches around my back for my dress's zipper. Just halfway down, the zipper catches, but Ryan tears through it anyway. He can't wait, and neither can I.

I whine as he lifts me onto his lap, one leg on each side of his waist. He palms the small of my bare back while the other forces my lips to his. "I think I'm obsessed with you," he breathes into me.

I'm obsessed with me, too.

Warmth grows between our legs, and I draw a quick breath when I feel him growing hard against me. With my arms around his neck, I drag my body over his and whisper, "I want it."

"How do you want it?"

"From behind," I exhale between moans. "Bend me over the table."

In one swift motion, Ryan turns me over the coffee table. I spread my arms over the table, sending a glass shattering over the hardwood floor. I feel Ryan yank my thong down to my knees. A whimper escapes my lips when I feel the length of him slowly make its way inside me. I bite my lip to keep from shouting as he grips the curve of my waist with one hand and my hair with the other.

Ryan pulls my hair, lifting my chin, and that's when my eyes lock on the screen.

I taste Ryan. I smell Ryan. I hear Ryan. I feel Ryan.

But, I see myself…

on the T.V. screen.

And I come quicker than I ever thought I could.

"It's my birthday on Monday," Ryan says as he makes his way to the front door of my apartment. "My parents wanted to take me out, but I told them I might have other plans." He raises a brow. "Am I crazy for wanting to take you out to dinner for my own birthday?"

I laugh while opening the door. With the side of my head pressed against the door frame, I mutter, "No dates, remember? We set boundaries for a reason."

He rolls his eyes, stepping into the hall. "All I want for my birthday is to cross just one boundary. Nora, it's one date. Just dinner, you and me. I'll even make the reservation. All you have to do is show up."

"It's Monday night. You know we're filming the next

episode."

"You've already done so much for Mendax, and you've been working overtime. Roth will let you take one night off."

I bite my lip, then exhale, "One date. Only because it's your birthday. But you have to make the reservation, and we meet there."

Ryan throws celebratory fists in the air, then leans against the door frame. "I always knew you had a heart, Nora *Bennett*," he teases.

I struggle to hide my smile. "Don't push your luck."

CHAPTER SEVEN

JOSEPH

"Dad, I think it's great that you're getting laid tonight," Stevie says from the bedroom.

I cringe at my reflection, then cock my head back to face him. "What did you just say?"

Stevie's eyebrows draw apart. "Did I say something wrong?"

I set my comb down, then place my hand on the bathroom door frame. "You're 11. Do you know what 'getting laid' even means?"

"I heard a kid say it at school." Stevie adjusts his glasses, pondering my question. "It means going out on a date."

A laugh escapes me. "That's… that's exactly what it means." I face my reflection and yank the comb back through my gelled curls. "I'm gonna ask you one more time. Are you sure you're okay staying home alone tonight?"

"Yes, I'm sure I can spend a couple hours alone in our own house. Stop worrying so much."

Stevie twirls his brand-new wheelchair in a circle. It was the first purchase I made with the cash Nicky gave me. He's been in it for two days now, and I still haven't gotten used to it. The sleek design, the adjustable features, the way the light reflects off the polished steel and aluminum. A newfound confidence is now working through Stevie, and I couldn't be happier for him.

After dousing my neck and chest with cologne, I crouch in front of Stevie and place my hands on the chair's armrests. "You're my kid. I have every right to make sure you'll be okay without your old man."

"You do realize you're a kid, too." Stevie places his tiny hand on my shoulder. "You're just a kid with a kid."

My eyes lock on Stevie's for a moment. For most of his entire life, I've seen his mother in him. But, I hear myself in the way he talks. "*I'm a kid with a kid.* You're clever." I stand over him and wink. "Just like your dad."

KNOCK! KNOCK! KNOCK!

Stevie rolls his eyes, then turns down the hall. "Tell Ava I say hi and to enjoy getting laid!"

I shush Stevie while making my way to the front door. Before opening it, I send Nicky a text.

JOSEPH: You'll keep an eye on Stevie?
NICKY: Yeah, got you covered

Nicky and I have grown closer over the past few days. Sure, he's paying me a shit-ton of cash under the table for this case, but I'm starting to think we can eventually, maybe, possibly, by some chance, become friends. Besides Ava, I've never trusted anyone enough to keep an eye on my kid while I'm out. But Stevie is getting older and it's time for me to put myself out there, whether it be making friends or going on dates. I guess tonight I'm taking a chance on Nicky *and* in myself dating again after five years.

I take one last look at myself in the entryway mirror. My curls are slicked back behind my ears, my mustache neatly trimmed above my upper lip. My new gold chain peeks through my new dress shirt that's been tucked into my new slacks. I know what you're thinking… I bought a lot of new things and I bought them pretty quickly. Besides Stevie's new chair, I must say that I'm the most proud of my brand-new… front… door.

I gently caress its smooth round knob that's cool to the touch. On the first try, it glides open on silent whispers, showing no signs of restraint like the door before. Its sweeping arc speaks of hope, promise, and change, as I… as I… *Am I really this fixated on a door right now?*

"You fixed it!" Ava shouts, her eyes wide open. She throws her hands in the air. "You fixed the door!"

I'm caught by surprise as she leaps into my arms. A moment passes before I let myself receive her affection. As we stand locked in each other's arms, I accept the fact that her embrace serves as so much more than a mere embrace. It speaks volumes of validation that I'm doing something right after all these years of focusing on what I've done wrong. Sometimes, it's nice to be reminded that you're worth something, even if it's not a whole lot.

Ava pulls back, the two of us still locked in each other's arms like we were the other night in my living room. Her eyes flick between mine, the two of us content with nothing but each other's presence. It's in her gaze that I see the path forward. It's not a straight path or one with arrows showing me exactly where to go. It weaves among other paths, rising and falling. Regardless, it's an opportunity to move forward. Maybe, I'm able to give love a chance after all these years of closing myself off from it.

Ava's dress is a warm canvas of flowers complementing her tan complexion. Finding it hard to keep from staring, I slowly reach into my pocket and pull out a set of car keys. It takes her a second to realize what this means.

"You *didn't*…"

I smirk. "Listen, it's nothing nice, but it gets the job done."

She shakes her head, unable to suppress her joy. "I don't care about the car, Joseph." Her hand meets mine. "I care about the man driving it."

◆ ◆ ◆

I open the restaurant door for Ava and we're consumed by posh laughter and luxury. I'm a fish-out-of-water in a restaurant this nice, growing more uncomfortable with every step I take toward the hostess. The young girl scans me from head to toe before continuing her conversation with another hostess. I want to say something witty like I normally do, maybe try to impress Ava by making our presence known. But my wits have been replaced by an extreme case of first-date jitters. I clear my throat, and the hostesses look my way. "I made a reservation?"

"Name?" one of them scoffs.

"Joseph Verita."

The hostesses scroll through a list of names. After a silent beat, they both look up at me. "You're not on our list."

I narrow my eyes at them. "Not on the list?" It suddenly dawns on me that I forgot to make the reservation. *Joseph, you fucking moron. There you go again.*

I fold my lips between my teeth, twiddling my coin in my coat pocket with my sweaty fingertips. In a last-ditch effort to save my date with Ava, I catch a glimpse of the name, "Bennett," written near the top of the list. "Ah, that's right! I forgot we booked it under *your* last name," I lie to Ava, then glance back at the hostess. "Bennett. Party of two."

Ava nods, the hostesses now eyeing us skeptically. "Right this way," one finally mutters. She leads us, menus in hand. As Ava and I follow from closely behind, I become more comfortable with the fact that we don't belong here. Frankly, I don't want to belong in a place like this with these pretentious elites in their overpriced clothing and obnoxiously loud jewelry. I would much rather be eating pizza in my tiny kitchen with Ava and Stevie. And I'm pretty sure Ava would want the same.

"Enjoy," the hostess exhales, setting our menus on the table.

I pull Ava's chair out, then guide it underneath her as she sits. This is the first date I've been on since before Stevie was born. *Do guys even pull chairs out for girls anymore?*

"Such a gentleman," Ava whispers playfully as I sit across from her.

The candle between us highlights the gleam in her eye. I can finally appreciate the effort she put into her appearance for our date tonight. I'm just so used to seeing her in her everyday clothes. She smiles. "Bennett, huh?! How did you think of taking someone else's reservation so quick?"

I shrug and flash Ava a cheeky smirk. She laughs, and before we know it, we become one with the moment. Even amid a setting so foreign to us, we find peace in the now. The world around us dissolves as we share stories and reminisce about simpler times. We learn more about each other than I thought we would.

Ava wants to be a writer and I want to renovate the house.

Ava plans to start a charity one day and I plan to move to the West Coast.

"The West Coast?!" Ava shouts between sips of wine. "Like 'California' West Coast?"

I shrug. "New York isn't what it used to be. I can't raise Stevie in a place where crime is through the roof. Not to mention all these people out and about glorifying that new show." With my elbows now resting on the table, I whisper, "That show Stevie was talking about at dinner the other night... What's it called? Good or Great?"

"Greater Good." She shivers as the words leave her lips. "Have you seen it yet?"

Chills run down my spine as I recall watching the recap of the last episode. I remember the man standing center-stage as he was lifted with the noose around his neck, the crowd cheering as he's introduced to Death on live television. The memory is so vivid, I'm watching the scene play out before my very own eyes. Even in my mind, I can't get myself to look away.

"I've seen a bit of it," I mutter, my vision blurry until I shake my head. "How could they put a show like that on T.V.?"

"No traman nada bueno," Ava whispers under her breath.

I pinch my eyebrows together. "Was that–do you speak Spanish?!"

She places her hand over her mouth. "Sorry, it just came out!"

It dawns on me that Ava has been Stevie's nanny for a while now, and I hardly know anything about her. I've been so stuck in my own world, going through the motions while raising an early adolescent child. I find comfort in remembering that learning more about someone is what dating basically is. *Woah, I'm dating Ava.*

"Don't be sorry," I laugh. "What'd you say? Teach me."

"No traman nada bueno," Ava says slower this time. She looks both ways before whispering, "They are up to no good."

I look both ways, too. "Who is up to no good?"

She shrugs. "Whoever made the show. Back in the country my family came from, the news would create these wild distractions to keep people from seeing what was happening behind the scenes. There is a lot of money to be made off of people who can be easily manipulated."

"And people wonder why I keep the T.V. unplugged," I mutter.

Ava sighs. "It's just scary to see what terrible things the world has numbed itself to."

I nod. How the hell am I supposed to keep raising a kid in this broken world where people are killing themselves on live television while the crowd cheers like it's some kind of game. My stomach tightens at the thought of someone I know standing center-stage on Greater Good.

I run through the scenarios, my mind drawn to the morbid display. Ava slitting her wrists as the people cheer, Stevie blowing his brains out as the crowd roars, me getting burnt to a crisp in an electric chair before a standing ovation. My mind is pulled into a morbid abyss of sickening scenarios. No matter how hard I try, I can't get myself out. A cool breeze sweeps the back of my neck, and I feel the weight of Death lightly enveloping my shoulders with its wiry fingers.

"Are you okay?" I hear Ava's voice, but I can no longer see her. Death threatens to pull me from the table. *Death is here.*

"I'll be right back." I jump to my feet, the chair skidding out from under me.

I'm overwhelmed by my own anxiety as I make a beeline for the restroom. I avoid eye contact with each person I pass, wondering if they notice me trying to outpace Death. My heartbeat doubles along with the rhythm of my footsteps. I weave through restaurant-goers and waiters alike, my gaze glued to the restroom door. I throw the door open and shove it closed, pressing my back against it as if Death is going to barge in after me. There's nothing in the restroom but a stall, sink, urinal, and smooth jazz playing in the background. I attempt to calm myself down. *Get it together, Joseph.*

My breath steadies as I approach the mirror and take a long look at my reflection. When I hear the door swing open, I lower my head and rinse my hands under the sink. The sound of dress shoes clicking against the tile fills the room until the shoes stop at the urinal behind me.

ZZZIP!

The man unzips his pants and the two of us are now standing with our backs to each other. We both let out a loud sigh.

"Long day?" the man asks, staring at the wall.

I laugh under my breath. "Guess you could say that."

I half-glance at the man as he zips up his pants, flushes, and stands over the sink to my right. "Same. I've been seeing this girl who stood me up tonight," he exhales, fixing his hair in the reflection. "It's complicated–I mean, she's complicated."

"Life is complicated," I admit, splashing cold water on my face.

The guy smirks. "She's obsessed with her work."

"That's not such a bad thing."

"You don't know what she does for work." He pumps soap into his hands and begins lathering. "If you knew what she does, you would be worried how she's capable of obsessing over it."

"Do you see any kind of future with her?" My eyes meet his through the reflection. There's deep thought behind them.

"That's the thing," he sighs. "Since we met, I've fallen more in love with her by the day. But ever since she got pro-moted at work, she's changed. It's gotten to a point where not only do I not see a future with her, but I don't see a future without her either."

I know nothing about this poor guy, but I want to help him. I want to lend him some life-changing advice about how it's been tough for me to see my own future since I lost my wife. It's odd not being able to see or look forward to what could lie ahead. Being a father, I should be able to offer him some type of wisdom, but I'm used to giving advice to 11-year-old kids through bedtime stories, not men in public restrooms post-panic attack.

"If it's meant to be, it will be," I say hollowly as we dry our hands. It's the best I can come up with, given the circum-stances.

The man laughs. "On top of her standing me up, someone stole our reservation. That has to be a sign that it's not meant to be."

My eyes widen. *If this guy's last name is Bennett, I may owe him an apology for stealing his reservation.*

Before I can confess having committed my restau-rant-crime, he continues. "I told the restaurant to let the couple take our table. It's not like I need it. She isn't coming, so I'm just gonna head home."

I do my best to take his mind off the table topic. "This girl you're seeing… Why couldn't she make it out tonight?"

"She's working. I was hoping she would take one night off to celebrate my birthday with me," he says, fixating on his reflection. He turns to me and laughs. "Last we spoke, she was going to. I guess she decided otherwise."

"Well, Happy Birthday, kid. It could be worse. You could be 37 years old and on your first date in five years, like me."

He tilts his head. "Damn. This might sound rude, but I would've assumed a guy your age is married."

"I was." I slip my hand into my pocket, twiddling my coin. "I should get back to my date. Keep your head up. I'm sure your girl will come around."

"What's your name?" the guy asks like it matters.

"Joseph."

He extends his hand for me to shake. "I'm Ryan."

"Best of luck, Ryan."

Ryan's gaze softens. He gives an unsettling nod and turns back to the mirror. Before I head out the door, I catch a glimpse of his face through the reflection, the light shining over his saddened expression. I see a young man wallowing in his loneliness. I don't know his story, but I recognize his demeanor. I get it. I've been there and I'm fortunate to have made it out alive. I can only hope that he does the same.

Ava's smile brings me peace when I return to the table. "Everything okay? I was starting to worry."

I sit, feeling more comfortable in my skin than I was earlier. "Everything is great," I exhale. "Sorry, it's just been a while since I've done…" I point around the restaurant. "All of this."

The moment I set my hand on the table, Ava holds it. She tightens her grasp, locking eyes with me. It's in her eyes that I find the courage to seek love again. I loved my wife with all my heart, and when I lost her, I wasn't willing to love her any less to love someone else. But, maybe I don't have to love her any less. Maybe a heart can grow larger. Maybe a heart can grow in order to make room for new people to love. That way, I don't need to love my wife any less. I will love my wife the same, while I open myself to loving someone new.

The rest of our date goes smoother than I thought it would. And as we arrive at Ava's apartment doorstep, I don't think I'm ready to say goodbye. She picks up on it, a trace of reluctance manifesting in her voice as she says, "Same time, tomorrow morning."

I love hearing her say the phrase because it brings promise of a new day spent together. Her grip on my hand loosens, and I realize this could be my chance. *Kiss her, you idiot.*

Before we let go, I tighten my hand around hers, then pull her into my chest. With our hands locked, I caress the back of her head and our lips meet. Her lips are a promising oasis in a desert of lost intimacy I've wandered for far too long. I feel her arms tighten around my neck, and I'm reminded of what it feels like to take a chance on love.

When I pull back, I dip my forehead to hers. "Same time, tomorrow morning," I whisper.

Ava beams up at me. "I like saying it, but I love hearing you say it."

I already look forward to saying it again tomorrow.

I'm on my way home from Ava's when I notice the streets are desolate. The usual city hustle has been replaced by an eerie emptiness, the towering skyscrapers devoid of life. My car is the only one on the road. No honking horns, not a single pedestrian in sight. It's as if Manhattan took a collective breath, holding it in anticipation of something about to happen.

I flip through radio stations, waiting to hear a radio host address the city-wide silence. The streetlights I drive under, ones once casting a warm glow, now flicker and cast long shadows dancing along the littered sidewalks.

Where is everybody?

I finally land on a radio station, the host's enthusiasm nearly blowing out my speakers as he shouts, "And I'll tell you, tonight is the best night of the week, y'all! Greater Good, let's go!"

I flip the channel. "¡Pronto, Greater Good comenzará!"

I flip the channel. "How do you think tonight's winner will take their life? Bullet through the head? You know what would be cool? Setting someone on fire. Call that a 'slow burn,' get it? They should—"

I flip the channel. "Hope you got your watch parties ready because tonight's episode is going to be wild!"

I mute the radio, my eyes panning left and right as I drive up the road. I notice large groups of people gathered in bars and in their living rooms, their faces lit by their T.V. screens. *Is* that *where everyone is right now? Inside, watching Greater Good?*

As I make a right onto 5th Avenue, I notice a crowd gathered on the side of the road. I cautiously pull up to the curb, far enough to see the commotion without being affected by it. People are climbing over one another to be noticed by somebody standing outside the building entrance. I take one last visual sweep around the block. Nobody is in sight except for the herd of people crowding the regal lobby doors.

Curiosity seeps into the confines of my mind, encouraging my hands to open my car door. As I step around the front of the car, I can make out the people's shouts.

"*Pick us! Please, pick us!*"

"*We got here first! We deserve seats!*"

"*I've been camped out here since last night!*"

Their passion and determination fuel my curiosity even more, pulling me toward the back of the crowd. "This is bull-shit!" a man groans to my right. Sweat glistens over his forehead, evidence of the struggle he's undergone for who knows how long. He looks rough around the edges and reeks of cheap whiskey and diesel.

"What's all this about?" I ask him.

He waves his hands in the air, trying to get the attention of somebody standing at the building entrance. Without looking at me, he mutters, "Greater Good. This is the entrance for people who want to be in the live studio audience."

"The show is open to the public?!"

"Yup. We'll get in if we're lucky." He curses over the people in front of him. "And it ain't lookin' like we're getting lucky tonight."

A breath escapes me as I'm shoved from behind. In the couple minutes I've stood behind the crowd, more people gathered behind me, forcing me to become one with the crowd. I feel pressure from all angles now, with nowhere to look but up. My eyes land on large luminous white letters at the top of the building, spelling out: MENDAX.

I'm suddenly thrust forward with the crowd. Standing between two security guards, a man stands by the lobby doors with a shirt that reads, "CREW MEMBER." The crew member waves us in one at a time, counting us off one by one. He taps my shoulder as I'm forced through the front door with the current of bodies. "137," he says sternly, tapping my shoulder. He continues as people flood in behind me. "138, 139, 140…"

Adrenaline courses through my veins as people rave about what's to come. We're herded like sheep without a shepherd into the television studio, my fellow sheep making their predictions as to how the winner will commit suicide on tonight's episode. They continuously commend the show's creator for her creative brilliance, while I can hardly process what's happening as I'm forced through a fluorescent-lit hallway. I felt sick to my stomach, watching the last episode's recap in my living room. *How will I stomach watching this live?*

"Let me out," I demand aimlessly. "I want out!" Nobody responds, and the entire crowd goes silent as the people in front of me stop. We bump into each other, all coming to a halt in the crammed hall. In an instant, the hall goes pitch-black, causing some people to cheer while others question what is about to happen.

An elevated L.E.D. screen at the end of the hall brightens the room, depicting a woman of bewitching beauty. Her short black hair frames her face, her alluring eyes captivating the crowd around me, including myself. A chilling familiarity lingers between the woman and myself as I listen to her opening remarks.

"Welcome to Greater Good, the show for the morbidly curious! My name is Nora Fictus, and I am the creator of the experience you are about to take part in." The crowd erupts in a deafening applause as she continues. "Now, you all play a vital role in the success of tonight's episode. On each side of the stage and on the backs of the seats you'll sit behind, you're going to find 'prompter' screens. Besides enjoying the production, you are required to follow the prompters' commands, whether it be to laugh, cheer, clap, or gasp. If you do not abide by these prompts, you will be removed from the building. Enjoy the show, and be aware… Death is in the building!"

The screen fades to black, and as "GREATER GOOD" appears on the screen, the crowd continues to cheer and applaud. Nora's final words cling to my soul… "*Death is in the building.*"

A chilling breath tickles the back of my neck. I look over my shoulder and witness Death's ethereal presence. It glides above the back of the crowd, an eerie stillness in its wake as it looms to the front of the hall. People pay no mind as if they don't see Death the way I do. And maybe they don't.

Death's shadow creeps over me, acknowledging me but only for a moment. Its existence, more potent and omnipresent than ever, continues with us into the television studio. We enter to the left of stadium-style seating that rises to the studio's back wall. In the front of the room, a stage with vibrant orange accents depicts a set straight out of the 70s. The orange accents contrast the black walls and ceiling, pulling everyone's attention to the stage the moment we sit down in the audience section.

To my demise, I'm seated in the back row next to the sweaty man I stood next to outside. Whiskey and excitement radiate from his pores as he gets situated in his seat. I notice three plush orange chairs placed evenly across the stage, each facing us. Behind the chairs, the wall of a screen reads, "GREATER GOOD."

"Joseph, what have you gotten yourself into?" I whisper under my breath.

The audience claps as the woman from the hallway screen arrives through a side door, escorted by her security team. She's wearing an orange blazer and slacks, her jet-black hair slicked straight back, revealing the orange hoops hanging from her ears.

A haunting familiarity still hangs over me as she casually waves to the crowd and walks up the stairs and into a room behind us. There's a wide window next to the door that closes behind her. *She must run the show from up there.*

The lights around us dim except for the ones illuminating the stage where crew members prep the show's host. The screen built into the seat in front of me reads, "GET READY TO APPLAUD IN 3… 2… 1. APPLAUSE."

We obey, and as if on command, the host delivers her opening lines with overflowing enthusiasm. "Good evening, and welcome to Greater Good, the show for the morbidly curious! Death is in the building! And it's prepared to take the life of tonight's winner in exchange for bettering the lives of others. Each contestant has already decided where their cash prize will be donated, and it's up to *you* to decide which contestant will receive that prize. Now, let's meet our first contestant!"

The prompter prompts us, flashing: APPLAUSE.

We obey.

The screen behind the stage reveals an edited segment of a

woman talking about her life. She's sitting in a dimly-lit room, her eyes glossy. Sitting on her lap is a child no older than 10. The child's skin is flushed, the top of her head just recently shaved. With the help of the host on-screen, the woman shares the story about her daughter's fight against cancer and how they can't afford to pay her medical bills.

We watch attentively, sympathy washing over us like gentle rain on a warm summer day. When the lady finishes her story, she's introduced onto the stage, where she sits in one of the orange chairs. Two more contestants occupy the screen shortly after her, one of them sharing their story about living with Schizophrenia and the other sharing their story about not recovering from being wrongfully imprisoned for 30 years.

After being drawn in by the stories of each contestant, I'm brought back to the present moment when the host announces that it's time to vote. The screens behind each seat reveal three portraits, one for each contestant. Whispers fill the room as audience members debate over who deserves their vote.

I lean toward the man next to me. "The one with the most votes is supposed to kill themselves right in front of us?"

"That's right." He nods, then whispers, "Hopefully it's a slow death. I drove six hours to see this shit live." He itches the thin hairs on his double chin, debating who to vote for.

My stomach tightens as I lock on to the screen in front of me. The contestants are each smiling in their headshots. Are their smiles sincere? These people are sons and daughters of parents somewhere out there. Are they really willing to kill themselves right here, right now?

I fold my lips between my teeth, refusing to place a vote. I don't want to play a part in this and I refuse to do Death's bidding. A few minutes pass, and the crowd's whispers have silenced. The contestants sit anxiously in their chairs on stage, the host casually scrolling through her phone near one of the cameras as if it's just any other day on the job.

The room shakes as an announcement is made over the intercom. "AUDIENCE MEMBER 137, YOU ARE THE ONLY VOTER REMAINING. PLEASE PLACE YOUR VOTE."

Heads around me turn left and right. People start to look back at me, and my heart plummets when I see "137" engraved in my armrest.

Shit.

The man's whiskey-stained breath repulses me as he hisses, "Just vote for the schizo. The world needs less of those freaks."

My hands shake as people whisper about me. Their voices grow louder, most of them urging me to hurry up. I stiffen when I realize I'm causing a commotion by simply refusing to participate. Security guards toward the front whisper to one another, then glare in my direction. I suck in a deep breath. Upon exhaling, I vote for the contestant with Schizophrenia.

PING!

The lights dim once more, and the host takes center-stage.

I'm officially one of them. I'm one of these sick and twisted individuals. Here I am, among the crowd, taking part in this sick game–taking part in Death's bidding. Sheer panic works its way through me as the winner is announced. The crowd cheers for the schizophrenic before the prompters even tell us to. As the man stands and embraces the host, celebrating his victory, I ponder how the world has gotten to this point. Humanity has stooped low in the past, but this is a level of depth that I couldn't fathom until this point.

Death looms over the crowd, manifesting on and around the stage before me. It cloaks the man as he spreads his arms and closes his eyes, taking in a moment that will be his last. The man to my right removes his hat and places it on his lap. He holds back a grin as people continue praising the winner.

"And how does it feel being tonight's winner?!" the host asks the winning contestant.

He raises his chin, locking eyes with the spotlight shining from above. "My life is misery," he breathes into the microphone. "So, I will end it with pleasure."

The stage in front of the winner slowly splits down the middle. A bathtub rises from below until it's elevated a few feet above the stage. Two broad crew members stand on each side of the winner, prepared to assist him into the tub. Without hesitating and with a smile on his face, the winner allows himself to be placed in the tub.

The crowd goes silent in eager anticipation for the climax. I want to look away. I want to keep from poisoning my mind with this visual. But I can't. Death pulls at my attention with its inevitable force. It wants me to watch, to witness its masterpiece. The crowd grows louder as a golden hairdryer is lowered from the ceiling above.

"They're gonna electrocute him," I exhale under my breath. I look right at the man next to me. "They're gonna…"

My heart drops at the sight of the man's gaping mouth. His arm is extended over his gut, the hat in his lap slowly moving up and down as he pleasures himself to what's happening on stage. I clench my jaw. I'm frustrated, repulsed, and flat-out disappointed in everything that's led humanity to this disgusting low point. I always knew there were sick people out there, but I never realized the level of sickness that lurks in the minds of some people in this world.

With the little strength I have left in me, I force myself to my feet and hurry down the staircase splitting both sections of the audience. Nobody looks in my direction, their eyes glued to the bathtub on center-stage. I keep my head down. The crowd roars, and I see sparks fly across the stage in my peripherals. The applause is loud, but I can still hear the sizzling and popping coming from the bath water.

Look, Joseph. You want to look.

"Look away," I command myself.

I reach the foot of the stairs and make a hard left. With my right hand held up, I shield myself from seeing the spectacle unraveling on stage. People cheer, people shout, people praise the morbid display. Their energy radiates, and I use it to thrust myself through a group of crew members and out the emergency exit doors. The night's chilling breeze wraps me as I sprint to my car parked down the road. In a mere blink, I'm holding my door handle. I blink again, and I'm driving. A third blink, and...

"Joseph?" a voice says.

Tears trickle down my cheeks as I gasp for air. I don't know if I'm crying because I'm mad at the world or just relieved to be away from that demented display. Regardless, I haven't cried like this in a long time and I don't give a damn who sees.

"Joseph," the voice says again calmly.

I'm looking at the floor below my knees. *I'm on my knees.* I'm breathing shallow breaths that don't go any deeper than the back of my throat. *I can't breathe.* So, I surrender. "Help me, please."

"Just breathe, Joseph." There's that voice again. "All you have to do is breathe."

All I have to do is breathe.

I inhale, I exhale.

I inhale, I exhale.

It's not until I find my rhythm that I realize I'm in a church. My eyes trail up from the floor to the stage in front of me. Just above the stage is a colossal cross that stretches up to the ceiling. A blue light shines from the ground up, highlighting the polished wood the cross is made of.

I run my sweaty palm over my shirt while standing to my feet. A silhouette appears to my right, and as it gets closer, the blue light reveals that it's Pastor Ben. My voice pierces the silence. "Sorry if I startled you, Pastor Ben. I... I don't really know how or why I ended up here."

"I told you to call me Ben, didn't I?" Ben calmly strokes his beard, taking another step toward me. "And I run a church in the Bronx, Joseph. You're not the first person to randomly barge through the front doors. They're unlocked for a reason."

I let out a laugh in an attempt to hide my confusion. The only reason I step foot in this building once a week is to hear how bad other people's lives are. I'm not religious, I don't pray, I don't take part in any of this stuff. So, out of all the places I could've ended up tonight, why did I end up here?

Since Ben has been present, a sense of calm has washed over me, smoothing over the jagged edges of my disturbed mind. The scent of polished wood and the feeling of tranquility envelop me at once, detaching me from the nightmare I somehow managed to escape. That's when I realize…

It's silent.

And there's no trace of Death or its whisper.

I let out a long exhale, admitting defeat. I never thought it would come to this, but now is a better time than ever to take Ben up on his weekly offer. "Listen, Ben. If the offer still stands, I'd like to grab that cup of coffee with you."

Ben smiles.

I cradle my coffee mug between my palms, watching the steam rise from the surface. We're in a janky diner a couple blocks from the church, one that seems to have been frozen in time. A neon "24 HOURS" sign flickers over the worn tile, the air thick with the scent of fried food and cheap coffee.

"So, what brought you in tonight?" Ben pours enough sugar in his coffee to give Willy Wonka a toothache.

I sigh. "You're gonna think I'm crazy."

He begins stirring his coffee. "The most influential people in history were considered crazy before they were considered brilliant or courageous."

"I don't see myself being brilliant or courageous any time soon."

"Sometimes simply *living* is an act of courage." Ben's words are simple, but the meaning behind his words is riddled with complexity. "I'm not going to think you're crazy. You have my word, Joseph." He flashes a warm, encouraging smile, the lines crinkling beside his sympathetic eyes.

I tap my coin against the table's edge, contemplating the most sane way to voice my struggles. "I sort of hear Death," I mutter.

Ben blinks at me. "You hear Death? Like, it's saying something to you?"

"It's a whisper," I exhale, leaning forward. "I hear it in the silence or when my mind focuses on something morbid. It starts off as a whisper, then becomes this dark force that weighs me down." I pause for a reaction, and Ben simply nods for me to proceed. "Lately, it's been happening more often and I can't seem to shake it."

He narrows his eyes, genuinely interested in what I have to say. I haven't even gotten to the root of my problems, and I already feel like I'm growing. All these years sitting in that support group circle, refusing to address my brokenness. *It's my turn to be fixed.* Ben takes a sip of his sugar-filled coffee. He cringes at the taste, sets the cup down, then adds more sugar.

"Jesus," I mutter toward the now-empty sugar container.

"What about Him?" Ben teases while stirring. He looks up at me and winks. "See what I did there?"

"Very funny," I exhale.

Ben loosens his grip on his mug, and his eyes meet mine. "When did you start hearing this whisper?"

"It started five years ago," I sigh, clinging to my coin. "When I killed my wife and took away my son's ability to walk." I pause, waiting for him to judge me–to call the police or make a run for it. Instead, he nods, and his nod is all I need to pour my heart out in hopes that I get fixed.

I start with the night I ruined my life and met Death for the first time. "Five years ago, my wife, son, and I got dinner in Jersey. My wife, Elizabeth… she was a foodie. She loved trying new restaurants and I found this one 45 minutes up north, so we made the drive. It was a regular night, a night like any other. Nothing special…"

My words are cut off by the lump in my throat. Ben patiently waits as I take a sip of coffee and continue. "I was a corporate lawyer at the time, representing businesses on Wall Street. I hated it, the mountains of paperwork and watching rich guys get away with murder just because they were rich. The day you hear what these billionaires do behind closed doors is the same day you learn who the real criminals are. Anyway, I wasn't happy working with these corrupted suits, so I drank. And I drank. And I drank.

"When it was time for us to drive home that night, Elizabeth told me she should drive, and I took offense. I found it insulting that she thought I had let the liquor get the best of me, but she was right. I was arrogant and told her I had my booze under control when I didn't. I was so rude and obnoxious, and she still didn't get upset with me. Instead, she did something worse. She trusted me." My hands caress the mug. It's hot, but I need to feel the burn. "I remember we were on this long, winding road, coming home. Stevie, my son, was asleep in the back seat. I was so confident, Ben. In that moment, I could've sworn I had everything under control, but that's what happens when you're too far under the influence. What you see and feel becomes an illusion. We were on a two-lane road, but I started to see four."

Ben narrows his eyes at me, slowly nodding for me to keep sharing until I can't anymore. Despite the struggle, I suppress my tears and keep going. "We were on the road until we weren't. I remember coughing from the smoke rising in and around the car after it stopped rolling. The right side was smashed against a tree. I still have no idea how long we were sitting there, but I was woken up by Stevie crying. It was this piercing, deafening scream, but I had never been so happy to hear it because it meant he was alive. As I came to, the left side of my face was almost completely numb except for this trickling sensation running down my cheek and neck from all the blood." The tip of my finger traces my scar. "I looked at my wife, who was turned away from me. She was facing the tree we hit.

"I wanted to hear something from her–anything–and I did. In the faintest whisper, she said, 'Stevie.' I unbuckled my seatbelt to get to her and that's when I saw that the distance between the center console and her door was a foot at the most. She had been completely crushed. With another breath, she said Stevie's name again, and I knew what she meant. She wanted me to save Stevie because it was too late to save her. So, I climbed in the back and pulled Stevie from his seat.

"When I got out of the car, I shouted that I would come back for her. I told her to stay awake, though she was already drifting. Ben, when I looked back at what was left of that car, my wife wasn't alone. I saw Death towering over the car, cloaked in darkness. I saw Death with my very own eyes. I watched Death creep into the car, wrap my wife in its chilling embrace, and take her with it. At the time, I thought I was still drunk and maybe I was. Maybe it was all a part of the illusion. Regardless, I ran back up the hill. I stopped the first car I saw, gave them my wallet, and begged them to take Stevie to the nearest hospital while I went back to save my wife. Thank God they took him. They saved his life, but he was left paralyzed from the waist down.

"As for me, I went back down to the car. I climbed through the driver's side, and when I got to her, I knew she was already gone. Death beat me to her, and I'll never forgive myself for letting that happen. I sat there with her lifeless body for hours until I… until I realized that if the police found me with alcohol in my system, I could be in prison for the rest of my life. Stevie wouldn't have a dad. No dad, no ability to walk. I did the unforgivable. I ran as far as I could, and by the time they found me in the next town over, I was sober, and they ruled me running as a result of the concussion I suffered. I was off the hook, but I've been on Death's list ever since. I hear its whisper in the silence. Death doesn't speak actual words, but I know it's coming for me.

"I moved Stevie and I out of Manhattan after that. I became a criminal lawyer to find good in people who did bad things because part of me thinks there's good in me even though I did a real bad thing. Truth be told, I don't deserve to live. Most of the time, I actually invite the thought of ending my life rather than living with the guilt."

When I finish speaking, Ben is still looking at me the same way he did when I started. He's the only person besides me who knows why I don't deserve to live, and yet, he still looks at me like I *do* deserve to live.

Ben tilts his head, transferring empathy through his gaze. "Thank you for sharing your story with me, Joseph," he speaks softly. "I'll start off by saying that you deserve to live. I'll say this again... *sometimes simply living is an act of courage*, so be proud of yourself for living courageously. I know you may not be asking for it, but being the pastor I am, I'm going to lend you my perspective." He pushes his coffee aside, lacing his fingers together over the table. "God kept you alive because He's not finished with you, so don't think for a second that *you* are finished with you. I've been a pastor long enough to witness how the more a person struggles, the more that person is called to accomplish. You've struggled a great deal, and I truly believe that God is calling you to accomplish something great."

Ben's words engrave themselves into my heart. He leans forward, gripping my forearm tightly. "There is a spiritual battle happening all around us at all times. Angels and demons are fighting for your mind every waking second of the day, even in your dreams. Forces of good and evil will compete for your eyes, mind, and body. At the end of this war between good and evil, our souls will be claimed. And believe it or not, you have a say in who will claim your soul based on the decisions you make."

I blink at him. "I have a say? How can I have a say in a matter that's so much greater than me?"

"You have a say every day." Ben points to the side of his head. "You just need to pick your path. Evil manifests itself in various forms, one of them being Death. Joseph, I urge you to pick the path that leads to *life*. God gave it to you for a reason. Don't let Death steal it before God calls you to do something great." He gently caresses my shoulder, smiling. "I've prayed for you every day since you started coming to Positive Pathways. Do you mind if I pray for you now?"

My tears begin to fall, knowing someone I've avoided every week has kept me in their prayers. How could I have been so closed off to life but so open to Death all this time? I begin to regret not speaking up in my support group. Ben deserves better than the silence I've given him. Hell, *I* deserve better.

We lower our heads, and Ben prays. "Lord, I thank you for my friend, Joseph. Listen, he's been hurting for a while now, and I ask that you provide him with the healing he is looking for. Remind us that when we seek healing, it doesn't always happen right away and it isn't always in the way we want to be healed, but rather the way we need to be healed. You have worked miracles in my life, and I humbly ask that you show Joseph a bit of that light you've shown me. He has struggled tremendously, and I know it's because You're calling him to something great. Give him grace, peace, and love as he continues to carry out Your will. Only You know how bad we need it. Amen."

For once in my life, I feel an ethereal presence working through Ben–a whisper, but it doesn't belong to Death. It belongs to a being greater than Death, and I know it's in my best interest to listen.

"Amen," I whisper before looking up. "What happens now?"

Ben chuckles. "You go out there and live."

CHAPTER EIGHT

NORA

Ryan is going to kill me.

It's 7:30a.m., and I'm clinging to a pink box filled with Ryan's birthday cake as my driver pulls up to his apartment. It's times like these that make me wonder if I'm taking my career too seriously. I've become so invested in Greater Good that I forgot I made plans to celebrate Ryan's birthday with him last night. I should have at least had the decency to remember it was his birthday when all he wanted was to celebrate with me.

As I pass a group of kids on the sidewalk, I notice them watching Greater Good on one of their phones. At this point, it doesn't surprise me. Greater Good is the most Googled T.V. show on the internet. Since I was on Danny Davis's talk show, I can't even buy a bagel without someone asking for my autograph.

I use the spare key Ryan gave me a while back to enter his building. When the elevator opens, my eyes land on a poster advertising Monday night watch parties on the building's rooftop: "ENJOY GREATER GOOD WITH THE GREATEST NEIGHBORS."

When the elevator opens, I fix my hair in my phone

screen's reflection, then knock on Ryan's door. *Eyes, chin, shoulders.* My posture follows. After a few knocks, the door opens to a view I never get tired of–shirtless Ryan. I'm at eye level with his bare chest, and while I want to straddle him in this hallway, I manage to lift the box between us.

I try to appear as cute and innocent as possible. "Happy Birthday?" The words leave my lips in the form of a question. "Don't hate me."

Ryan rubs his sleepy eyes with his palms before turning back into his apartment. I take it as a cue to follow him inside. My eyes pan around his apartment, and it dawns on me that I haven't been here since we first met. He's always made an effort to come see me. It's not a spacious apartment by any means, nor are there any decorations. It's a minimalist's paradise.

An empty glass, half a bottle of whiskey, and an empty pizza box are spread across Ryan's coffee table. Judging by his appearance, there is no way he plans to go to work today. He sprawls himself on the couch, wearing nothing but his gray sweatpants. His messy hair hangs over both sides of his emotionless face as he glares at me from across the room. *He doesn't give a shit about the cake I got him.*

"I'm sorry." I set the cake box on the kitchen counter. "You can say it, I'm a bitch for standing you up last night."

Ryan leans forward, resting his chin on his fist. He stares at the blank T.V. screen in front of him. I assume he's choosing his words carefully before he speaks. Maybe I *have* been too focused on work because his disappointment in me is coming across as a shocker. There wasn't a person in my life who gave a shit about me besides my dad, who I lost a long, long time ago. Since then, feelings have become foreign to me.

Being raised by a man who hunted for sport taught me more valuable lessons than I could count on one hand. One of those lessons involved never needing to depend on anybody but myself for anything. The idea of depending on anybody–especially for love–never seemed appealing. Love won't immortalize me. Fame will. Love dies with the person. On the other hand, fame will live on longer than the person's lifetime. So, why would I ever settle for love?

While still staring blankly at the screen, Ryan says, "My birthday is beside the point, Nora." He looks up at me. "I'm in love with you."

His words force me back a step. Falling for each other wasn't even a boundary we set because we both considered it impossible from the beginning. Or, at least, I considered it impossible. "I'm–you can't…" I stutter. "You can't be in love with me."

Ryan buries his face in his palms. "I know we set boundaries. I know we agreed that all this would ever be is physical, but that was years ago. I know, deep down, that what I feel toward you is more than physical. This is real." Warmth flows through me as I catch a glimpse of his light I was once familiar with, the same light that dissolved when Greater Good first aired. "You know what we have is real, and you're wrong. I can be in love with you. I've been in love with you for a while now."

I see a sense of hope weaving through his iris. I wonder what he sees in mine. I wonder if he sees my potential the way Samuel does. I wonder if he sees how devoted I am to building a legacy on my own. I wonder if he sees how in love I am with my craft and what I've been called to accomplish by Death and how loving him back is exactly what I need to avoid right now.

I pinch my eyebrows together. "Why now? Of all times, why are you telling me this while Greater Good is taking off?"

Ryan stands, his face softening as he steps closer. "Ever since you created this show, you haven't been the same. Mendax, the fame, even Roth… they're consuming you. I see it when I look at you. I feel it when I touch you." He caresses the side of my face with his palm, which I'm quick to push away. "You're taking this whole morbid thing too far. You've gone cold."

"We can't be anything more than what we already are," I state dryly.

His face flattens. "What are we then?"

"We're nothing. You're my assistant."

Ryan clenches his jaw and I instantly regret saying the words, because it's a lie. *He's more.* For the first time since we met, he turns his back on me. A part of me thinks it could also be the last time, and as harsh as it sounds, I'm okay with that. I have no choice but to be okay with that. I'm shooting for the stars while this boy is down on his knees.

Ryan sits back down on the couch. "You're all I have." He looks up at me, a few strands of long brown hair hanging over his disheartened face as he adds, "If it's not now, it's never."

The sincerity in his voice bangs on the door to my heart. For a split second, the thought of letting Ryan in crosses my mind, and I'm forced to consider that it's possible for me to receive and return love. I'm also forced to consider that I've been dealt a hand already, and unfortunately, the cards I can play won't win love, a family, or anything in between. But I can play to win the crowd's praise, to use the gift bestowed upon me by Death.

I check my phone for the time. Samuel is expecting me at the office within the hour. "If this is how it needs to be, then it's never."

Ryan doesn't react. I take one last look at the pink box lying on the kitchen counter. While gently sliding it in his direction, I leave him with, "Take today off."

◆ ◆ ◆

Every head turns toward me the moment I walk into Samuel's office. The black marble flooring continues up each wall except for the glass wall separating his office from a view of Times Square. The enormous screens mounted on nearby buildings cast vibrant colors through the windows. Men and women are scattered around the room, the air thickened by an unsettling energy.

Samuel motions for me to sit. "Where have you been?" he asks, checking his watch.

"Family emergency," I lie.

As I sink into the seat next to Samuel, his black eyes burn a hole in my cheek. *Family emergency*? I'm such a dumbass. A few nights ago, I told him I don't have or even want a family.

Regardless, he ignores my response, addressing the group with a lifted chin. "Show Nora what you just showed me," he demands one of the tiny men standing near a flatscreen T.V.

As the man presses a series of remote buttons, I scan the room and pick up on an aura of power and influence. The men and women scattered around the room are a blend of calculated ambition and mystery. They carry themselves in a way that mirrors Samuel's authority, their true expressions masked behind practiced smiles.

I watch them whisper among each other, their voices weaving webs of deception and manipulation. Ever since I've let Death work through me, I've become more in tune with forces beyond human comprehension. It's evident that these people have the same gift.

A still image of a man with his head down pops up on the screen. The man in the image is using his right hand to cover his face as he walks away from the... wait... that's my stage.

"During the peak moment of last night's episode, a man walked out of the live studio audience," Samuel states, disappointed. "We haven't been able to identify who this man is yet."

I remain fixated on the image of the man, his slouched posture hiding his face as he looks away from the winning contestant on stage. "Why does it matter? He's just a random guy in the audience."

Samuel folds his thin lips between his teeth. Without saying a word, he nods to the man controlling the T.V., who pulls up a video of an internet influencer in his bedroom.

"Who's the kid?" I ask.

Samuel sternly points at the screen. "Watch."

"Wassup widdit?!" the kid in the video shouts at the camera. "Finally, somebody steps up against this satanic show! This man's got some serious balls for protesting in the middle of the show, and we can't let him down, y'all. We need to back this guy, whoever he is. Greater Good needs to be put to a stop before–"

The video pauses as Samuel raises his hand. He looks at me for a response.

"This kid thinks that a man leaving mid-show was an act of protest?!" I laugh. "The man obviously couldn't stomach the show's climax, so he left. That's not protesting. There isn't a single Greater Good hater out there."

"Show her the next video," Samuel blurts out.

A few buttons are clicked, and a podcast set is displayed on the screen. "So, let's talk about last night's episode of Greater Good," the podcast host tells her guest.

"Hell yeah," the guest replies. "It's amazing how theatrical they make these suicides. A golden hairdryer lowered into a bathtub. That was fucking nuts!"

The host nods. "It was insane. But real quick. I wanna talk about this guy who walked out during the show." Another image appears on the screen, an image of the man leaving the studio, captured from a different angle. The host looks directly at the camera. "For those unaware, this guy made a huge statement by leaving during the most exciting part of Greater Good last night. It doesn't seem like he was trying to make a scene, but I don't know, it's just crazy because a lot of people would kill to see this show live, and he's walking out during the best part."

"So true," the guest chimes in. "I didn't even think there were people who disliked this show. They're making the world a better–"

Samuel raises his hand, and the video pauses. The room is silent, the men and women patiently awaiting my response.

"Am I missing something here?" I ask. "I don't see what the big deal is."

"These two videos alone have over 300,000 views since they were posted today." Samuel's face turns to stone. "That means people have seen this 'man leaving the show' over 300,000 times. In most of the videos being posted, they're labeling him as a protestor standing up against Greater Good. That doesn't seem like a big deal to you?"

I tilt my head, staring at the still screen. Greater Good has amassed hundreds of millions of views in the weeks we've aired. We're only a handful of episodes into this season, and we're already being nominated for a list of awards industry-wide. *So what if some guy walks out during the show and a few hundred thousand viewers see it?!*

"We're the number one show in the country," I declare. "Is this guy really a threat to us?"

The people look to Samuel for a response, but not just any response. They expect a specific response, one that I don't seem to pick up on. Whatever it is they get, I don't. And they want him to hammer the message into me until I do.

"I know you've never performed at this level before, Nora. You don't fully understand your calling yet, but what you need to understand is that you're gifted like everyone else in this room."

Thoughts run through my mind as I process what these people's gifts could be. Do they hear the whisper, too? Do they also do Death's bidding?

Samuel continues. "We're not just in the entertainment business. We're controlling the minds of the masses. We're controlling the crowd." He starts pointing out the people in the room. "Each person here plays a part in dictating how the crowd views the world through narratives we embed in our viewers' minds."

While I've heard Samuel refer to the narrative before, this time is different. As the words pour from his mouth, the energy in the room intensifies. It's a dark energy fueling my ambition as I open myself to Samuel's words. Shadows dance along the silhouettes of the individuals in this room, each embodying darkness that transcends their personas.

"What's the narrative?" I ask.

Samuel stands and places his wiry fingers atop his desk. "The point of us instilling our narrative through our media is to control the population, to keep the crowd under our influence. Greater Good is the perfect way for us to desensitize our viewers to violence and death, making it easier for us to weaken their wills. For thousands of years, elites like us have used morbid curiosity to suppress the lower-class majority of the world—also known as 'the crowd.' Take the Romans and the Colosseum, for example. The Roman elites made people fight to the death in front of the crowd to distract them. While the crowd was distracted, the elites made decisions for their own gain behind the scenes. Our aim is to manipulate the crowd's moral compass, allowing us to gain control over their minds and actions. When they don't know right from wrong… when they have no ambition… when they have nothing to live for… they're ours to control."

I struggle to keep my jaw from dropping. *I'm controlling the crowd.* Ryan had told me from the beginning that he didn't think this was right, but he doesn't see that I'm more than just a showrunner now. I'm controlling the crowd, weaving our narrative through the minds of the masses.

Samuel raises his arm toward a man sitting on a nearby couch. "Dr. Bane…"

Age has etched itself deep into Dr. Bane's round face. Thin strands of gray are neatly combed over his liver-spotted head, the skin on his neck folding over his shirt's collar as he opens the folder in his lap. "Since the show has aired, we've seen a spike in suicide and crime cases across the country. Domestic abuse, assault, reports of road rage, all increasing by the day."

Samuel chimes in. "Proof that the crowd is losing the ability to tell right from wrong. We're turning the people against each other. If they're too busy turning against each other, they'll never turn against us. The world becomes what it watches. Win their eyes, and you will win their minds."

Samuel's wisdom slithers into my mind, his voice laced with insidious allure. The words he speaks infect my confidence like a virus. I'm being handed the power to control the population, to influence the world. I wanted fame. I wanted power. But I'm being offered even more. I'm being offered the world.

I remember Ryan accusing me of not being the same since this all began. A part of me knows he's right and has been all along. I've changed, but not for the reason he thinks. *I'm greater than I once was.* "So, what do we do about this protester?" I ask.

Samuel gestures to a woman in the back of the room. "Donna, owner and founder of MediaFlow, today's top social media platform."

Donna's expression is frozen and unyielding, revealing serious signs of botox. She remains in a cross-legged position, her essence alone demanding authority. "It's an easy fix. We'll skew the social media algorithms to only show content favoring Greater Good."

"What does that mean?" I ask, leaning forward.

"It means we will put an extra boost behind any pictures or videos that show Greater Good in a positive light."

Samuel places his hand on my shoulder. "This is how we control the narrative," he whispers. "The world only sees what we want them to see."

"Should we also boost content that showcases this protester in a negative light?" Donna asks.

"Not yet. I would rather people not be aware that he exists at all," Samuel replies. "But let's all be aware of what this man looks like." He lifts his chin, and the screen is turned on again, portraying a pixelated image of the man sitting in the crowd. The man's curly hair has been gelled back, a jagged scar etched along the left side of his face. "From now on, I want to collect the contact information of every audience member who attends the live show. This will not happen again."

I hear Samuel's voice, but my eyes are fixated on the image of the man on the screen—a threat to the legacy I'm building. The scar along the left side of his face, his stubble and slicked hair. I know this man, whether it be from another life or the one I'm living. I just can't pinpoint who it is... *not yet.*

CHAPTER NINE

JOSEPH

"I tried to kill myself a few weeks ago," the lady to my right blurts aloud. Ben and I are the only ones looking at her while the rest of the support group looks in other directions. The flickering lights throughout the church basement emphasize the bags under the lady's eyes as she continues. "I walked in on my husband with another woman. We were married for a decade, and now I'm forced to question how real that decade was. I usually eat lunch near work, but that day, I went home for lunch. The house was quiet, but I heard this faint sound from our bedroom while chopping onions. It's funny how in that moment, as soon as I heard the noise, I knew he was fucking some other woman in our bed.

"I considered leaving instead of confronting them. I almost convinced myself that if I didn't see it, it wasn't actually happening. But I just had to see it for myself. I was so jacked up on adrenaline at that point I only remember bits and pieces. I remember seeing the door hanging open like they didn't even consider the possibility I'd walk in. I remember seeing her naked back bent over him as he lay under her. I remember him seeing me from around the curve of her waist. I remember looking at her and knowing exactly why he would sleep with this woman–she was young, hot. Then, I remember him calling me crazy for holding the knife in my hand." The lady laughs under her breath. "I didn't use the knife. I dropped it and ran out of the house. I knew it was going to fuck with my head, and lo and behold, I down a handful of Xanax at my sister's house, I blink, and then I wake up in the hospital."

Ben listens attentively from across the circle. With his fingers laced over his knee, he opens his mouth to speak but is cut off by another group member.

"Do you still think about killing yourself?" the guy asks.

"Every now and then, the thought crosses my mind."

"I've been thinking about committing suicide, too." The guy's hollow gaze hovers around the group. "There's that show, Greater Good. If you're gonna end your life, might as well be for something. They give whoever you want a whole lot of money for ending your life on the show. If you got kids or family you want to give money to, you should consider being on it. I know I'm considering it."

"There are viable options," Ben interjects cautiously. "There are plenty of different ways to seek help before considering such a thing." He faces the lady. "Your feelings of sadness and betrayal are normal responses to an experience as traumatic as the one you faced. I can't tell you how to live your life, but there are ways that are proven to fight this attack on your mental health–prayer, journaling, mindfulness exercises. Sometimes, healing doesn't happen overnight. It's a process that requires building trust and mental strength. I encourage you all to please keep from watching morbid shows like Greater Good. Evil works its way into your mind from all sorts of angles, and you should steer clear of the forms it takes on."

The group remains unfazed by Ben's response, each person avoiding eye contact. *Say something, Joseph.* I witnessed the evil myself. I witnessed it firsthand. Chances are, I'm the only one in this room who was a part of the live studio audience. If anyone can testify to Greater Good's toxic effects on the mind, it's me.

"Pastor Ben is right," I mutter, my voice cracking. Everyone turns to me, and the silence is deafening. "I saw the show live. I was in the audience. If 'evil' is the right way to describe it, there is a whole lot of evil working through that show."

Ben gives me a subtle, grateful nod. It's the first time I've spoken since joining Positive Pathways. Backing up Ben is the least I can do after our conversation the other night in the diner. While there hasn't been much growth since my first group meeting, hearing my voice echo across this church basement is a huge step. *And I kind of like the sound of it.*

Ben smiles. "You know I'll pick up the phone any time you call. If any of you ever find yourself in a dark place, please don't hesitate to reach out. I also leave the church doors unlocked, so know you're always welcome here. Would anybody like to pray us out before we call it a night?" He glances at me, and I instantly shy away. *Let's not get too far ahead of ourselves, Ben.*

A group member raises their hand, and after Ben nods, they begin. "Dear God, thanks for another day. Thanks for putting up with us and for helping us find a way. Even when we don't know where we're headed or why we're here on this planet, we trust that you got your hand on us. So, um… yeah. Keep guiding us, and we'll just keep going, I guess? Amen."

After a few silent beats, Ben says, "That was wonderful." He adjusts his glasses, his radiant eyes panning around the room. "We'll see you all next week."

The group members stand and pack their things, some with renewed hope and others just as lost as they were when they arrived. My one conversation with Ben has helped me more than the entire year of group sessions I've sat through. As weird as it sounds, letting someone in on the worst moments of my life felt good. It felt so good, I've thought about talking to Ben again since we parted ways Monday night. Something attached itself to me that night, something I need more of. Where else to go but...

"Coffee?" I ask Ben while helping him stack chairs.

He grins. "Well, I'd be honored."

◆ ◆ ◆

"Why do you like this diner so much?" I ask Ben after the waitress hands us menus.

"It's simple," Ben replies, dumping sugar in his coffee. I lean forward, waiting for him to continue. He doesn't.

"That's it?" I ask. "It's just 'simple?'"

"Yep." Ben stirs through his mountain of sugar. "There are five items on the menu, a couple sodas, and cheap coffee." He lifts the mug to his lips and raises his brows. "And I sure love my coffee."

I squint at him, trying to see what he sees in this place. The floor is sticky, there are rips in the booth cushions, and there's a jukebox in the back of the diner that doesn't even work. Ben is either blind or has extremely low standards.

"I'll explain," he says, picking up on my confusion. "Everywhere you go, you're told that you need better things. The world says you need a better car, you need a better house, you need a better-looking face. Places like this old diner are testaments to the fact that we don't need 'better.' We already have more than we need." He sips his coffee. "This diner has been in business for over 60 years. They haven't changed the menu..."

"They haven't changed the booths either," I interrupt, picking at one of the holes in my seat.

Ben smirks. "This old diner is a reminder that we don't need all the fluff the world is trying to sell us. The truth is that material possessions of this world will never be enough. There is beauty in the simple things; you just need to focus on that beauty. Otherwise, you'll miss it because you're too distracted chasing something 'greater.'"

"I never saw it like that," I admit. "All this time, I've only focused on the negative. There was always something wrong with my house, I was screwing up my court cases…" I lower my head. "I'm the reason my son is in a wheelchair."

Ben taps the top of my hand. He speaks each word with conviction, stating, "It's like I said last we spoke, Joseph. You need to pick your path. You can be upset with what's wrong with your house, or you can be grateful that you *have* a house for things to go wrong in. You can fixate on the court cases you screw up, or you can celebrate the ones you *win*. You can blame yourself for your son not being able to walk, or you can thank God that your son *survived* the accident."

I clench my jaw, nodding as Ben's words are engraved into my heart. "You're right," I exhale. "You're so right. I've seen the world through this lens of negativity since I can remember. I was just on the wrong path."

"It's not your fault." Ben peeks over the waitress's arm as she pours us more coffee. "It's just the world we live in. Our minds are everything. And yet, we poison our minds with sick T.V. shows and twisted influences. These big corporations and T.V. networks manipulate the crowd into believing their lives aren't worth living. They're manipulating them into believing that nothing will ever be good enough. And as a result, people of the crowd are giving up on life before they even discover what they were born to accomplish."

A shiver travels down my back at the thought. All these years, Ben has seen one broken person after another come through Positive Pathways, seeking a support group. It's not our fault that we're broken; we're just the product of a broken world.

I raise my chin. "All these years, I've been looking for the will to live in a dying world."

"We live in the devil's world, and it's by God's grace that we're able to make it out."

"The show," I exhale. My elbows hit the table, startling

Ben and some nearby customers. I lean forward, whispering, "I didn't mention this last we spoke, but that new game show, Greater Good? Some people from the group were talking about it tonight. Ben, I saw it. I saw it live, and it was… it's evil, I tell you. It has Death written all over it."

Ben shuts his eyes, lowering his head. "It pains me to see others in pain, and it kills me to know that people are killing themselves. The world has changed a lot over the decades, but one truth will always hold up—*you were born to live.*" He points to my chest and narrows his eyes. "Don't you ever forget that. It's God's timing, not anyone else's. I sleep like a baby every night knowing that when it's my time to go, it will be by God's will."

I want to believe what Ben is saying. I want to possess the light he embodies and the grace he carries with his words and actions. But I met Death the night of the accident and watched it take my wife away from me. Death warned me that it would return for me, and I fear it's a bit too late to switch paths. "What about Death's timing?" I ask, my voice quivering.

"Death was defeated," Ben declares. "Death was defeated when Christ rose from the grave."

"I know Death, Ben. I've been trying to shake it since that night."

Ben smiles. "Death has no power in the presence of God, Joseph." He reaches forward and places his hand on my shoulder. "Try letting God into your heart, and I promise that things will fall into place. People of this world will preach of a false 'greater good,' but true greatness comes from above. Don't take the path leading to death. Take the path that leads to life."

My entire life, I chased what the world told me to chase while living in this constant cycle. I became a slave to the legal system, a slave to the programming of society. When I unplugged my T.V. five years ago, I did it to hide from the news headlines about the accident. Little did I know, I was dodging a twisted narrative that served to keep people like me from breaking this cycle I've been enslaved to.

But what if there is a way to break this cycle?

What if the true good comes from a being greater than Death?

What if the true good comes from God?

And what if meeting Death strengthened my position against it?

Maybe, I'm being called to fight for more than just the lives of criminals.

Maybe, I'm being called to fight for the lives of the broken.

◆ ◆ ◆

The door slides open as I enter the gas station store. I nervously flick my gold coin in the air, then catch it in my sweaty palm. While I came for Stevie's Kit Kat like I always do, a more important matter needs to be addressed. Now that I'm Nicky's lawyer, I need the cashier to drop the charges.

"How you doin', Joseph?" the cashier greets with a warm smile. I force a grin, my stomach tightening as I prepare to tell him that I'm siding with the criminal who robbed him, regardless of the gun being fake.

"Is that him?" a voice whispers. I look up from the candy section and see two men peeking over the shelf. I make eye contact with one of them. His eyes widen, and he ducks behind the shelf. "It's him! That's the guy."

Me?

In my peripherals, two silhouettes appear at the end of the aisle, separating me from the cashier. I slowly face the two men who glare in my direction. They stand side by side, their figures polar opposite. One is lanky and the other is stubby, his gut reaching toward me like he's in his third trimester.

I turn away, my eyes grazing over the shelves as if I didn't notice them staring at me. I walk the opposite way and turn down the next aisle. My eyes are on the cashier at the end of the aisle until the two men step between us again.

"Hey, buddy!" the lanky one shouts. "You're that guy from the show, aren't you?"

I look over my shoulder, then back at them. "You talkin' to me?"

Lanky and Stubby take a few steps toward me. Based on the tone behind the few words spoken, I can already tell they don't like me. Usually, lawyers have to keep their heads on a swivel in public places if they prosecute criminals. But I *defend* criminals. I shouldn't have anything to worry about, but these guys are starting to give me a reason to worry.

"I'm sorry. Do I know you?" I ask as they now stand only a few feet away.

"You're the guy protesting Greater Good."

Stubby reveals a picture on his phone of a man walking with his back to a stage. The man in the picture is covering the right side of his face, looking away from the stage where—wait. My breath hitches. *The man in the photo is* me.

It's a photo taken by someone in the audience. My head is down, but the scar along the left side of my face is exposed by the camera flash. Behind me, the winning contestant is being electrocuted by the golden hairdryer that was lowered into the bathtub.

"Where did you find this picture?" I whisper, looking up at the men. Lanky raises his phone, the light shining in my face as he records me. I stutter-step backward. "Hey, what're you—"

"Ayo, fuck this guy! It's the guy trying to take down Greater Good!"

Before I can say a word, they shove me to the floor. Now standing over me, they record me as Lanky shouts, "How you gonna fuck with a show that supports suicidal people?"

I raise my hand, shielding my face from the phones that keep getting closer. My body tenses as the front of a shoe digs into my ribcage. I absorb the blow and brace myself for another kick.

CHK! CHK!

Silence follows the sound of a gun being cocked. The two men slowly lower their phones and turn to the cashier behind them. The cashier raises his gun between them. "Get out of my gas station before I pop two caps in you for messin' with Joseph."

A nervous gulp forces its way down my throat. The men scurry past the cashier and out the door, muttering profanities under their breaths. My chest rises and falls with every heavy breath once trapped in my chest.

Who were those guys?
How did they get that picture?
Why do they think I'm protesting Greater Good?

I've lived my entire life without being recognized, and I prefer to keep it that way. I don't do well with T.V., phones, and all that other crap most people submit themselves to nowadays. I hear stories about clout-chasing, fame-hungry people looking for attention on the internet and never considered becoming one of them anytime soon.

"You alright, Joseph?" the cashier asks as he helps me stand.

"I'm good, I'm good," I reply, dusting off my coat. My eyes drop to the shotgun resting in his old, shaky hands. "Well, that's new."

The wrinkles beside his eyes introduce themselves as he smiles. "I brought it to the store the day after I got robbed! You saved my life, you know. If that filthy scumbag ever comes into this place again, I'll put a bullet in that hollow head of his."

The hairs on the back of my neck stand when I remember why I'm here. We head to the front counter where I place the Kit Kat bar. I wait for him to slide the shotgun under the counter before I say, "Listen, Anthony. I sort of need a favor. It's important."

"Anything you need, Joseph," he chirps.

"That robber who stole from you a while back? I'm kind

of, well… I'm defending him."

A line shows between Anthony's furry brows. "Defending him in court? You're defending the criminal who robbed me?"

"It's a bit more complicated than that," I manage. "If you haven't already, you and your lawyer will soon get the case file. When you read over it, you'll see that the gun was fake. I know my client didn't steal a whole lot of money from you, and without his intent to actually cause harm, I was hoping–"

"The gun was fake?" Anthony interrupts, looking down.

I nod. "An airsoft gun spray-painted black."

His face flattens. "I see you every day. Regardless of the gun, why would you represent someone who stole from me?"

"I was nearly broke when I agreed to defend him. You know I have a kid to provide for. If I had a choice, I wouldn't, but I don't have the luxury of choosing. Look, all I need is for you to drop the charges on your end. If you understood why he did it, you might even have some sympathy for the guy."

Anthony raises his hand to silence me. "Is what they said true?"

His sudden change of tone catches me by surprise. "Huh?"

"Those two guys that were here earlier… is what they said true? Are you trying to take down Greater Good?"

I fold my lips between my teeth. An urge manifests within me to own the fact that I'm becoming the face of some sort of movement. I can't help but think that it ties back to what Ben said about me being called to something great. With my heart being pulled in this new direction and the good that can come from it, I find myself more confident than ever before.

"It's true," I state. "I'm gonna take down the show."

"You're doing God's work, you know." Anthony sighs, fixating on the Kit Kat bar between us. "I'll lose more money going to court than I lost from the robbery. You lawyers are the real criminals with how much you charge," he exhales. After a silent beat, he adds, "If you give me your word that you'll fight this show and all the evil it stands for, then I won't testify."

I crack a smile. "You have my word."

I love how I can open my front door without nearly breaking my shoulder. I love how the house smells like a home-cooked meal as I hang my coat on the hook in my entryway. I love seeing Ava wave to me from the kitchen before I enter Stevie's room. I love that Stevie's already tucked into bed, reading under the lamplight.

He looks up at me and squints through his lenses. "Hey, Dad."

I sit on the edge of his bed and swiftly pull the Kit Kat from behind his ear. "How'd that get there?"

Stevie rolls his eyes. "Magic?"

I nod while tossing the Kit Kat on his lap. "How was school?"

"Meh."

"Meh?"

"Yeah," he exhales, replacing his book with the Kit Kat bar. "Mikey tried to pop holes in my wheels again today."

"I thought he stopped!"

"He never stopped," Stevie sighs. "I just stopped telling you about it."

I look at the brand-new wheelchair I got him. Not a single trace of Mikey's pen. "Well, it looks like Mikey failed."

"It's still annoying!" He throws the Kit Kat bar across the room. "They just won't stop. No matter what I say. No matter what I do."

I hear the frustration in his voice, the anger. "I can talk to the school," I reason. "They can catch Mikey in the act. He'll get in trouble for how he treats you and finally stop."

"That will only make things worse," Stevie murmurs. "Everyone is still talking about that show, Dad. Our teacher played an episode for us in class, and I think I want to be on it."

I suck in a quick breath, my heart now in my stomach.

"Your teacher what?!"

"We watched an episode of Greater Good, and I think I want to be on the show. I see how hard you work. I know you could use the money. You could get a big house with Ava and not have to keep looking after me anymore."

Anger and sorrow intertwine within the depths of my being. My anger is fueled by the thought of Stevie's school feeding them this morbid garbage and poisoning their minds. My sorrow is fueled by my own son wanting to end his life for his father, who is also the reason for his pain and suffering.

I grab his little hand in mine and look him dead in the eyes. I can't be angry with him because it will only feed his frustration. I can't be sorry for him because it will only feed his self-pity. Therefore, I choose to be hopeful.

"You listen to me," I say. I quote Ben as if he's speaking through me. "You were born to *live*, Stevie. We could have died the night of the car accident, but we didn't, and it's because you and I are being called to something even greater than Greater Good. We're being called to fight it. And that's exactly what we're gonna do."

Stevie simply nods, unfazed by the promise I just made. I get comfortable next to him, and the two of us lie together until I feel his body loosen to the rhythm of sleep. I silently slip out of the room, doing my best to keep my cool. A fire has started within me, craving something to burn. I won't deny that taking down Greater Good is my calling. After the past few days, I'm more than willing to accept it. It's time to silence Death, once and for all.

"Nicky?" I whisper into my phone.

"What's up?" he answers, half-awake.

"I need your help…"

CHAPTER TEN

NORA

I used to wonder what it was like to be immortal, and now I'm starting to believe I am *immortal.* As security opens the door to my Escalade, I step out to an ocean of screaming fans. Their bodies remain behind the metal barriers, their phones held high enough to catch a glimpse of me in my Celine dress. To be worshiped by the crowd in such a way is a rush I may never grow tired of. To these nobodies, I am somebody. Their screams make me feel like a goddess–divine. This reaction to my arrival at Mendax can only mean that my name will live long after Death takes me because Greater Good will live forever.

Eyes, chin, shoulders. The bottom of my black flats land on the orange carpet. I adjust my jet-black mini dress that stops at the top of my thighs, the white collar popping against my black hair that's been freshly cut. I gracefully lift my chin left and right for the photo op, giving the press just a little bit more of me but never all of me.

The Escalade door shuts behind me, and I strut up the orange carpet and into Mendax. The lobby is a bit quieter than it was outside, lending room for me to think clearly. I haven't seen Ryan since the morning we spoke at his apartment. I haven't called. I haven't made the slightest effort. I mean, how could I? I'm a busy woman. He sadly wasn't able to comprehend that, and he's lost me because of it. I tell myself I shouldn't pity him because he could've had what I was willing to give him. Maybe it wasn't much, but even the slightest bit of me is more than any man can handle.

As I make my way through the lobby to the control room, I notice a man being detained by police near the entrance. A zip tie binds his wrists behind his back, his nose dripping blood over his white T-shirt that reads, "LOOK AWAY."

"What's his story?" I ask one of the crew members escorting me.

"Some protester," she scoffs.

I flatten my dress with my palms.

A protester? That's a first.

The control room is silent upon my arrival, a sign of respect or fear or both.

"Are the contestants being prepped in the green room?" I ask, looking through the window at the set. Audience members funnel into the studio, finding their seats in the stands. "Tonight's winner is in for a real treat."

I spent the past few days putting together tonight's suicidal display. I've been adamant about the displays becoming more theatrical, more dramatic. Based on the polls we received from the public, everyone agrees we need to go "more morbid." While the live suicides have been morbid, we received complaints that the deaths are "too quick" or "borderline painless." Samuel and I agree, and tonight, we intend to take it to the next level. *Slower. More painful.*

The door opens, and the crew members stand as Samuel enters the room with two security guards at his sides. The guards remain by the door as Samuel stands in front of the wall of screens. His black eyes flick to me, the orange and blue lights highlighting half of his leathery face as he says, "I have a good feeling about tonight."

I smirk. "It's showtime."

GREATER GOOD

EPISODE 3

3 SPOTLIGHTS ILLUMINATE 3 PLUSH ORANGE CHAIRS
ON STAGE. AN UNSETTLING PRESENCE MAKES ITSELF
KNOWN AS THE L.E.D. SCREEN BEHIND THE CHAIRS
READS, 'GREATER GOOD,' IN BRIGHT ORANGE LET-
TERS.

DOROTHY (voice-over): On tonight's episode of Greater Good, three contestants will
share their stories—the hardships they have
faced and what has led them to their breaking
points. We've hand-selected these contestants
based on their generosity and willingness to
take their own lives on live television tonight, giving the winner's cash prize to their
family estate or charity of their choice!

70S MUSIC PLAYS AND THE AUDIENCE APPLAUDS AS
DOROTHY MEADOWS ENTERS FROM STAGE-LEFT. DORO-
THY MEADOWS RAISES HER HANDS, WAVING ENTHUSI-
ASTICALLY TO THE LIVE STUDIO AUDIENCE.

DOROTHY (now standing center-stage): Good evening, and welcome to Greater Good, the show
for the morbidly curious!

AUDIENCE APPLAUSE EVENTUALLY FADES.

DOROTHY: Death is in the building! And it's

prepared to take the life of tonight's winner in exchange for bettering the lives of others. Each contestant you will meet tonight has already decided where their cash prize will be donated, and it's up to *you* to determine how much that prize will be and which contestant will receive it. Now, let's meet our first contestant!

DOROTHY MEADOWS TURNS BACK TO THE L.E.D. SCREEN. ON THE SCREEN, A VIDEO PLAYS OF CONTESTANT #1 IN AN INTIMATE, DIMLY-LIT STUDIO ROOM.

DOROTHY: Can you start by telling us a bit about yourself?

CONTESTANT #1: My name's Janice. I'm 42 years old, and I've been dealing with a difficult situation for some time now, I… I walked in on my husband having an affair, and it's been hard for me to try to get over it.

DOROTHY: Can you recall seeing signs that your husband wasn't being faithful before you walked in on the affair?

CONTESTANT #1: I noticed a while back that he was spending more time on his phone. He went on more "walks" alone or spent late nights "at the office." I had a feeling something was happening, but I played dumb. I chose to be ignorant. Then, when I saw it happening right in front of me in broad daylight, in our own bed, it was like my whole world shattered in an instant. I just turned and ran.

DOROTHY: What was your lowest point throughout this entire ordeal?

CONTESTANT #1 (sniffling): It was the silence that followed. I tried to commit suicide shortly after at my sister's house. My family and friends were there for me and still are, but I just can't shake the image of my husband of 10 years embracing a woman the way he had once embraced me. It's when I'm alone I hear this voice telling me that my marriage was a lie… that my entire life is a lie and I have nothing to live for. I have no idea what to believe anymore. My husband was my everything.

DOROTHY: Sad. That sounds so incredibly difficult. Have you sought help during this mental struggle?

CONTESTANT #1 (nodding): I've been attending a weekly support group at some church in the Bronx, but it wasn't enough. Nothing will ever be enough. 10 years. I'm too old to start over and have kids now. My marriage was a lie for 10 entire years, which I will never get back.

DOROTHY: What have you planned to do with your winnings, given you win the most votes tonight?

CONTESTANT #1: If I win, I want the money used to create a foundation that supports people who have experienced infidelity and betrayal. I want to provide them with resources, counseling, and a safe space to heal and rebuild their lives. No one should go through this pain alone, and I want to make a difference for others facing the same struggle.

L.E.D. SCREEN FADES TO BLACK. CONTESTANT #1 ENTERS STAGE-LEFT TO AN APPLAUSE FROM THE LIVE STUDIO AUDIENCE. CONTESTANT #1 WAVES CHEERFULLY TO THE CAMERA AND TAKES A SEAT IN THE ORANGE CHAIR ON STAGE-LEFT. THE SCREEN BEHIND CONTESTANT #1 DISPLAYS A PICTURE OF CONTESTANT #1.

DOROTHY (standing behind CONTESTANT #1 with hand on her back): We feel for you, Janice. We commend you for your bravery and willingness to take your own life for a good greater than yourself.

DOROTHY (to camera): And now, let's meet our second contestant.

A VIDEO PLAYS ON THE L.E.D. SCREEN, REVEALING CONTESTANT #2.

DOROTHY: Can you start by telling us a bit about yourself?

CONTESTANT #2: I'm Raquel. I'm 18. I'm from

Boston, and when I was 12, I was in a very, very bad car accident that left me with third-degree burns covering most of my body and, well… my face, obviously.

DOROTHY: If you're comfortable sharing, can you tell us about the accident?

CONTESTANT #2: I don't remember a thing. I was in the car with my friends, and I swear that I just blinked and woke up completely bandaged in a hospital bed. I have burns and scars all over my body, especially my face. That moment ruined my life. I was told that when the car caught fire, my friends were able to get out fine, but I was still unconscious. They left me there to burn.

DOROTHY: Raquel, I'm so sorry. What terrible, terrible friends. When did you realize the impact of your burns on your life?

CONTESTANT #2: I knew before the doctors took the bandages off. High school was the worst of it all. Other kids wouldn't look at me. Teachers gave me A's out of pity. I was only comfortable inside of my room because my parents let me get rid of all my mirrors.

DOROTHY: What was the lowest point during your recovery?

CONTESTANT #2 (sniffling, holding back tears): Looking in the mirror for the first time and being scared of my reflection. You don't know what it's like to not recognize yourself. I never came to terms with my own face being taken from me. I wish I would've died that day.

CONTESTANT #2 BREAKS DOWN IN TEARS.

DOROTHY: What do you plan to do with your winnings, Raquel?

CONTESTANT #2: I want the prize to go toward making a foundation that gives support and treatments for burn survivors. No one should feel alone or hopeless on their journey to recovery the way I have.

SCREEN FADES TO BLACK. CONTESTANT #2 WALKS ONTO STAGE-LEFT TO AN APPLAUSE FROM THE LIVE STUDIO AUDIENCE. CONTESTANT #2 TAKES A SEAT IN THE ORANGE CHAIR ON CENTER-STAGE. THE SCREEN BEHIND CONTESTANT #2 DISPLAYS A PICTURE OF CONTESTANT #2.

DOROTHY (standing behind CONTESTANT #2 with hand on her back): We feel for you, Raquel. We commend you for your bravery and willingness to take your own life for a good greater than yourself.

DOROTHY (to camera): And now, let's meet our

third and final contestant.

VIDEO PLAYS ON L.E.D. SCREEN, REVEALING CON-TESTANT #3.

DOROTHY: Can you start by telling us a bit about yourself?

CONTESTANT #3: My name is Ryan, and I work for Mendax.

DOROTHY: What's your story, Ryan?

CONTESTANT #3: I'm in love… in love with a woman who will never love me back.

DOROTHY: Wow, a true Romeo. Can you tell us a little bit about your Juliet?

CONTESTANT #3 (face softening): We work together. Since we met, I've spent almost every day by her side, and I learned quickly that there is no place I'd rather be than beside this woman. I don't know life without her. I don't *want* life without her.

CROWD OOH'S AND AWE'S.

CONTESTANT #3: She's hard-working, disciplined, ambitious. She's so invested in her career, which is great, don't get me wrong. It's just... what I didn't realize until recently is how willing she was to let her career consume her. I'm worried about her, but she doesn't want me around. And I can't live without her, so here I am.

DOROTHY: Well, chances are she's watching right now. Before we discover the results that decide tonight's winner, what would you like to say to this woman?

CONTESTANT #3 PAUSES FOR A MOMENT.

CONTESTANT #3 (looking above the audience): Don't let them change you. I know the real you is still in there somewhere, and it's always been more than enough. I hope you realize that before it's too late.

CAMERA FEED CUTS TO STATIC SCREEN FOR A SPLIT-SECOND, THEN CUTS TO THE CROWD, THEN CUTS TO VARIOUS FLICKERING ANGLES OF THE STAGE.

DOROTHY (with finger on earpiece): Whoops! Looks like we're having some technical difficulties...!

"GET OFF OF ME!" I scream, clawing at the security guard.

"Woah! Woah!" The crew members dodge my flailing arms and legs. I slam my hand over the control panel. The screens along the wall flicker and glitch as people around the control room try to calm me down. A second security guard locks his arms around my legs.

"Not Ryan!" I shout. "Samuel, stop the show! Ryan can't win!"

Security pins me to a chair in the corner of the room while the crew members continue operating the screens. One of them speaks into their walkie-talkie, "Dorothy, you have the go-ahead to get the third contestant up on stage."

"Samuel, do something!" I beg, tears trickling down my cheeks.

Two pairs of heavy hands keep me pinned to the chair. I catch a glimpse of Samuel standing at the window, watching the show go on. "Ryan is a distraction, Nora," he states without turning. "If you understood the potential of what you're being called to do, you wouldn't let your assistants disrespect you the way he has."

"Disrespect me?" I ask. "What are you talking about?"

"A few days ago, he came to me saying Greater Good is changing you for the worse."

I shake my head, my shallow breaths becoming sobs. *Ryan was just trying to protect me.* "Pay him out or send him away. Please, anything but death."

Samuel sneers in my direction. With two long steps, he closes the distance between us. "There it is." His breath is chilling as his lips graze my neck. "There lies your weakness. You were called to do Death's bidding, and you answered your call. I will not let what we've built be destroyed by some boy with a crush. Don't you get it? Our influence on the world is at stake."

His wiry fingers wrap my arm, and he yanks me to the window, forcing me to watch Ryan walk onto the stage. His grip on my arm tightens as every screen on set displays the voter options.

"He won't win," I mutter, my breath fogging the glass.

Samuel snickers. Remnants of Death linger on his tongue as he says, "The crowd doesn't actually have a say. They never did and never will."

My heart plummets. "The votes aren't actually count-ed...?"

"*We* control the narrative," he whispers. "We would be damned if the crowd actually had a say in who wins."

Tears continue down my cheeks, a result of the physical pain from Samuel's suffocating grip and the emotional pain of seeing Ryan look at me through the glass I stand behind. It's in his gaze I discover my own truth. *I love Ryan. I've* always *loved Ryan.*

"I'm sorry," I whisper. "I'm so, so sorry."

Ryan's face shows across the L.E.D. screen, the prompters flashing, "APPLAUSE." The crowd obeys, cheering for Ryan as he steps forward alongside Dorothy. Three crew members enter from stage-left. One sets a chair in the middle of a plat-form while the others bolt the chair to the ground.

Ryan is carefully guided into the chair, his hands tied behind his back and fastened to the chair's backside. A glass dome lowers itself over Ryan, and as the crew members bolt the dome to the stage, Ryan looks up at me again, this time apologetically.

A metal pipe is lowered from the ceiling, and I wince before the boiling water even touches his skin. Hot enough to leave blisters but not hot enough to kill him–the perfect tem-perature to boil him alive until he drowns. I watch him scream in agonizing pain, the veins in his body protruding from his once-smooth skin as it starts to boil and blister. The crowd cheers louder than ever before, standing from their seats to marvel at Ryan's impending death.

My strength is depleted more by the second, and I have

no choice but to call on the one constant who has given me strength since the beginning of it all. To whom can I call out to in my distress but Death?

I pull my forehead from the window, inviting Death into the confines of my soul. I yearn for the strength to see the greater good in Ryan's death so that he doesn't die for nothing. I need the spiritual strength to play my role in Death's plan, to focus on the call I've answered without Ryan trying to pull me away. Death's presence gradually fuels me with the morbid tolerance to witness it take Ryan before my very own eyes. I surrender myself entirely to Death's will, once and for all. *I do it for Ryan.*

I no longer fight to look away.

And as if on cue, Samuel releases me.

Losing Ryan has to happen.

It's for my own greater good.

MENDAX NOW OFFERING
"GOLDEN GUEST PASSES"

Tuesday, August 5th, 2019

The popular television show, 'Greater Good,' has just introduced an unprecedented opportunity for its dedicated fans. The show, known for its heartwarming acts of self-sacrifice and transformative experiences, is now offering exclusive 'Golden Guest Passes' that provide lucky recipients with a guaranteed spot at the front of the waitlist to be a contestant on the show.

Greater Good has gained a massive following since its inception last month, captivating audiences with its heart-wrenching stories and ending displays that allow contestants to positively impact the world.

With the introduction of the 'Golden Guest Pass,' the show is giving its viewers a chance to experience the magic firsthand. These coveted passes provide immediate access to the show, bypassing the lengthy waitlist and ensuring a prime position for participation as a contestant. It's a greater opportunity for fans to step onto the Greater Good stage and become a catalyst for positive change.

To be eligible for a 'Golden Guest Pass,' fans are encouraged to engage with Greater Good through various social media channels and participate in interactive events that will take place at schools, hospitals, and other institutions around the country. These engagement activities will not only boost the show's reach to receive more donations to the winning contestant's prize but also provide opportunities for fans to connect with like-minded individuals who share their willingness to take their own lives to make the world a better place.

In addition to bypassing the waitlist, 'Golden Guest Pass' recipients will receive V.I.P. treatment throughout their time on the show. They will have the privilege of meeting the renowned show's creator and now-Executive Producer, Nora Fictus.

The introduction of 'Golden Guest Passes' is an ingenious move by the creators of Greater Good to reward their dedicated fan base and create an even stronger sense of community. By offering this unique chance to step into the limelight, the show is emphasizing its commitment to empowering individuals and inspiring positive change.

MENDAX NOW OFFERING STUDIO TOURS:
Get a Glimpse Behind the Scenes of Greater Good!

Wednesday, August 6th, 2019

Calling all Greater Good fans! Prepare to have your dreams come true as Mendax, one of the leading T.V. networks [known for its latest hit, Greater Good], has announced the launch of exclusive studio tours. This exciting opportunity allows fans to go behind the scenes and witness the magic that unfolds on their favorite T.V. programs while the cameras aren't rolling.

The network, renowned for its captivating production and philanthropic efforts, recognizes the unwavering support and enthusiasm of its dedicated fan base. In an effort to further engage with viewers and provide a unique experience, the network has opened its doors to offer intimate glimpses into the inner workings of its studios.

The studio tours promise an immersive journey through the heart of television production. Fans will have the chance to explore the meticulously crafted retro set, witness the intricate stage designs, and discover the cutting-edge technology that gives life to death.

During the guided tours, fans will also have the opportunity to meet and interact with various production team members, including Executive Producer Nora Fictus and show host Dorothy Meadows. It's a rare chance to gain insights into the creative processes that shape their favorite show while getting up close and personal with the talented individuals responsible for their favorite on-screen moments.

To ensure every fan gets a chance to partake in this exciting experience, the network has established a reservation system for the studio tours. Tickets will be available online, and fans are encouraged to book in advance due to the expected high demand.

DISCLAIMER: THE T.V. NETWORK'S STUDIO TOURS ARE SUBJECT TO AVAILABILITY AND MAY HAVE SPECIFIC GUIDELINES AND RESTRICTIONS. PLEASE REFER TO THE NETWORK'S OFFICIAL WEBSITE FOR FURTHER DETAILS AND RESERVATION INFORMATION.

CHAPTER ELEVEN

JOSEPH

"Are you fucking with me?!" Nicky snaps while pacing around my kitchen. "You couldn't wait until after my case to pick up a side hustle this big?" He stabs my face with his girthy finger–only, it's not my face. It's a picture of my face on a paper flyer lying on the table. "These flyers are all around the city, man."

I take a long sip of coffee with my back against the re-frigerator. My eyes trail down to the flyer. The upper half of the page is a still image from the video of me leaving Greater Good. This image is the clearest I've seen since those two goons at the gas station brought it to my attention. The image on the flyer reveals the scar along my left cheek as I shield the right side of my face from the stage. Below the image and in all caps letters are the words: LOOK AWAY.

I shrug. "I mean, that could be anybody."

"No offense, but your face is pretty fucked up, Joseph. You ain't foolin' nobody with that scar."

"Wow," I exhale. "That might be the nicest thing you've ever said to me."

Nicky yanks a chair from under the table and plops himself down. "And you wanna get me involved in this? What even is this?!"

"I think it's a movement," I say, itching the side of my head. "I was approached the other night in a gas station by some guys who called me a protester. Looks like now I'm being used as some kind of... symbol? I don't know." I pace from one side of the kitchen to the other. "Look, I told you what happened. I left during the show, and next thing I know, I'm being noticed by those guys at the gas station. I really think I got a role to play in taking down this show. Nicky, my 11-year-old kid said he wants to be on the damn show himself. My 11-year-old kid, talking about committing suicide on live T.V." I lean forward, placing both palms flat on the table. "Think about your wife–"

"She's ain't my 'wife,'" Nicky snaps.

"Okay, your girlfriend–"

"She ain't my 'girlfriend.'"

"Whatever the hell you wanna call her!" I shout. "She has your kid inside of her. She's about to bring your baby into this world where people are shoving suicide down kids' throats like it's candy."

Nicky keeps from making eye contact, but I notice his hard expression soften. I slide the flyer toward him. "Yeah, I got a fucked up face, sure. But it's *my* fucked up face these people are using, not yours. And I guess it's all over the internet and now posted all over town. Regardless, it's a chance for me to make a difference and your chance, too." I sit, narrowing my eyes at him. "You're not a criminal. You're providing for Tanya and a baby that will be here before you know it. Let's make the world just a little bit better for our families, Nicky."

Nicky folds his lips between his teeth, his eyes finally landing on mine. He twists his jaw and releases a few cracks before muttering, "What do you need me to do?"

I smirk. "Show me how to use social media."

"Show you how to...? Bro." A line shows between his

thick brows. "You own a phone and don't know how to use social media?"

"I use my phone to call and text people because that's what a phone is for."

Nicky rolls his eyes. "Whatchu need social media for?"

"The people already know my face," I explain. "They already gave us the name, 'LOOK AWAY.' The movement has a face and it has a name. The only thing left is a voice. If we get on the internet, we can spread the word like wildfire."

"You want clout," Nicky states.

"I want clouds?"

"*Clout*," he groans, holding back a chuckle. "You want views, likes, fame."

"I want to be an influence."

"Same thing." He pulls out his phone, dials a number, then lifts it to his ear. "If it's clout you want, I know somebody who can get it for you."

"Clout," I repeat, the words scraping against my tongue like sandpaper. "Yeah, let's clout it up."

Nicky slowly shakes his head at me, waiting for the call to go through. "God, it sounds so cringy when you say it."

"Clouty clout," I tease. "Joseph, the clout king, comin' for the clout crown."

He cackles, pressing a palm over his face. The two of us laugh and I feel the light veil itself over me, despite the dark I've let consume me for the longest time. I feel Death at a distance, allowing me to breathe again.

There's a chance I might be on the right path for once.

It's early afternoon when the doorbell rings. It's only been half an hour since Nicky made the call. The call was brief, which makes me think the person at the door is either good friends with Nicky or not a busy guy because of how quick he got here.

I open the door to a teenager with arms so bony, they might as well be toothpicks. His hair has been permed into tight curls hanging over his forehead. After inhaling a drag of his green e-cigarette, he exhales a cloud of smoke into my face. "Wassup widdit, Nicky?!" he greets in a high-pitched tone. *Was that English?*

I flinch as Nicky lunges forward to hug the kid. The two couldn't be more different, and they hug like they've known each other for years. As they pull away from each other, Nicky pats the kid on the back so hard I'm almost positive I heard something crack. "This is my little cousin, BizKit."

I pinch my eyebrows together, confused. "Biscuit?"

"BizKit," the kid corrects me. "It's like 'biscuit,' but with a *Z* and a *K* in the middle." He lifts his chin, still thinking this through. "And without the *U*."

"So, not like biscuit at all," I reply coolly.

Nicky's cousin ignores me, strutting into my house and toward the kitchen. "Ayo, this place is off the chain, fam!" His voice gets quieter the farther he gets. "I'm diggin' the orange plaid."

"I'm sorry, but how is this kid supposed to help us?" I ask Nicky, the two of us standing side by side at the doorway.

"BizKit is a social media wizard," he replies, placing a heavy hand on my shoulder. "He's got millions of followers online. Every Hip Hop artist in the Bronx goes to him for their music videos and to get advice on how to go viral. You want clout? BizKit will get you clout."

Nicky and I have to walk through a cloud of e-cig smoke to get into my own kitchen. I blow it out of my face to see Nicky's cousin taking a selfie with my T.V. "Is this vintage?" he asks without looking up from his phone. "My followers are asking where they can get one."

I ignore his question. "Why do people call you 'BizKit?'"

"Because I'm always making that bread. Like, you know… always making that money!" He gives Nicky a fist-bump.

"I don't think a biscuit is a type of bread," I reply.

He ponders my comment before lifting his phone to his lips. "Ayo, Siri. Is a biscuit a type of bread?"

A colorful sound wave appears on his phone's screen. Through the speaker, a female voice responds, "*A biscuit can be considered a type of bread. However, biscuits typically have a different texture and recipe compared to traditional bread.*"

Nicky's cousin smirks up at me. "You hear that? I'm a different texture compared to the traditional. That's facts." He winks, then slips the phone into his pocket. "Nicky, you obvi haven't told this boomer about me yet. My name's Kit, but I go by BizKit because it's weird and people like weird shit. It's verbal clickbait."

"What's clickbait?" I ask.

BizKit lets out a patronizing laugh. "My guy, clickbait is what baits you into clicking on something! It tricks you into engaging with a video or a photo." I process his explanation, confusion etched all over my face. "Look, it worked like a charm on you," he continues, making his way to my refrigerator. "You first heard my name five minutes ago, and you've been thinking about it since. Now, here we are still talking about it. BizKit is the bait. You clicked, and now you're engaged."

Holy shit. I've known this kid for five minutes, and he's already proven his ability to get my attention and keep it. Here I am, fixated on this kid's internet alias, which is exactly what BizKit wanted in the first place. This kid is exactly what the Look Away movement needs.

"Just call me 'Kit,'" Kit says while opening the fridge. "No beer?"

"Beer?! You're a kid!" I snap.

"Joseph's been sober five years," Nicky chimes in from the couch.

"Bet." Kit takes a drag of his e-cig. "And I'm no kid. I'll be 19 in a month." He hops onto the couch from behind. "Alright, let's talk. Now you know who I am and I know who you are."

"You know who I am?" I ask, pulling up a chair from the kitchen. I sit halfway between the couch and T.V., my eyes flicking between Nicky and Kit, who take up the whole couch. "What do you know about me?"

"I'll tell you who you are based on what I know. You're a good-looking guy in your late thirties from the Bronx. You got a rad scar, kind of like Harry Potter–it's giving 'chosen one.' Nicky told me you got a kid in a wheelchair and that you're a lawyer who is mad witty and you're quick with your hands– magic tricks and shit. Recently, you went to see Greater Good live, and you were filmed and photographed leaving mid-show. Since then, those videos of you looking away from the stage went viral, making you the face of this 'Look Away' movement for people who want to take Greater Good off of T.V. Am I wrong?"

Nicky and I shake our heads.

He continues, using his hands to paint an imaginary picture. "Okay, broski. I told you who you are. Now, I'll tell you why the world needs you. Since Greater Good aired its first episode, my followers have been messaging me, opening up about how they're depressed and some have even considered committing suicide. They're brainwashed, reaching out to me for help. In the past month, I personally know a handful of kids who have taken their own lives. They all had one thing in common–they were big fans of Greater Good." He jumps to his feet and paces around the living room. "If we can turn you into an influencer who chooses *life* over death, your platform might actually be able to save people from Greater Good's tainted influence on them."

"Exactly!" I raise a palm toward Kit. "That's exactly what we need to do!"

Kit sits on the couch and places both hands on my shoulders. "Picture this–you, Joseph. Your nickname? *'Life's Life-*

line.' You become a prophet preaching the greatest good there is, which is life itself. Right now, the big media networks are losing all their viewers to social media influencers like me. They're desperate to keep the crowd's attention, which is why they're getting away with a show like Greater Good. Call me a conspiracy theorist or call me crazy, but all these media titans and big companies have worked together for decades to keep the people of this world depressed and distracted. They've tested the crowd for decades, seeing how much they can get away with. And what we're witnessing is the greatest test of our generation. That's where you come in. We use your face and voice to expose Greater Good for what it truly is, a ploy to keep the crowd from seeing the beauty life has to offer."

Nicky and I exchange a wide-eyed glance. The passion in Kit's voice radiates, his vision fueling a fire within my soul I never knew existed. A month ago, I was scavenging for cash, wallowing in my own misery. Now, here I am, becoming an influence for the Look Away movement, a movement I started without even realizing it. It's all coming together without me hardly putting in an effort. Now, I'm forced to consider the effect of me putting all my effort into this thing as "Life's Lifeline." It's got a nice ring to it, doesn't it?

Kit takes a long drag of his e-cig and exhales a cloud of smoke between us. When it clears, Kit's eyes lock on mine. "Don't move." He points his phone at me, and the camera light turns on. "What do you want to tell the people who watch Greater Good?"

My heart begins to race. My eyes pan around the living room as I ponder where to start. Nicky and Kit eagerly await my response. I've never been asked to speak in front of a camera. My body tenses and my breaths become shallow until Nicky gives me an encouraging nod. I inhale, then exhale until my nerves calm.

I tuck a few curls behind my ear, then clear my throat. "M-my name is Joseph Verita—"

"Don't stutter," Kit hisses.

I blink at him. "My name is Joseph Verita. I'm a lawyer–"

"You're Life's Lifeline," Kit hisses again.

I narrow my eyes at him before looking back into the camera lens. *You got this, Joseph.* I close my eyes, remembering Ben's words: "*You've struggled a great deal, and I truly believe that God is calling you to accomplish something great.*"

I open myself up to the ethereal presence I felt working through Ben that night in the diner. Its warmth flows through me, filling me with a new form of confidence and clarity.

I exhale, refusing to let years of struggling go to waste. "My name is Joseph Verita, leader of the Look Away movement. For years, Death has stood at my doorstep. I've struggled in ways others could never imagine, and I know there are people watching this who have struggled in ways I could never imagine." I lean toward the phone, resting my elbows on my knees. "I've met Death. I've seen how Death works, and believe me when I say Death is working through Greater Good. I saw it with my own eyes when it took my wife five years ago. Since then, Death has lingered, trying to convince me that my life is not worth living. It's been tough, but I managed to look away and you can, too." My voice raises, overflowing with conviction. "So, I beg you! Don't give in to your morbid curiosity because Death is using it to take over your mind. Stop watching before it's too late. Death is coming for your mind and it all starts with your eyes, so please… *look away.*"

The living room is still, silent. The camera light turns off, and Kit lowers his phone onto his lap. His jaw is hanging toward the floor. Nicky leans back, grinning cheek to cheek. "Damn," he mutters with a look of appreciation. "That's some good shit right there."

"You're him," Kit adds, turning the phone screen toward me. "You're the guy the world needs right now."

I see myself on the screen, the video filmed vertically. I'm perfectly centered, sitting on the folding chair in the middle of my living room. Orange plaid covers the wall behind me, the color popping against the black screen of the vintage T.V. set. The plug hangs from the back of the T.V.

I see myself again, this time in a new light.

I see a leader...

Life's lifeline in its fight against Death.

"You think you can work with that?" Nicky asks Kit.

"Easy," Kit replies. "I'll run Joseph's social media accounts and get my crew to share and blow up his profiles. They'll repost at all the best times and with the right captions and hashtags. We can work around all the antics these media companies will use to try to silence us. Joseph will be all over the internet in no time."

SLAM!

We jump at the sound of the front door shutting. Nicky and Kit look at me for direction, but it's too late.

"Joseph?" Ava chirps from the hall. She stutter-steps into the kitchen. "Oh, h-hi! Sorry, I didn't know we had guests."

Stevie rolls into the room behind Ava. His eyes widen at the sight of Nicky. "Dad, I didn't know you had friends." He gasps at the sight of Kit. "BIZKIT?!"

Kit turns to me with a smirk on his face. "Clickbait," he mouths before turning back to Stevie. "Wassup widdit?!"

I roll my eyes.

"Wassup widdit! I'm a huge fan! Everyone at school watches your videos," Stevie replies, his eyes filled with admiration as Kit high-fives him. "Dad, your face is all over school! Everyone is talking about you."

Ava subtly lifts a handful of Look Away flyers from his backpack. I flash a not-so-confident smile, my eyebrows raised. "Oh, would you look at that?"

Stevie excitedly makes his way to the center of the living room beside me. "Are you guys friends of my dad's?"

Nicky looks at me for a response.

I shrug. "You obviously already know BizKit. This is

Nicky. He's my clien–"

"Friend," Nicky interrupts. "I'm your dad's friend."

I smirk at his reply. This might sound weird, but I want Nicky to call me his friend again and again. Do friends even do that kind of thing? Call each other friends over and over? If not, then they should start. It feels good... *having friends.*

Nicky extends his massive hand toward Stevie. "I'm also your neighbor. What's up, little man?"

"Sup," Stevie shakes his hand, smiling ear to ear. "Are you guys staying for dinner?"

Everyone in the room turns to me. I bite my lip, contemplating an answer. It was only a matter of time before Ava and Stevie met Nicky. Kit is a rare breed I'm still trying to understand, but Stevie already seems to idolize the kid. *Ah, what the hell...*

I stand from my seat. "You're both staying for dinner." As I step around the couch, I give Nicky a nudge. "Invite her."

He turns away, attempting to hide his grin.

"Everybody stay put!" Ava announces. "I need to pick up more food."

"Bet!" Kit shouts while kicking off his shoes. "Grab some beer, too, will you?"

Nicky smacks him beside the head, causing Kit to cough on his own e-cig smoke. "This ain't your house."

Stevie giggles at the two of them bickering. I catch up to Ava a few steps from the front door. "A couple beers for them is fine," I whisper, handing her cash.

"You mean a couple beers for your *friends*?" she corrects me with a wink.

I blush, holding back a laugh. "Yeah, a couple beers for my friends."

Never in a million years did I think I would be having dinner with this many people in my kitchen. The five of us laugh and marvel at the stories shared between the group. From stories about Kit meeting obsessed fans to Nicky getting drunk with his parole officer, the moment is far from dull. Stevie's googly eyes widen every time Kit makes pop-culture references that go right over my head. I study his fascination and respect for Kit. All I could ever ask is for Stevie to look at me the same way. I'm not jealous. I don't get jealous. If anything, I'm inspired to make a name for myself in the public eye like Kit.

The room goes quiet at the sound of a knock on the back door. Nicky stands and opens it. Tanya's bulging belly is the first to slip into the room, then her pretty face. "How's everyone doin'?" she greets warmly. "I know it's not much, but I brought dessert." She holds up a–well, she holds up what looks like a cake. It's a valiant effort at baking a cake, that's for sure.

Ava leaps out of her seat to take the cake off Tanya's hands. "It looks wonderful! You must be Tanya. I'm Ava. So nice to finally meet you."

"Pleasure is mine," Tanya replies smoothly. Nicky is timid as he helps Tanya into her seat.

I clap my hands, then hand her a plate. "The party has arrived!"

She laughs. "I already know you bunch are up to no good with BizKit in the house."

"Me? Up to no good?" Kit smirks. "If fighting the most powerful T.V. network in the country is no good, then I'm the baddest there is." He points his fork in my direction. "All because I'm working for Life's Lifeline over here."

Ava turns to me and tilts her head. "Life's Lifeline?"

"The leader of Look Away, the movement," Kit replies while chewing. "We're gonna take down Greater Good and breathe life back into this bitch!"

"Easy, Kit," Nicky mutters, giving Kit a side-eye.

"Is this about the flyers?" Ava asks me, worried. "You're going to play the role these people are giving you?"

I fill my chest with air. Before I can answer, Stevie shouts,

"So, it *is* true! You're gonna protest the show! Dad, that's so badass! Everyone's talking about you at school, you know. I mean, most of them don't like you for going against their favorite show, but who cares what they think? Fuck their opinions!"

"Hell yeah, little man," Kit squeaks, giving Stevie a high-five across the table.

"Language," I warn Stevie sternly. "And yeah. I'm gonna take down the show." My eyes lock on Ava's. Her eyebrows draw apart, a look of unease. "I'm doing this for the people who don't think life is worth living," I assure her. "I'm gonna show the broken people in this world that it's not too late to be fixed the way I've been fixed."

Ava nods, though she is far from assured that I'm making the right call. I catch Stevie looking at me the way he looked at Kit earlier, his gaze filled with admiration. I lift my chin, my eyes hovering over the table. "Support me or not, I think this is it. This is my calling. I've felt it pulling at me since the night I walked out of that show, and I can't shake the feeling no matter how hard I try," I confess.

"I support you." Everyone turns to Stevie as he straightens himself in his chair. "You promised me you would fix my chair, and you fixed it. You promised you would fix the front door, and you fixed it. Since Mom died, you've just felt bad for yourself and this is your chance to stop. You can even get other people to not feel bad for themselves at the same time. This is your chance to fix the whole world."

"I support you," Ava adds cautiously. "You know I've always supported you. I just hope you know what you're up against—the media and whoever is running Greater Good."

I place my hand on hers and give it a squeeze.

"I got your back," Nicky says from across the table. He wraps his arm around Tanya, then adds, "We got your back."

Kit blows a few rings of smoke over the table. "You know I support you, Mr. Lifeline."

My arms are covered in chills, the appreciation and love bouncing off the walls. This is the most people I've had in this house, and it pains me to imagine having any less in it. I used to tell myself I didn't deserve half as much as I have right now. Maybe that's true, but regardless, I intend to be grateful for what I have now.

"Where do we start?" I ask Kit, who's fixated on his phone.

"We already started," he replies without looking up. "What we filmed of you today is an amazing start. Over the next few days, I'll show you the ins and outs of social media. We'll get content of you talking about Look Away, and I'll teach you how to connect with your followers. But first…" He slides his phone across the table, and I stop it under my palm. "We need to get you back inside of Mendax."

I lift the phone, reading the headline written across a graphic posted by Mendax: "MENDAX NOW OFFERING STUDIO TOURS: Get a Glimpse Behind the Scenes of Greater Good!"

CHAPTER TWELVE

NORA

Over the past three days, I've thought about committing suicide more often than I probably should. I never thought I'd actually go through with it, but lately, I find myself flirting with the idea. It's as if the thought of suicide replaced any thought of Ryan, so let's just say I actually think about suicide a lot.

Since Ryan took his life, there's just no point...

No point in romanticizing him, so instead, I romanticize my own death...

No point in wishing he was here, so instead, I wish I was there...

Wherever "there" is...

Wherever Death takes us when it's our time to be taken.

I exhale a cloud of smoke over the rooftop ledge. The early afternoon sun casts beams of light through a tapestry of fluffy clouds. The air carries a gentle breeze, just enough to create a soothing ambiance around my troubled mind. I ash the tip of my cigarette between remnants of my last two cigarettes. *Three cigarettes in half an hour*. I reach into my purse and pull out the fourth.

"Is this how you'll take me?" I whisper through a cloud of

smoke. Death doesn't answer. Death hasn't answered since it took Ryan from me. I lean against the ledge, my elbows resting along the concrete slab. "So, this is the price I pay for fame."

My eyes land on the security guard standing halfway across the rooftop. Since my rise to fame, I've gotten used to being followed by security. But ever since the protests began, the security guards are starting to feel more like parole officers. It's as if they're not just here to protect me. They're here to make sure I don't do anything stupid. For example, jumping off this ledge.

"If I jumped, do you think they would accuse you of pushing me?" I ask, smiling cheek to cheek. The security guard remains straight-faced. "I wonder what 'the narrative' would be." I roll my eyes, looking out over the ledge. "*Nora Fictus jumps off of Mendax Productions rooftop. The show's creator now a victim to the same morbid curiosity that gave her every-thing she thought she wanted.*"

I laugh under my breath. Having achieved everything I set out to achieve in such a short time makes dreams seem danger-ously underwhelming. Money, fame, power. I have it all. I can buy whatever I want. I can do whatever I want. And here I am, doing what I used to do during my lunch breaks with Ryan, but without Ryan. Would I give up fame for just one more lunch break with Ryan? Thinking back on those late-night pillow talks, "Nora *Bennett*" doesn't sound as bad as I made it out to be. That thought alone makes me question whether or not my deal with Death was a bad one.

I wonder what the rich and famous do when they reach this point. Seek more money, fame, and power? Will it ever be enough? Will I ever be satisfied? I shiver at the thought that crosses my mind, the thought of seeking help. No, no. It's too late to seek help. I tried to seek help once after losing my dad. I joined one of those depressing support groups in the Bronx, and it only took me a few weeks to learn that nobody will ever care for your well-being as much as you will. I'd end it before I try to seek help again.

"The next studio tour is in ten minutes." The voice blends with the breeze. I turn to see Samuel walking out onto the rooftop. "I insisted on coming to get you myself. I wanted to check on you."

I blow a strand of hair out of my face. "I'm fantastic," I lie.

Samuel leans against the ledge next to me. At the casual lift of his chin, the security guard leaves us alone. "I knew he was more than your assistant."

I look up at Samuel, mid-drag of my cigarette. Since our relationship began, I denied that Ryan was more than my assistant. I denied it to myself. I denied it to Ryan's face until he died. I've rerun each act of denial in my head since I witnessed Death steal him from me in front of the entire world on a platform I created. What's the harm in one more act of denial?

"Ryan was just my assistant," I exhale, hoping if I say it enough, I'll one day believe it.

Samuel laughs under his breath, his eyes flicking to mine. "Regardless of what he was to you, he went over your head to speak to me." He takes a subtle step around me. "He accused me of brainwashing you."

I remember Ryan trying to tell me the same, from him noticing I was changing to the looks of disapproval he gave me when the show first aired. He just never saw the bigger picture. He never felt the impact we're making on the world. It was obvious he wasn't on board with what we were creating, but he wouldn't kill himself over it. I know Ryan was never suicidal, so why would he feed himself to the monster he wanted to rid the world of?

"Who cast Ryan to be on the show?" I ask Samuel. The answer is in his eyes, but I want him to say it. I want him to admit that he signed off on it, that he planted the seed in Ryan's mind. Frustration builds in my tone. "Samuel, why did he agree to be a contestant?"

"He was given a pass."

"Given a 'pass?'"

"*The* pass."

"The Golden Guest Pass," I exhale. "But we didn't go live with the passes until after Ryan's episode…"

"The pass needed to be tested before we went live."

I imagine the golden envelope left at Ryan's apartment door, the golden ticket inside reading, "*Your call to a greater good has been answered.*" I envision the raised lettering of the description underneath the bolded line–the same description I signed off on just last week: "*This Golden Guest Pass guarantees you a priority contestant spot on Greater Good's upcoming episode. Present this pass at Mendax's studio doors, and you will be given special treatment prior to your courageous and selfless act.*"

I imagine Ryan opening his apartment door to see the envelope shimmering between his feet. He reads, "MENDAX," inscribed over the smooth surface. Struck by curiosity, Ryan brings the envelope to his living room. He sits on the couch, setting the envelope on the coffee table. I can picture Death slipping into Ryan's apartment in haunting silence as he opens it.

Death transcends upon him, making the walls appear to close in as the gold hue shines across Ryan's face. He doesn't realize it, but his mind becomes a battleground, despair locked in a relentless struggle with hope. Death whispers softly, seducing Ryan with the illusion of relief from his emotional torment, replacing his light with its abyssal darkness.

He could have had me.

He *did* have me.

But Death convinced us otherwise.

Not only did Death convince Ryan that he would never have me, but Death convinced Ryan that I belonged to Death itself. The sad truth is that it's true. I sold my soul for fame and fortune. I gave my life to Death in exchange for a shot at immortality, and it cost me a shot at love.

I lower my head upon realizing who the pass was signed by. My pen danced along the surface of the Golden Guest Pass contract, allowing Mendax to put my signature at the bottom of every pass Mendax gifted to a candidate. On the bottom of the golden pass, written in black ink, were the words, "*THIS PASS HAS BEEN PERSONALLY ISSUED TO YOU BY NORA FICTUS, CREATOR AND EXECUTIVE PRODUCER OF GREATER GOOD.*"

My stomach tightens. "You knew Ryan was vulnerable because he was losing me. And you had the pass sent to him in my name."

Samuel's back hunches as he lowers himself to my height. His face is inches from mine as he states, "I'll say this one more time, Nora. You were called, and you answered. There is no going back now, not with what now lives inside you." A crooked smile spreads across his leathery face. "You will continue to get everything you have ever wanted and more from this world. The people who gathered in my office the other day—do you remember their names?"

I remember the meeting I was late to after visiting Ryan, the darkness weaving in and around the crooked faces in that room. "I remember meeting with them about the protester," I say. "But I don't remember their names."

"Exactly," Samuel states. "We are the most powerful people in this world, Nora. And we don't need recognition to possess the power we have. The idea for Greater Good wasn't yours. It was Death's. You were called, you answered, and now you carry Death with you. Death works through you the way it works through us, which means you can access the most powerful people and their resources. You will be tempted by people like Ryan, who will try to pull you away from your calling. They will try to convince you that what you're doing is wrong, but I assure you that the more you lean into this, the more you'll understand the greater good in what you're doing."

I lower my head until Samuel's wiry fingers lift my chin. "We have big plans for you," he says softly. "You will be happy to hear that we secured Madison Square Garden for the next episode of Greater Good. We'll be broadcasting live from an arena that holds over 20,000 people, with you hosting center-stage."

My heart nearly leaps from my chest. "I'm... hosting?"

All I've ever wanted was to be on-screen. While I reached this level of fame from simply creating Greater Good, this is now my chance to make sure the entire world can put a face to my name.

Samuel is right. I've worked too hard to let Greater Good slip through my fingertips. I've gained too much to consider Ryan a true loss. I made an irreversible deal with Death, and now that Death has held up its end, I need to hold up mine by continuing to do its bidding. Being Greater Good's creator, Executive Producer, and now host, I refuse to let anybody get in the way of Greater Good.

Death called.

I answered.

Eyes, chin, shoulders.

I walk up the bright hall, my posture straight as an arrow. My orange heels click against the black marble floors, my skin glowing after being pampered by the hair-and-makeup team for the past hour. It was my idea to show face on studio tours Mendax is now offering to the public, an idea I'm already starting to regret. The number of protesters on the streets is quickly rising, and the studio tours give us a chance to show that at the end of the day, we're "just a harmless T.V. network."

It's sad to see our haters not understanding that we're helping people. From giving suicidal people a platform to donating their cash prizes, we've only set out to help the community. Sure, there are two sides to every story, but one is often wrong. Soon, the protesters will see how wrong they are, and the tours will help them realize that. With the public now being exposed to how Greater Good is filmed and produced, it will shed a new light on the production. If the tours are done properly, we can convince the public that we're just like them.

When I arrive in the control room, I'm greeted by two crew members standing stiffly. "The group was just escorted through the green room," one of them says. "They should be coming out of stage-left any minute."

"Wonderful," I reply. "Loosen up a bit. We want these people to see that we're human, too."

I look over the wall of screens showing different angles of the set, backstage, and audience sections. The movement on the screens depicts a small group being herded out of stage-left like sheep. The guide escorts them up the staircase dividing the audience section. As security opens the door, the group funnels in and marvels at the wall of screens behind me.

"Remember to refrain from taking photos and videos!" the tour guide reminds the group.

"Good afternoon," I greet warmly. The group naturally forms a half-circle around me, standing wide-eyed. Their intrigue fuels me, and I feel as if I'm hovering over them even though we're eye to eye. Despite my not needing an introduction, I give myself one anyway. "I'm Nora Fictus, the creator and Executive Producer of Greater Good!" The group is speechless, which is a response I've gotten used to. With my palm raised toward the screens, I continue. "We have eyes on every centimeter of the set, from backstage to center-stage, up to the very last row of the audience. It's my job to make sure we're getting the best view at the best time so that our viewers can witness the beauty displayed at—"

"No phones!" the tour guide shouts.

I fold my lips between my teeth, blinking at the group. The handful of people in the front row smile and nod, lending me their full attention. I notice a few heads in the back looking in different directions.

I clear my throat. "As I was saying, these screens allow us to see everything happening in the studio all at once." I turn to the crew member manning the control panel. "Give us *3*." A red light blinks on a screen labeled *3*, which films a widescreen angle of center-stage. "Now, give us *11*." A red light blinks on screen *11*, which shows a close-up of the front row of the audience section. "You see? And just like that, we're able to switch–"

"Sir!" the tour guide shouts. "No phones used inside the building!"

I clench my fist. "Who the hell is using their phone?!"

"It's the man in the back," the tour guide hisses.

People in the group turn their heads, looking for "the man in the back." All eyes land on a man wearing prescription glasses. His hair curls over the sides of his face, which is freshly shaven despite the thick mustache growing along his upper lip. Upon realizing everyone is looking at him, he looks back over his shoulder.

I roll my eyes. "It's *you*, sir. There's nobody behind you."

The man shakes his head. "That, uh… wasn't me. Can't be me."

"What's that in your hand?"

He looks down at the phone in his hand. "I… wait… oh, oh! You meant no phones at all! I'll just put it away."

"Confiscate it," I command security.

The security guard grabs the man's shoulder and swipes the phone from his hand. The man reaches for the phone and…

SMACK!

His face is palmed by the guard before it's pinned against the wall. His glasses break into two pieces and fall to the floor. "Ow! Okay, yep. That hurts," the man mutters against the wall.

"Has everyone in this group signed an N.D.A.?" I whisper to the tour guide.

"Yes, before the tour began."

"Before the tour ends, remind them that they signed away

their ability to talk about what happened during the tour, this included."

The tour guide nods and then addresses the group in a perky tone. "Right this way, everyone!"

"Except you," I state, pointing at the man still pinned against the wall. "You stay here."

The group funnels out the door behind the tour guide. I flash the crew members an irritated expression, signaling them to leave with the group. They obey. The screens flicker, casting lights across the security guard and man's backs.

My heels click against the concrete floor as I approach them. "You have a lot of nerve, breaking one of the main rules after getting the opportunity to meet me like this." With my hands behind my back, I puff out my chest. "Let him go."

The man sucks in a few deep breaths as he's released from the wall. He jerks his torso, releasing a series of cracks in his back, then kneels over his broken glasses to try to fix them.

"We'll be keeping the phone," I say. I lower myself to look at his face, but he looks away. "Look at me. What makes you think you can break the rules in my studio?"

He slowly stands to his feet, the two of us now face to face. The left side of his face begins to swell under poorly applied makeup. As the screens along the wall flicker, I notice a jagged scar peeking through the makeup coating the left side of his face. *I know that scar.*

"You," I whisper, stutter-stepping backward. "You're him. You're the one who walked out of my show. You started the fucking protests!"

He places a gentle palm on his left cheek, then rubs the concealer that once covered his scar between his fingertips. Deafening silence overwhelms the two of us when his eyes meet mine. It's in this very moment that we both realize… we've already met… a month ago… *at a gas station.*

"Wait, I know you," he whispers. "I helped you break into your own car."

My eyes widen. "You're the lawyer–Joseph." With my palm pressed against my racing heart, I tilt my head. "You're the one behind the protests…?" Joseph stands so still it becomes evident his hands are shaking. The shock within me threatens my confidence, but I force it down. With my jaw clenched, I step forward. "You fucking nobody. You think you're brave. You think you can walk into the empire I'm building and get some kind of dirt on me with your little phone?" I snarl, forcing my nail into his chest. "You think you can make a difference? You're naive like every other mindless idiot watching the shows we make."

Joseph winces as if my words are literally getting through to him. I raise my voice with every word I speak into existence. "We control the narrative. It's ours to do whatever the fuck we want with, and all you poor fucks will do is watch because that's all you're good for… being manipulated. I promise you, Joseph. Whatever you plan to say to talk people out of ending their pathetic lives won't work. We already control the crowd. Go home and mourn your dead wife because she's the only one who will have given you the time of day when you finally do yourself a favor and end your hopeless, mediocre life."

Joseph's face is emotionless. I question whether or not he's even breathing until he suddenly sprints out the control room door. The security guard doesn't react, still stunned by my speech.

"Let him run," I exhale. "We have his phone. He doesn't have shit on us."

I stick out my palm as I sit in a nearby chair. The security guard hands me the phone, and I press the button to open the screen. It doesn't turn on. I press again. It doesn't turn on. I press again. It doesn't…

"It's dead?" I whisper under my breath. My jaw drops. *It was never alive in the first place.*

No, no, no.

"It's a decoy phone." I jump to my feet. "It's not the

phone he was using! It's a fake phone it's–he was recording everything with another… HE HAS ANOTHER PHONE!" I slap the security guard's arm. "CALL EVERYONE!" I scream, shoving him out the door and down the stairs. "DON'T LET JOSEPH OUT OF THIS FUCKING BUILDING!"

CHAPTER THIRTEEN

JOSEPH

"HOOAAGGHH!" I vomit between my car and the curb.

"Woah! Woah!" Nicky shouts from the driver's seat.

I can't help it. The anxiety, nerves, and energy drained from me after everything that just happened. I let it all out on the pavement. I was face to face with Nora only a minute ago, and now here I am, standing outside of Mendax. I sprawl myself across the back seat and shut the door. "Drive."

Nicky steers the car from the curb and weaves through traffic. I lower myself below the windows to keep from being noticed. As we turn right on to a busy street, I peek my head up to see the Mendax building now far behind us. I let out a sigh of relief, sitting up. "I can't believe it actually worked."

Nicky catches my eye through the rearview mirror. "What the hell happened in there?"

"I got it all," I say between quick breaths. "Photos, videos, my conversation with Nora."

"What?!" Kit's head peeks out from the passenger's seat. "You talked to Nora?!"

"Every word she said to me in the control room. I pressed *Record* and kept the phone in my pocket." I wipe the sweat from my forehead, then hand my phone to Kit. "You were right, Nicky. The fake phone worked. I pretended to be using it, and they didn't search me after confiscating it."

"Knew it!" Nicky laughs, tapping his heavy fist against the steering wheel. "I told you, it works every damn time. I use that trick on the police all the time."

I roll my eyes. "Hey, easy with that crime-talk. I'm still your lawyer."

"For one more day," Nicky smirks at me through the rear-view mirror. "When you win my case tomorrow, I'll be a free man!"

Nicky's voice is brimming with joy. I smile, though I'm unsure of what will happen when this case is over. I've grown comfortable having Nicky around. Despite the heat we've been under with his upcoming court hearing and Look Away, I like to think we're on the verge of becoming good friends.

"You fucking did it," Kit says with my phone pressed against his ear. He looks over his shoulder at me. "Keeping your phone recording in your pocket when you met Nora was genius! I'm listening to the conversation, and this chick is a straight-up *witch*."

As Nicky and Kit scroll through the photos and videos I took throughout Mendax, I reflect on how everything has fallen into place up to this point. I've spent all week with Nicky and Kit, getting more comfortable in front of the camera, sharing a hopeful message with a world that now knows who I am, Nora included. I'm on the brink of exposing one of the most power-ful networks, forcing me to consider that I'm risking my life. But I'm risking my life to earn the reward of helping others see what I see, which is a life worth living, regardless of how broken we are.

◆ ◆ ◆

After a long night of recording and editing the Mendax

footage, Nicky and I make our way to the courthouse the next morning. I make it a point for us to get there early. I like to think I've come a long way since the last time I saw Judge Bailey, and I want to prove to her that I'm a changed man. "I can't believe my suit fits you," I tell Nicky from the driver's seat.

"It doesn't." Nicky looks down at the dress shirt I picked out for him. Given the width of his chest, the shirt buttons could burst any second. He couldn't look more uncomfortable, and I can't tell if it's because his hearing is today or the suit he's wearing is trying to suffocate him. He itches his bare face. "Man, I haven't shaved since I was 13. I feel like a kid."

I laugh under my breath. "Believe me when I say that judges note every detail behind a case. That includes your appearance and the effort you put into it."

"The only thing this judge is gonna notice is how small this tie is on me." He chuckles as he lifts his tie, then lets it fall halfway down his shirt. I feel bad for making Nicky wear one of my suits, but I've been in Judge Bailey's courtroom enough to know that she appreciates the effort. Nicky is making that effort, which will only strengthen our case.

I tap his chest with the back of my hand. "Hey, I let you wear your sneakers. I didn't have to do that."

"You didn't have a choice! My foot is four inches bigger than yours."

"Size is irrelevant."

Nicky laughs. "In jail, you learn that size is very relevant."

We make our way into the city, and I merge into the flow of traffic. The city's energy surges around the car, the symphony of car horns and distant sirens competing with the smooth jazz on the radio. I'd be lying if I said I wasn't nervous about today. Cases are always based on the facts, and while I have the facts, there is always an off-chance that the jury can be swayed in any direction.

"You nervous at all?" I ask with my eyes on the road.

"Nah, I know you got me."

I smile. It's nice to feel trusted. The people I represent don't trust me the way Nicky does and I don't always trust those people the way I trust Nicky. Every case I've been a part of has gone down the same way. The person gets into legal trouble, they give me a call, we meet in public a few times, we have our hearing, I win or I lose. Nothing special, just the routine. It's the job, and I just do my best to get the job done. I'm paid regardless, sometimes more for proving my client's innocence... even if they weren't. But, Nicky? Nicky is different. I've seen a side of Nicky I wasn't supposed to see and Nicky's seen a side of me he wasn't supposed to see. So, I guess you could say this case is personal.

"I'm nervous about being a dad."

Nicky's words catch me by surprise. "Being a dad?" I ask. When you look at a guy as strong and tough as Nicky, you don't think he could get nervous about anything. "Why are you nervous about being a dad?"

Nicky anxiously tugs at his shirt sleeves. "I ain't ever had a dad. I sure as hell won't know how to be one." He flashes me a half-glance. "You seem like a pretty good one. I've been watchin' the way you are with Stevie."

I fold my lips between my teeth, his words penetrating the indifference I feel most of every day. Being a good dad is never something I actually sought to do. It's more of something I've become. Being Stevie's dad is simply something I am. Do I think I'm good at being a dad? No chance. I guess it just comes with the effort of raising your kid. You don't choose to be a dad, let alone a *good* dad. You become a dad, and you do your best in hopes that your kid will one day appreciate all you've done.

"What happened to your dad?" I ask.

"Wish I could tell you. He was never in the picture. My ma wasn't the best neither. She was always on the corner or shootin' up in the living room in front of me, Kit, and the other kids living in our apartment."

A pit forms in my stomach, picturing Nicky, Kit, and other kids seeing their mom drugged up or selling her body for cash. "Well, look at it this way. You get to set the bar however high you want to. You get to raise your kid to be a better person than you, your mom, and your dad combined. It's up to you. You get to pick your path."

"You don't get it, man. I can't be a dad. Tanya is having this baby soon and I got a criminal record that goes on for days. Ain't nobody gonna hire a bad dude like me. And I don't know any different from the life I'm used to, anyway."

I pinch my brows together. "What do you mean?"

"I've never made a clean dollar. I make my money the only way I know how to make it–by breaking the law. How am I supposed to provide for a kid?"

"That can all change today, Nicky. We'll figure something out. We'll get you a clean job making clean money for you, Tanya, and the baby." I finish my statement, wanting to bite my tongue. *Dammit, Joseph. There you go again, taking on responsibilities you can't afford to take on.*

Nicky looks forward, his posture reflecting serious doubt. While I want to give him the pep-talk he needs, I'm starting to think his fragile demeanor will win Judge Bailey's sympathy, so I keep my mouth shut.

"Holy shit." I slam on the brakes, my car stopping within a foot of people weaving between moving traffic. "Get out of the way!" I shout, my hands raised. They ignore me, joining a crowd of people walking up the road and along the sidewalk.

Nicky's head swivels left and right. "What's happening?"

"No," I whisper under my breath, checking the time. We're due in court sooner than I would like to be. I catch sight of a few signs held above the bobbing heads making their way up the road. "Is this some kind of protest?"

I spot the courthouse in the distance. The crowd's density thickens at the foot of the stone staircase in front of the tall, white building. My mind races as I think through different outcomes. I refuse to settle for the outcome where I walk into this courtroom late *again*. I refuse to hear the security guard remind me that I'm late *again*. And I refuse to let my friend down.

"We're getting out," I declare, my eyes fixated on the courthouse.

Nicky's eyes widen. "You wanna ditch the car?!"

"We don't have a choice. Get out and guide us to the curb. I'll park the car, and we'll run the rest of the way."

His eyes light up at the opportunity to do what he does best, which is intimidate others. With a smirk on his face, he says, "Alright, fuck it." His pants are so tight they almost rip as he throws the door open and stands outside the car. He barricades the car to my right, towering over the hood and extending his palms in the driver's face. "My buddy's switching lanes."

The driver lays on the horn but lays off when Nicky clenches a fist. He allows me to switch lanes as if it's his choice. Nicky walks to the next lane and does the same, then again until I park along the curb. I grab my briefcase from the back seat and shut the door. "I'll be honest," I exhale, combing through my greasy curls. "I didn't think that was actually going to work."

We merge into the river of people walking along the sidewalk. They talk among each other, their random conversations mixing with the sound of distant chants I can't make out yet. Nicky effortlessly parts the crowd for me, the two of us forcing our way toward the courthouse.

"Excuse us!" I shout, compensating for Nicky's ferocity. "Pardon us! Sorry!"

"Don't apologize," Nicky mutters back to me. "You have somewhere to be and these people are keeping you from it."

He shoves a man out of the way. "Easy, pal!" The man nearly drops his sign, stumbling to his right. As we pass, I catch a glimpse of his sign, the large letters beckoning for my attention as they spell out, *"LOOK AWAY."* The moment we make eye contact, he lowers his sign in shock. "It's him," I hear him say as we continue on our way. "He's here!"

A few heads in front of us turn back at the commotion. Eyes widen at the sight of me behind Nicky as he continues parting the crowd. I can't help but look back at these people, picking up on expressions of admiration and respect.

"It's Joseph!" a woman shouts.

"He made it!" another adds. "Life's Lifeline, baby!"

"Did I miss something?!" I say to Nicky's back. The lifted signs face me as the people do, some with printed photos of me captured from videos we've posted, and others displaying my quotes…

"*YOU WERE BORN TO LIVE.*"

"*LIFE > DEATH.*"

"*LOOK AWAY.*"

"*LOOK AWAY.*"

"*LOOK AWAY.*"

As Nicky and I continue through the crowd, my heart pounds. My thoughts form a blend of disbelief and gratitude. I've become an overnight sensation, an icon for a movement that celebrates life against the backdrop of a television show glorifying death. Everywhere I turn, I see my face lifted high, conveying messages of hope and resistance. It's a moment of sheer humility because never in my wildest dreams did I imagine being cherished by so many, let alone cherished by my own self.

I struggle to process this newfound fame as we make our way to the courthouse. It's through the cheers and genuine praise that I find the strength to carry the weight of the responsibility I've accepted. I credit the moral goodness I've opened myself up to, acknowledging that I didn't get to this point alone.

I find clarity amid the chaos in this city as I'm welcomed by it for the first time. Sure, I'm on the path to the courthouse, but I'm also on a path transcending the boundaries of being a once-suicidal criminal lawyer. I've been entrusted with the power to be a force for true justice, an agent for change, *a lifeline for Life itself.*

Nicky no longer needs to move people out of our way. The crowd parts for us now, making it easier for us to walk up the stone steps. The white columns of the courthouse stand tall above me. Its presence once intimidated me, but with the validation of my new identity, I've outgrown the intimidation.

A wall of police officers stands at the top of the stairs. A few recognize me and open their stance for us to pass, but the crowd buzzes behind me, their praise motivating me to face them. "Wait," I tell Nicky.

I slowly turn to look out over the stone steps. People from all walks of life are gathered, packed below me as they wait for me to speak. Confidence forms with every breath I breathe. Phones are lifted high, all pointed in my direction. I spot pictures of my face along with the now-iconic picture of me leaving the show.

After clearing my throat, I shout, "I, uh… I wish I could find the right words to express how grateful I am right now!"

The crowd roars, giving me a few crucial seconds to collect my thoughts before I continue. I look up, begging God to guide me through this, to speak through me. A sudden wave of clarity washes over me, words and ideas eager to be spoken over the crowd. "I'm Joseph. Many of you know me as Life's Lifeline, the leader of Look Away!" The crowd cheers. "Before I get in there, I wanted to take a moment to say that we're not too different, you and I. We're broken. To some degree, we aren't happy with ourselves or the life we live. You see, Mendax knows that about us. They know that we're broken, and they're trying to convince us that life isn't worth living so that they can decide our fate for us. The sad part is that it's working. Suicide and crime rates are higher than ever, and that's exactly what they want because if we're too busy worrying about ourselves, we won't have time to worry about the true evil Mendax is pushing! Listen, the truth of the matter is that we're all going to die, but that's only because we're fortunate enough to live. We didn't earn life. We didn't do anything to deserve it, which is what makes it a gift." I pick a phone to lock my eyes on. "Death has cloaked itself in the form of entertainment. Mendax is doing Death's bidding. Don't be fooled. Don't be misled. Look away!"

The people below me erupt, lifting their signs and posters high. A surge of energy flows through me, provoking me to lift my arms and wave. I feel empowered, strengthened, *chosen*.

My eyes fixate on a woman in the crowd. She lifts her right palm to her face, shields her eye, and looks away. *It's the same motion I made the night I walked out of Greater Good.* I make the same motion over the crowd, and as I look away, I turn back to Nicky. He flashes me a smile, but it dissolves when he looks up over my shoulder. He points to the top of a nearby building where a woman in an orange shirt is standing on the ledge.

I notice another woman step onto the ledge of the neighboring building. Her orange shirt pops in contrast to the gray sky above. To my left, two more people in orange shirts stand on the ledges.

The people on the rooftops all look my way seconds before...

"NO!" I scream. "DON'T..."

They gracefully lean forward, throwing themselves off the buildings bordering the crowd. Their bodies flatten themselves against the pavement at different times, and upon hearing the loud cracks of their now-shattered corpses, the crowd's cheers become deafening screams.

POP!

A crackling sound sends the crowd into a panic.

POP! POP!

People run in different directions, and in an instant, a peaceful gathering becomes a feud of flying fists, smoke, and fireworks as people in orange shirts spring from the crowd. Orange becomes all I see as a man lunges toward me, his fist barely missing my cheek. "FUCK YOU!" he screams, his eyes tainted by pure hatred.

The police around me seize the man and charge down the steps, wielding batons they use to beat innocent and guilty people alike. I stand stunned, eyes fixated on the back of the man's orange shirt that reads, "THIS IS MY GREATER GOOD."

Nicky throws his arm around me and then guides me through the entrance. As the stone floor becomes tile and the screams are muffled, my mind is spinning, hands are shaking, heart is racing. I realize that if I'm going to become the influence I set out to be, it comes at the price of becoming a target.

◆ ◆ ◆

"You've become quite the celebrity over the past few weeks, Joseph." Judge Bailey's voice bounces off the wooden walls as she enters the courtroom with commanding grace. Dressed in a black robe, she ascends the wooden steps to her elevated bench as we stand out of respect for her authority. She sits and subtly gestures for us to sit, too. Her lazy eyes land on mine. "It's nice to see your dazzling personality being recognized for once."

I sit casually, twiddling my coin to keep my hands from shaking. "I'm just happy to give the people something to talk about," I manage coolly.

Judge Bailey lowers her chin, observing me from above her glasses. "So, you like what the people have to say about you?"

"I've heard nothing but positive things." *Though I just witnessed hell on Earth.*

"You must not watch the news then."

"Watch the…" I pinch my eyebrows together. "I'm on the news?"

"Anybody who owns a T.V. knows your name by now. You've been mentioned in almost every news headline today."

My heart plummets, and an audible gulp gets stuck in my throat. I've been so focused on my name circulating social media that I haven't thought for a second that it might have landed on the news. I pull a handkerchief from my coat and pat my forehead, fighting off a cold sweat.

The last time I appeared in a headline on the news, I was in my living room shortly after the accident. I came home from the hospital one night to pick up some of Stevie's toys. Before leaving the house, I noticed the T.V. in the living room was on. I remember slowly walking in, feeling the presence of some-body–some*thing* watching the news. It was the first time Death was in my home after it took my wife. It turned my attention to the screen, and I read the headline written under aerial shots of the car wreck: DEVASTATING CAR ACCIDENT CLAIMS LIFE OF A WOMAN, LEAVES CHILD'S LIFE IN CRIT-ICAL CONDITION. I pulled the plug from the T.V. without hesitation. Before Stevie was even able to come home after months of physical therapy, I had already sold the house to pay off the medical bills and bought our house in the Bronx. Little did I know that night was only the beginning of my relation-ship with Death.

"Forget what they're saying on T.V." Judge Bailey's voice brings me back to the present moment. "Whether or not I agree with them is beside the point. I swore an oath to judge your case based on facts alone, even if the world wants *you* behind bars for trying to cancel a show created to help people."

I narrow my eyes at her, then hold my tongue. Judge Bailey has been brainwashed along with the millions of other Greater Good viewers. I don't want to ruin our chances of win-ning this case before it even begins, so I keep my mouth shut.

I place a comforting hand on Nicky's shoulder, remind-ing him he's in good hands. He nods, keeping his eyes fixed on the table below him. Nicky's spot is a difficult place to be, fighting for his freedom a couple of months before his first kid is born. Out of all the criminals I've taken a stand next to, he's the only one I've grown close enough to feel. I feel for Nicky, a man simply trying to navigate the trials of life while seeing the world through a lens tainted by crime.

"Alright, let's begin," Bailey sighs. "Mr. Verita, I trust you're prepared to present your defense today?"

I straighten my stance. "Indeed I am, Your Honor."

"With the commotion you have caused outside of my courthouse today, I would like to cut right to the chase so we can get everyone out of here safely. Your client stands accused of armed robbery, even though the gun in question was later proven fake. How do you plan to navigate this delicate situation?"

"Your Honor, the evidence will demonstrate that my client, Nicky Williams, was not the perpetrator but rather a victim of severe mental distress which led to chaotic circumstances. I intend to present compelling witness testimonies, including my own account as a witness."

Judge Bailey raises her eyebrows, adjusting her glasses. Whispers flood the room from behind me as the crowd processes my statement. It's not often that a victim of a crime is also the defendant of the criminal behind the crime. My eyes pan around the back of the courtroom as the crowd's eyes fall back on me. I notice a familiar set of eyes staring from the second row, eyes belonging to the person who can win this case for us.

"Hmm, I *thought* I saw your name a few times in the case file," Judge Bailey mutters. "I thought your name listed as a witness was a mistake. You don't think your involvement will compromise your ability to represent your client?"

I casually stroll around our table, weaving my coin between my fingers. "Your Honor, my dual role in this case may be out of the ordinary, but it has also allowed me to form a unique bond with Mr. Williams. It has given me a perspective that no other witness can provide. I know my client isn't innocent, but—"

"Your client committed armed robbery, Mr. Verita."

"Forgive me, Your Honor, but my client was not armed. The gun was fake, and he had no intent of hurting anybody. The fake gun was just as much of a weapon as a pencil could be."

"Whether the gun was real or fake, the gas station cashier was forced to comply with Mr. Williams' demands."

I look around the room for Anthony, the cashier. A sigh of relief escapes me when I realize he didn't show after all. "That's right," I say, suppressing my gratitude toward the only man who could take Nicky down. "I understand that. According to New York's Penal Law 160.05, it should be decided that Nicky here is guilty, but under the third degree. With no intent to cause harm and having stolen no more than a hundred dollars in cash, I humbly ask that you reconsider his sentence from imprisonment to house arrest along with a rigorous community service program."

Judge Bailey laughs. "You want me to minimize his sentence to nearly nothing?! Under what grounds?"

"Under the grounds of the gas station cashier refusing to testify *and* my first witness being the expecting mother of Mr. Williams' firstborn child." I open my stance, my eyes hovering over the crowd until I find the familiar set of eyes. "I would like to call Tanya to the stand."

I flash Tanya a warm smile. She stands with one palm pressed over the curve of her belly. Judge Bailey's eyes soften as she watches the bailiff guide Tanya to the witness stand beside her. She sits, the chair creaking beneath her.

"Can we find her a more comfortable chair?" Judge Bailey scolds the bailiff. "Go find her a more comfortable chair. For Christ's sake, the woman is pregnant."

Tanya is beating sweat, quivering in her creaking chair. I watch Judge Bailey grow more sympathetic toward her by the second, which was my goal since I came up with the idea of asking Tanya to be a witness. Tanya reaches into her bag and pulls out a loosely folded piece of paper. She clears her throat, then says, "If you d-don't mind, I prepared my words for to-day."

Judge Bailey respectfully nods. "Go right ahead, dear."

Tanya's shaky hands lift the paper, and though she's not the best reader, it strengthens our case all the more. "I understand that what Nicky did was wrong," she reads. "But I want to shed some light on the circumstances that… that led him t-to believe he didn't have a choice." Her eyes well up with tears. "We found out about the pregnancy seven months ago, and we were thrilled. But the reality of our financial situation set in. Nicky, the… loving and devoted partner he is, felt over-whelmed w-with responsibility. He needed to provide for me and our… our soon-to-be child."

The room holds still, awaiting her next words. A few tears trickle down Nicky's cheeks as Tanya continues. "With Nicky's upbringing and record, he can't find a job to make the money we need to pay for our child's needs. We're trapped, with no way to bring this baby into the world. Your Honor, I need you to understand the desperation Nicky faced. H-he believed that robbery was the only way to secure some quick funds. It was for our child."

The atmosphere is somber, the weight of Tanya's words resonating with every heart in the room. "I'm not defending his actions," she continues. "I'm just asking for leniency… to urge the court to consider the circumstances that led him astray. More time in prison won't help him. More time in prison won't help our baby. My Nicky needs leniency. He needs guidance and support. Please don't make me raise this baby alone."

She lowers the paper to her lap, her testimony lingering in the air for all to inhale. I study Judge Bailey's empathetic expression. Nicky uses his short tie to pat his cheeks dry while I hold back my smile. Tanya's tone, along with her fragile demeanor and shattered gaze—she delivered the speech I wrote perfectly.

With the gas station cashier's absence and after the testimonies spoken by Tanya, Nicky, and myself, the entire room was a puddle of sympathy and understanding. When I'm finished speaking, I sink into my seat beside Nicky. His large hand envelops my knee, and I turn to see him smiling thankfully. *Win or lose, we won.*

Judge Bailey flips through her notes. After a few silent beats, she looks up at me from over her glasses. "Mr. Verita, I must say I'm impressed. Partially by you, but mostly with the support you gathered in this case. Every time I've seen you defend clients in my court, you defended them with a surface-level obligation." Her eyes flick between Nicky, Tanya, and me. "But it's evident that you have done your research. You wrestled with not just what happened at the scene of the crime but also what led to the crime. I find Mr. Williams not guilty of the original charges against him." Nicky and I grab each other, preparing to celebrate until Judge Bailey shouts, "But…! Mr. Williams will be under house arrest for six months and will receive a strict community service program that must be approved by the court." She slams the gavel against the wooden block beside her. "Case dismissed."

We celebrate as people exit the room. Nicky lifts me up from my chair like I'm lighter than air. As we express an abundance of gratitude for each other, the near-empty courtroom becomes the scene of a sweet victory…

Or a tragedy in the making.

A WOLF IN SHEEP'S CLOTHING:
MEET THE MAN SABOTAGING GREATER GOOD

Saturday, August 10th, 2019

In a world where kindness and selflessness are celebrated, a dark and sinister figure has emerged, threatening to overshadow the good deeds of today's top-ranked T.V. show, Greater Good. Meet the enigmatic man who is quickly gaining popularity across social media, but beware, for his intentions are far from good.

While the T.V. show seeks to give meaning to the hurt and conflicted people of the world, Joseph Verita, cloaked in a facade of charisma, cunningly deceives the public with hollow pep-talks about his version of moral goodness online. A master manipulator, he is a wolf in sheep's clothing, exploiting the brave souls taking their lives on stage in order to serve his own sinister agenda.

As he gains followers online, his intentions become unclear, but one thing is evident: Verita cannot be trusted. He has stirred doubt and division as his protestors take to the streets, violently opposing a show that only serves to better the community. With each viral post and trending hashtag he and his entourage share, he manages to incite controversy and chaos, diverting attention away from the genuine efforts to make the world a better place.

While Mendax continues to shed light on those living in darkness, Verita spreads misinformation and mistrust, tarnishing the show's reputation and causing rifts within the community.

Beware the wolf in sheep's clothing, for his intentions are far from noble, and his actions threaten to overshadow Mendax's genuine philanthropic efforts that deserve our attention and support. Together, we can ensure that the true spirit of helping others prevails, undeterred by the shadow cast by this deceiver.

THE RISE OF A FALSE PROPHET:
What You Need to Know About Joseph Verita

As Joseph Verita spreads false accusations about Mendax's intent in creating Greater Good, it's best you know the truth. Verita has recently taken to the internet, sharing a conversation he allegedly had with Nora Fictus, Greater Good's creator. The self-proclaimed visionary has garnered attention by exploiting Mendax's philanthropic efforts, and now, he threatens the production by creating a fake audio recording he claims belongs to Nora Fictus.

Fear not, Greater Good fanatics. MediaFlow and other social media partners have run multiple fact-checks on Verita's content, concluding that his photos, videos, and recordings are fake.

While this false prophet's rise to prominence is marked by a combination of charisma and persuasive rhetoric, skeptics are raising concerns about the authenticity of his claims. An abundance of sources have reported that Verita has an extensive network of criminals throughout the state of New York. Authorities are monitoring the situation closely, urging the public to exercise caution if approached by Verita or any of his cult-like followers.

◆ ◆ ◆

"Man, I don't know about this," Nicky groans. The two of us stand in the middle of the vacant street, staring up at the church. "I've seen dudes do community service by pickin' up trash on the side of the highway. That's more my speed. Not this."

I squint up at him. "You're telling me you would rather pick up trash on the side of the road than mop floors in an air-conditioned building? Judge Bailey let you off easy. And I'll tell you, she didn't let you off easy because of you or me. She let you off easy because she felt bad for your kid. So, you don't get to be picky with how you serve. Just serve."

A few days have passed since the trial, giving us time to reflect on a successful case and go all in on Look Away. Kit has been working wonders, creating captivating videos of Mendax and myself. I'm still no internet expert, but with Kit's guidance and Nicky's support, the numbers continue rising.

Stevie and Ava are even taking part in the movement now. While most of the kids at Stevie's school voice their negative opinions of me, a small group of kids are actually fans of what we're doing. I know that ten times out of ten, Stevie will take that small group of kids over being alone the way he was before.

Ava has been helping me organize my thoughts into words, the two of us spending late nights writing scripts for the videos we make. The scripts are made up of personal accounts I've had with criminals I represented in the past. With Ava's passion for writing and my experience in shedding light on people who have seen the darkest of days, our message has blossomed into one of inspiration and hope.

I brought Nicky to Ben's church to fulfill his community service sentence. More importantly, I know that if Ben gets enough time with Nicky, then Nicky will no longer have doubts about being a good dad. If Ben could rid me of my self-doubt the way he did, he'll be able to do the same for Nicky.

It's the first time I've been to Ben's church during the day. The church is rundown–borderline abandoned–but the inside is serene. The warm-colored walls and tile floors blend seamlessly from the wide entryway into the sanctuary. The interior is traditional, with long wooden benches that stretch to both sides bordering the wide center aisle. Red, green, and blue hues seep in through the mosaics lining the walls while a center spotlight illuminates the large wooden cross above the stage in front of us.

My phone vibrates, and I see it's an incoming call from an unknown number. I decline the call, then slip the phone back into my pocket.

"I've never been inside a church before," Nicky says softly as we reach the front row.

"Positive Pathways meets every Thursday night here in the basement," I reply, our eyes fixated on the cross.

"What's Positive Pathways?"

"My support group. It's a couple hours of broken people talking about how broken they are."

"Does it help?"

"I like to think so." I turn to see his gaze narrowed in on mine. "I'm doing better than I was before I started coming."

"You think it'd help me?" Nicky's gaze hardens from the outside in, a depiction of the battles fought, mistakes made, and scars borne deep within his soul. Despite his lengthy criminal record, I know he's innocent on the inside. He's just a product of the environment in which he was raised. Like all the other criminals I know, he simply got lost somewhere along the way. *And the world shows no mercy on the lost.*

We turn our heads at the subtle sound of conversation near the church entrance. Ben is finishing a conversation with a professionally dressed woman who taps on the thick folder in her hand, then toward the rest of the sanctuary. Ben nods, and they shake hands. Once the lady leaves, Ben lowers his head.

My voice echoes across the empty church as I tease, "I didn't know you had a girlfriend." Ben is caught off guard by our presence, but after a moment, a warm smile spreads across his face. "Didn't mean to scare you," I add as we approach him.

"Good to see you, Joseph." He checks his watch. "Sorry to keep you waiting. I just received an unexpected visit."

"Everything alright?" I ask.

Ben nods, but it's not convincing. "She works with a real estate investor who wants to buy the church property."

Nicky and I exchange a look. Maybe I'm just paranoid, but my mind goes straight to Mendax keeping tabs on me. Now that they know who I am, who is to say they won't come after the people I know and the places I go? Regardless, I'll take payouts like this over death threats every day of the week and twice on Sunday.

"It was quite the offer, but I told her God's house is not for sale," Ben says enthusiastically. He extends a hand toward Nicky. "You must be Nicky!" I open my stance to a timid Nicky, and they shake hands. "Joseph told me you found yourself in some legal trouble."

Nicky's eyes flick to mine, then back to Ben's. He politely nods, making him appear smaller than Ben even though he's twice his size. "Y-yeah. I made a mistake and have to do community service because of it, and Joseph... I... we thought this would be a good place to start."

Ben patiently nods, doing what he does best... *listening.* He smiles up at Nicky, then says, "This is a great place to start, my friend. Joseph also tells me you'll be a father soon."

Nicky lets out a shaky laugh. "Kind of," he murmurs.

"What do you mean?" Ben asks.

"I'm not ready to be."

Ben steps forward and nearly stands on his tiptoes to place a comforting hand on Nicky's shoulder. "I hope you'll believe me when I say that God will never present you with a situation you can't handle. My bet is on your child becoming the blessing you never knew you needed. Take Joseph here for example. Just a month ago, he was the quietest in my Thursday night group. Now he's a celebrity fighting the good fight!"

"Nicky has played a big part in that!" I add, patting Nicky on the back. My phone vibrates again, and I'm quick to mute it without looking. "Ben, do you mind signing the court documents saying Nicky can do his service hours here?"

"Of course! Just show me where to sign, and we'll get you involved."

Nicky hands Ben the contract. As Ben looks it over, I pull out my phone and see a new missed call from Stevie's school. The atmosphere around me tenses as my paranoia kicks in. Stevie's school *never* calls me. With trembling hands, I call the number back. The world around me fades to the background as I hear the woman's voice. "Mr. Verita?"

"This is he."

"This is Principal Anderson here at Pioneer Middle School. We've been trying to reach you."

"What happened? Is something wrong?"

"Well, not exactly," she replies. "Stevie is here and he's alright. But we think you should come in because he's a bit shaken up."

"Shaken up? Why '*shaken up*?'"

"We found him a few blocks away from the school after lunch. He claims to have been escorted off campus by a friend of yours."

My grip on the phone tightens. Principal Anderson continues speaking, but I no longer hear her. I imagine Stevie being lured out of school by a stranger. I picture him innocently believing that whoever kidnapped him was actually my friend. I slowly turn to Nicky and Ben, the two picking up on my impending episode.

"Mr. Verita?" Principal Anderson's voice pulls my attention back to the phone call.

"Tell Stevie his dad is on his way." I hang up, and as I pass Nicky and Ben, I say, "It's Stevie."

"Everything alright?" Ben asks.

"I need to get to him now," I snap.

"I'm driving," Nicky says as we head for the exit. "I'll get us there faster."

Panic surges through me, not because Nicky is driving like a madman, but because I can feel in my gut that my son is in danger. My heart pounds with the car's erratic movements, my fingers clutching the edge of my seat as Nicky swerves. I scroll through the various scenarios in my head, each revolving around Stevie's life being at risk because of me.

What 'friend of mine' would visit Stevie?

Whoever they are, why would they take him out of school?

If their aim was to kidnap him, why did they return him?

My breath shallows as I come to the realization that their aim wasn't to kidnap my son. Their aim was to send a message.

Nicky's forearms are throbbing from his death grip on the steering wheel. We tear our way through the Bronx, each person we pass staring in awe. "Fucking red light," Nicky mutters. We stop near the intersection and notice a group of teenagers standing on the corner. They glance at us, then whisper among each other. Nicky leans over the steering wheel to get a look at them, then says, "I think they recognize you."

One of the teenagers slowly raises his right hand to the side of his face. He covers his right eye, shielding his view from me as he looks away. It's the same motion that lady made to me in front of the courthouse. I do it back to the teen, indicating that we're on the same side.

The light turns green and Nicky speeds through the intersection. "That signal y'all just gave each other… did you make that up?" he asks. "What was that?"

"Some lady did it the day I spoke outside of the courthouse. I did it back, and I think it's become some sort of symbol for the movement," I reply, slightly confused.

"I can't believe it," he exhales, his eyes fixed on the road. "By now, I know you're a leader. But what I just witnessed? That shit is different. You're becoming an icon."

"Sadly, becoming an icon comes at a price," I sigh as Stevie's school comes into view.

Nicky pulls up in front of the entrance. I fling the door open and sprint into the front office. A few ladies behind the front desk are taken by surprise as I struggle to catch my breath. "I'm Joseph, Stevie's dad."

"He's with Principal Anderson in her office," one of the ladies replies.

She points behind the front desk. As I pass them, I hear their slurs of disapproval. "That's the guy," they scoff. "He's the one on the news."

I couldn't care less. With the media's goal being to paint me in a bad light, I can't help but feel bad for the people consuming their lies. With my mind locked on Stevie's well-being, judgment has no effect on me. In fact, it's the opposite. I welcome judgment with open arms. If my name is on your tongue, it means I'm on your mind. And I'm starting to like that. *I was a nobody for so long, it feels good to be somebody worth thinking about.*

I knock before opening the principal office door. I lock eyes with two police officers, then Principal Anderson, and finally Stevie. A wave of relief washes over me, and I drop to my knees to hug him. It's the sight of my child, safe and unharmed, that makes the outside world irrelevant. In this moment, there's no movement that matters. There's no Greater Good that matters. What matters is that Stevie is safe.

A smile breaks across Stevie's face, and fear loosens its grip on my heart. "You alright?" I ask, grazing my thumb over his cheek.

"I'm fine. I'm alright."

I slowly rise to my feet. "What happened?" My eyes flick between Principal Anderson's and the police now standing by the door. "How could you let a stranger take my kid?"

The two officers hide behind still expressions and guarded responses. I pick up on a sense of reluctance to provide me with answers. I take a deep breath, my desperation to know who laid hands on my son becoming too much to bear.

One of the officers grips their baton, prepared to use it if I act out. "Sir, calm down," one warns. "We're going to need you to stop yelling."

"Yelling?" I ask calmly. "I'm not yelling."

The officer removes the baton from their belt. "I told you to calm down, or we'll be forced to arrest you."

With my hands raised, I reply, "I'm calm, I'm calm! What is this?"

"He's not doing anything wrong!" Stevie yells.

The second officer unclips her taser from her belt, stepping toward me.

"Stop," Principal Anderson states. The officers stop in their tracks, still focused on me. "I'd like to speak to Mr. Verita and his son alone, please. It will only be a moment."

The officers are reluctant to leave the room but eventually obey Principal Anderson's command.

I exhale a shaky breath. "Principal Anderson, you have to explain what's going on."

"I understand your frustration and confusion, Mr. Verita," she says calmly from behind her desk. She cautiously makes her way around the desk, separating me from Stevie. "I am just as frustrated. You know my students' safety is my priority, and I'm looking into this the best I can. But, there's a bit more to it."

Her eyes flick to the door, then to me. "A woman took Stevie away from the campus for a short time. Stevie said it was no more than 10 minutes. One of the teachers pointed out Stevie returning through the parking lot by himself. He doesn't seem fazed by the encounter, but he returned with this." She hands me a golden envelope. "It's… for you."

The envelope gleams in my fingertips, its surface reflecting the light with a captivating allure. I run my fingers over the smooth, gilded edges, the middle of its surface reading, "MENDAX." A chilling sensation spreads up my arms, reflecting the chilling mystery inside.

"The officers," Principal Anderson adds. "They showed up at the school before we even called them. It's like they knew it was going to happen. They didn't ask many questions about the lady who took Stevie, and they didn't take any notes. I think they're here for *you*. They might be looking for some reason to arrest you."

I lift my eyes from the envelope. A look of genuine fear is written across Principal Anderson's face, and I'm left to consider that she's right. After releasing the photos, videos, and voice recordings from inside Mendax, it would only make sense for them to silence me–to lock me away. They know where my support group meets. They know where Stevie goes to school. How many other messages will Mendax send before I feel their true wrath?

"We need to get out of here," I mutter. "But how am I supposed to get past a couple of corrupt cops?"

"Do what you've been doing," Principal Anderson says. "Record yourself. They won't get away with corruption if they have thousands of eyes on them."

"Genius."

I pull out my phone and begin live-streaming. I point the camera lens at myself, my face filling the screen as the number of viewers on the top right grows by the second. *27 viewers… 138 viewers… 897 viewers… 1,716 viewers.* The number grows, comments now flooding the bottom half of the screen…

"LIFE'S LIFELINE!"

"Look away gang"

"fuck u"

"you saved my life forreal"

I fix my eyes on the screen, speaking with conviction the way Kit taught me. "I'm gonna come right out and say it. Based on the response to my last video exposing more of Nora and Greater Good from the inside, Mendax is now threatening my family. I'm here at my son's school where I think they're trying to have me arrested so that I can't spread my message–a message you all know I'm spreading in your best interest." I flip the phone's camera, hand it to Stevie, then step into the camera's focus. "I'm taking my son out of school for his own safety. While we leave the office, he is going to film us peacefully leaving so you can all testify if we're falsely accused of anything. We are keeping calm, so if you see them apply unnecessary force, you're all witnesses."

Stevie points the camera at the door.

"Thank you," I mouth to Principal Anderson, knowing she can't fathom how grateful I am.

She nods, then slowly raises her right palm to the side of her face and looks away. Chills cover my arms as I'm reminded of the magnitude of this movement. From teenagers on the streets to school staff members, there are people among the crowd who are on my side. Mendax can threaten me all they want, but it only proves that what I'm doing is working.

I open the door. Stevie lifts the phone as I push him into the front office, the phone screen revealing staff and students standing idly by in the shadows as we pass. The room is silent, the atmosphere thickening with suspense as eyes flick between the officers, Stevie, and myself. Some teachers offer supportive smiles and nods. Others express looks of disapproval, leaving an unsettling undercurrent of judgment in the air.

One of the officers leans forward. Before he can step toward us, he's stopped by his partner, who notices Stevie recording.

"Not so tough now, are we?" I tease with a smirk.

The phone screen is now showing the two officers between the growing number of viewers and the bustling comment section. I can hardly make out the number of viewers, but as long as the people around us assume the public's eye is on them, we can't be touched.

"Smile, officers," Stevie teases the cops when we reach the exit. "We're live!"

They grit their teeth, remaining motionless as their eyes follow our every move. I never realized the power that comes with the eyes of thousands watching a scene unravel. After all, reality is a culmination of each unique viewpoint lending its weight to the truth. And as our viewership grows in this moment, so does the potency of truth in what's happening here and now. It's difficult to believe in something nobody has seen, as opposed to believing in something everybody has seen.

Nicky picks up on our urgency as I roll Stevie to the curb. He opens the door and lifts Stevie into the back seat while I load the wheelchair. "They don't look too happy," he whispers, starting the car. The two officers now stand behind the entrance doors, straight-faced. Eyes of students and teachers fill the windows on each side of them. "What the hell is happening to this city? Everywhere you go, people love or hate you."

"That's just about the truth of it." I lift my palm for Stevie to place my phone. I thank the viewers, end the live stream, and then crank my neck to see Stevie. "Are you okay? Tell me everything that happened."

Stevie's eyes drop to his lap. "There was this woman with short black hair. I couldn't get a good look at her face because she was wearing these big sunglasses and a hat."

"Did she threaten you?" my voice cracks. "What did she say?" Stevie winces at my words. It dawns on me that a mere change in tone can make kids think they're in trouble. I patiently watch him overthink his next words as if certain words are off-limits. "Stevie…"

"The lady was standing outside of my classroom when lunch started. I was the last to leave the room like I always am, and when she saw me, she seemed super happy. She was really nice, actually. I thought she was a teacher, then she told me she's an old friend of Mom's."

My heart drops, my stomach tightening into a rock at the center of my core. Stevie's mom didn't have many friends. And the few she had didn't live anywhere near us. For a woman to suddenly appear at Stevie's school, asking for Stevie, claiming to be a friend of his mother who died years ago–it just seems unlikely. My eyes fall to the golden envelope that rests in my fingertips.

"We only went a few blocks away from school," Stevie continues, his voice quivering. "She told me a couple stories about Mom, some from high school and others from Mom's old neighborhood in New Jersey."

"What was the lady's name?" I ask, my voice sharp. "Was it Nora?"

Stevie pauses. "I don't know."

I clench my jaw. "You just went off with a stranger without knowing her name?!"

"Joseph." Nicky attempts to calm me down while driving. "The kid was confused."

"You're not a father yet, so you don't get to speak on this." I point to the side of Nicky's face. "I raised my kid better than this." I glare at Stevie. "What's the matter with you? You know a lot of people don't like us, Stevie. We're a target! You know the risk I'm taking by being the face of Look Away?! I could lose everything! I could lose *you*!"

Stevie slouches forward, a layer of fog coating his glasses. "She said she knew Mom," he murmurs, defeated. "I don't even care what you think because I'm glad I got to hear stories about Mom that you never told me."

I pinch my eyebrows together. "I tell you stories about your mom all the–"

"You tell me bedtime stories about make-believe shit!" Stevie snaps.

His words are daggers of truth. Hearing your own kid curse at you is powerful. It's even more powerful when the cursing is justified. The truth is, I haven't spoken a word about Stevie's mom since she died. Instead, I tried to suppress the stories about her with illusions like bedtime stories and little magic tricks. I buried our memories under make-believe stories about superheroes, knights, and witches, all to keep me from falling back into the void that Death created with my wife's absence.

Our car slows to a halt in front of our house. I turn to see the worn brick exterior, the slender trees reaching for a sky draped in a blanket of clouds. Stevie's door opens and I see him prop up his wheelchair through the side-view mirror.

"Stevie."

"I can do it myself," he snaps.

For the first time ever, he sets up his chair without any help.

I open my door and pull out my keys. "At least let me–"

"Ava will let me in," he says, rolling himself up the ramp to the front door.

A sigh of defeat escapes me as I bow my head. "It never gets easier, you know." I sit back in the passenger's seat and flash Nicky a half-glance. "It's like a new challenge comes with every year that passes."

"I won't handle it any better than you," Nicky replies. "I know you lost your wife, but you never mentioned how it all went down."

"Five years ago," I exhale, tracing the stubble on my jaw. "The night I lost my wife was the same night Stevie lost his ability to walk." I silently pull out my gold coin, placing it on the dashboard between us. "I was driving drunk and got into an accident–drove right off the side of the road. One stupid decision cost me my wife, my son's legs, and my will to live."

Nicky squints at the coin. "You don't drink anymore because of that accident."

I nod. "It's one of the many ways I've tried to repent for the mistake I made. You don't know how tough it is to see your son become a reminder of why you want to live and die at the same time. If Death had taken Stevie from me that night, Death would've taken me shortly after. It's the pain I see him in that makes me want to die. But then there are these moments where he smiles. And I'm reminded of why I choose to live."

My vision is blurred behind tears that deserve to be set free. I can hardly see Nicky in my peripherals, but I feel empathy through his rugged exterior. "I don't know what it's like to be you," he says softly. "It sounds terrible."

I let out a laugh, letting a few tears fall on my lap. "Wow, thanks."

"Well, I ain't gonna sit here and tell you your situation doesn't suck because it does. But a good friend of mine once said, '*You were born to live.*' He would tell you the same. You were born to live, Joseph. You tell others that. Keep telling yourself. If you couldn't live with what happened to you, you would already be dead. But here you are living. So, keep on living."

I place a hand on Nicky's shoulder. "You're my best friend, Nicky."

He flashes a faint smile. "Just get back to work." He taps his massive finger over the envelope in my lap. "We have a war to win."

I wipe at my tears, then open the envelope's seal. As I slide out the golden paper, a tiny white card falls onto my lap. I pick up the card, my eyes widening at the sight of the elegant letters handwritten across the surface...

Joseph,

There are two sides to every story, and I know yours…
April 9th, 2014

Nora Fictus

A wave of terror consumes me when I read the exact date of my car accident. I drop the card, feeling the blood flush itself from my face. Does she know I was driving drunk that night? If so, how? The written note is only a few lines, but I dread the thought of what this could mean. If Nora knows the truth–if she knows I ran away that night, that I drove drunk and killed my wife and left my son crippled–she can bury me.

Sure, it could be a bluff. It takes a simple search of my name through Mendax's past broadcasts to find out that I was involved in that accident. At the time, the story Mendax reported was that it was an innocent car accident. But with there being "two sides to every story," Mendax can make up an even worse story if they don't already know mine.

I raise the golden paper that came with the white card, the top reading, *"Your call to a greater good has been answered."* The words below shimmer with a haunting allure, warning me that this is no ordinary letter. It's the Golden Guest Pass Mendax offers to priority candidates they are willing to cast as contestants on their next episode of Greater Good. My mind races with possibilities and consequences, and I suddenly find myself at a crossroads. Death's presence seeps through the car door, making itself at home in the back of my mind.

My thumb grazes over the raised lettering at the bottom of the pass: *"THIS PASS HAS BEEN PERSONALLY ISSUED TO YOU BY NORA FICTUS, CREATOR AND EXECUTIVE PRODUCER OF GREATER GOOD."*

I see this pass for what it is… a gift from Nora, a sick and twisted peace treaty. She's giving me an out before she leaks whatever information they have or make up about me.

Using this pass to get on Greater Good could be my last chance at repentance for ruining Stevie's life. Not only would I be a contestant, but I know that I would win. Nora would make sure of it. Plus, all of Greater Good's viewers know who I am. They all want me dead. I would sweep the other contestants, and the millions I make from ending my life could go to Stevie and Ava. The two could buy a home somewhere safe and far from here. Some of the prize money could go to Nicky, and he could use it to support Tanya and their kid. I could even donate some to Ben's church and Positive Pathways and...

"Joseph." Nicky snatches the pass from my hand. He leans forward, conveying resolute confidence in his voice as his words pull me from Death's grip. While stuffing the Golden Guest Pass in his pocket, he shakes his head, stating, "You were born to live."

CHAPTER FOURTEEN

NORA

"Is that a gray hair?"

I look up at my reflection, wide-eyed. "What the fuck did you just say?"

My makeup artist runs a brush over the back of my head. The light emitted from the mirror reveals hair strands of black and one gray in her palm. Our jaws drop as if it's the first time we've witnessed a sign of aging.

I tilt my head. "Impossible."

"There's more than one," she replies cautiously, sifting a handful of hair through her fingertips. She lets it fall against the back of my head. "Don't freak out. We can pluck them before you get on stage."

I fold my lips between my teeth to keep from hyperventilating. I want her to tell me she's joking. I want her and the rest of the hair-and-makeup team to tell me I'm radiating like they do every time I sit in this chair. I want to feel dangerous and powerful and youthful. Instead, I feel betrayed–not so much by her comment, but by Death.

"Have you been stressed?" she asks.

Me? Stressed?

I fixate on my phone screen, hearing the sound of roaring fans in the stadium just outside my room. The script for tonight's episode of Greater Good floods the screen. I've been reading it over since Samuel told me that Mendax now wants me to be the new host. With my reputation now overpowering the industry and beyond, it was only a matter of time before I claimed center-stage of the show I created. I saw it coming and embraced the opportunity with open arms, so I'm most certainly not "stressed."

My eyes meet the makeup artist's in the mirror's reflection. "I don't stress," I reply coolly.

She leans over my shoulder to grab a pair of tweezers. "You can talk to me, you know. I signed a million N.D.A.'s, so I'm forced to keep your secrets."

"I appreciate the reassurance," I mutter.

I scrunch my nose at the sudden pinch. She places a gray strand of hair on the countertop below the mirror. It mocks me, and before I can silence it, I feel another pinch. "So, you're not worried about that Joseph-guy?" She sets another gray strand next to the first. "It's kind of scary to see how much traction he's getting, even with the news bashing him over and over again. He was interviewed on this podcast my little brother watches." I wince at the third hair plucked. "I think his scar is hot, but my friend doesn't. I feel like it's this… like… damaged, bad boy vibe that–"

"SHUT UP!" I stand and snatch the tweezers from her feeble little hand. "I don't give a shit about what you think or what your little brother watches. Get the fuck out. GO!" Her face flushes, tears welling. "You heard me! Go. I'll do my own damn makeup."

I don't feel the slightest bit of remorse as the girl grabs her bag and scurries out of the room. When the door slams behind her, I notice I'm holding the tweezers like a weapon I intended to stab her with. With the tweezers still raised, I face my reflection. The truth is that I *am* stressed. Last week, Joseph almost ruined everything by leaking what I said to him during the studio tour. I was the queen of a castle I built with my own hands, and he snuck right in and exposed me for what I may actually be–*some witch.*

Since then, Samuel and I have conjured up a series of threats, none of them successful. We proved that we know where his little support group meets and where his kid goes to school. All of our media outlets are simultaneously slandering his name, and he still won't let up. With Samuel constantly reminding me that this Look Away movement needs to be stopped before it gets any bigger, I put together a last-ditch effort by sending Joseph a Golden Guest Pass. If that doesn't get through his thick skull, we'll be forced to prove that we know where he lives.

My eyes lock on the gray hairs that threaten my youth. They lie there, reminding me that despite my quest for immortality, I am, in fact, mortal. I have done Death's bidding, and for what? To be reminded that despite my loyalty and sacrifice, I will one day die, too?

The mirror cracks as I throw the tweezers at my reflection. The sound of the impact bounces off the walls, and when the tweezers land on the countertop next to the hairs, I look up to see the crack, which lines the left side of my face.

Even when I'm alone, I can't escape Joseph.

"Leave me alone," I hiss under my breath. With my palms pressed over the cold countertop, my breath fogs the mirror as I continue. "I'm not like you. I'm not a part of the crowd. I'm not broken. I'm more. I'm so much more. I'm…" *alone.*

Reality seeps into my mind like a distant echo, lingering at the outer rim of my consciousness. Everything I thought I was given–fame, wealth, and power–was never truly given to me. It was lent to me. The pleasures of this world don't belong to me. I'm merely borrowing them. If it's the universe that formed me from atoms, to atoms I will return. If it's God who breathed life into me, my breath He will take. The sad reality is that despite what I gain, become, or accomplish, Death will deliver me back to whoever created me.

I fall back into the vanity chair, wallowing in a pool of thoughts I've been suppressing for weeks. I imagine what Ryan would say about my performance. If he saw me right now, something tells me he wouldn't scold me, though that's what I deserve. Something tells me he would understand that I simply made a bad deal with Death. And even though I introduced him to Death, he would still feel sympathy for me. Deep down, I know that he would still love me despite my hurting him, and that's what hurts me the most.

The knocks on the door don't faze me in the slightest. "Nora?"

I look up to see Dorothy standing at the doorway. I brace myself for a jealous rant, a list of jabs and digs about how I snaked my way into her role as the new host. Even in the dimmed lighting of the green room, Dorothy glows. A pit forms in my stomach, knowing Dorothy's beauty was God-given. She didn't have to sell her soul or make a deal with Death the way I did.

I watch her pan curiously around the room. Her hair has been slicked into a low bun, a thin layer of orange eyeshadow popping in contrast with her tan skin. Regardless of her radiating beauty, she carries herself with less confidence than usual. "Hosting Madison Square Garden, huh?" she forces a smile. "That's... amazing."

Her words are genuine, making it harder for me to take part in whatever conversation this is. I almost wish she would scold me for stealing her job, for letting my career take precedence over what could have been a friendship between us.

She gestures toward the empty couch. "May I?" I nod, and she sits. "Samuel broke the news to me this morning. I'm happy for you, truly."

"Are you?" I ask skeptically.

It doesn't take an expert to know that being a professional

in the entertainment industry also means being a profession-al liar. Dorothy could be trying to throw me off just minutes before I get up on stage.

"Nora, you might have lost sight of this along the way, but we were always in this together," she continues. "I will never see you as competition, but I will say I am worried about you." She stands from the couch, her hand over her heart. "I haven't heard from you since Ryan died. It killed me to know that he was a contestant and I wanted to tell you before the show, but Roth wouldn't let me."

I begin to find Dorothy's presence unsettling. A spiritual force is working through her that threatens Death. *Don't let her distract you, Nora.* Death stirs unease within me, wanting me to rid myself of whatever spirit Dorothy is carrying with her.

"I'm doing alright," I say, forcing a smile. "Thanks for checking on me."

Dorothy frowns, picking up on my verbal dismissal. I would never tell her this, but I'm afraid that the more she speaks, the less prepared I will be to host tonight. She stands to her feet and nods respectfully. "They want me to be your understudy in case you're not able to host at any point the rest of the season. I came to tell you to break a leg." She places a hand on my knee. "And I never thanked you for casting me. So, thank you. Thank you for seeing something in me. And thank you for giving me a chance to prove myself. Regardless of what happens with Greater Good, I've always got your back," she adds.

I keep my eyes on the ground between us, refusing to show her a sliver of vulnerability. My peace returns when she finally leaves. Before the door shuts behind her, a crew member pushes it open.

"Sorry to bother, Nora," the crew member says. "Just wanted to give you the list of contestants so you can read up on them before you open tonight." He cautiously slides the single sheet of paper on the coffee table in the middle of the room.

Upon seeing the cracked mirror, he flashes a nervous smile. "I'll leave you to it."

I stumble to the couch and lift the paper. I drag my eyes over the random names of contestants until I get to the third name. Thoughts of Dorothy, Ryan, and all other distractions vanish when I recognize it. A crooked smile hugs the bottom half of my face when I realize the impact of tonight's show will be unforgettable, leaving a lasting impression on anybody supporting Greater Good or even Look Away. It'll be the most morbid display imaginable–the final blow–ending the war between Joseph and myself once and for all.

I laugh, gripping the edges of the paper in my fingertips. *Sweet Death, you've done it again.*

As I'm escorted by crew members from the green room, a surge of energy surrounds me. The dimly-lit backstage area is buzzing, men and women in black shirts and headsets moving swiftly to orchestrate the final preparations for tonight's spectacle. My heart rate accelerates when I hear the distant hum of the crowd from all around. It shakes the ceiling, walls, and ground below.

For the first time, Greater Good will be broadcast in Madison Square Garden, an arena seating 20,000 people, and I will stand center-stage. Mendax has never hosted an event this big, from today's biggest pop stars performing as our opening act to the grand suicidal display at the end of tonight's show. And I've never felt more alive.

The sound of conversations among crew members competes with the click of my orange heels while I walk up the narrow corridor. Security is glued to each side of me, their eyes vigilant for any sign of protest or disrespect. My tolerance for haters has only grown. If there's one thing I've learned, fame comes at the price of protest.

The dark walls are adorned with posters of iconic artists–

Midnight Mirage, Fai, Ani Black–the list of musicians and performers just keeps going. I imagine my poster up on this wall sandwiched between such talent, a reminder to all who come after me that by some chance, they might live up to "*Nora Fictus, Creator of Greater Good*."

"The opening act is finishing in five minutes! Let's get her mic'd up!" a producer commands a small group of crew members.

I'm guided into a wide space, the ceiling made up of transparent black panels and steel beams so low I can reach up and grab them. A small black box is attached to my black mini-skirt. "Does that bother you?" a crew member asks.

I shake my head. A makeup artist steps in front of me. With determined eyes, she applies last-second touch-ups. "No gray hairs?" I ask before holding my breath.

"No gray hairs," she replies, allowing me to breathe again.

Another crew member gently fastens a microphone to my ear. "Nora, give us a, '*Test 1, 2, 3.*'"

"Test 1, 2, 3."

The crew member looks over my shoulder at the crew manning the sound booth. They respond with a thumbs up. "Soundcheck complete. You got the green light!" I hear one of them shout.

Eyes, chin, shoulders.

After the approval of a few more producers and crew, I'm left alone on an orange platform. Since the moment my identity has been attached to Greater Good, orange has become my color. Trademarking a color is quite the power move. It's one of the many moves I take pride in having made.

My orange heels and the platform I stand on suddenly shimmer. At first, the light is a single beam until it spreads wide. I lift my chin, consumed by flashing lights as the ceiling above me opens. Crew members clap and shout praise as I'm raised above them toward the opening. The praise of my team and the increasing hum of the crowd fuel me more than ever before. I'm bolstered from all angles, confidence flowing through me as if it's been injected into my veins.

The platform rises higher and higher.

The audience roars louder and louder.

I spread my arms, engulfed by an ocean of worship as I'm lifted to center-stage.

It's showtime.

GREATER GOOD

LIVE AT MADISON SQUARE GARDEN ARENA

70S MUSIC PLAYS AS A SINGLE SPOTLIGHT ILLU-
MINATES NORA FICTUS RISING FROM THE GROUND
BELOW. HER BLACK BLOUSE AND SKIRT CONTRAST
THE VIBRANT ORANGE PLATFORM SHE STANDS ON.
AN UNSETTLING PRESENCE MAKES ITSELF KNOWN AS
THE L.E.D. SCREENS ABOVE HER READ, "GREATER
GOOD," IN BRIGHT ORANGE LETTERS. THE CHEERS
AND SHOUTS OF 20,000 AUDIENCE MEMBERS SHAKE
THE ARENA. NORA FICTUS STANDS STILL, HER HEAD
PANNING FROM LEFT TO RIGHT, AS SHE RELISH-
ES THIS EUPHORIC MOMENT. THE PRAISE CONTINUES
FOR NEARLY A MINUTE BEFORE SHE LIFTS HER HANDS
HIGHER WITH A CUNNING SMILE.

NORA: Good evening, and welcome to Greater
Good, the show for the morbidly curious!

THE CROWD'S ROAR BECOMES DEAFENING, CREAT-
ING A PHYSICAL SENSATION OF BEING ENVELOPED
IN SOUND. NORA FICTUS LOWERS HER HANDS, AND
THE ROAR BECOMES A LOW HUM AS PEOPLE SET-
TLE IN SHEER EAGERNESS FOR THE SHOW TO BEGIN.
NORA FICTUS STRUTS TO THE EDGE OF THE CIRCULAR
STAGE.

NORA: Death is in the building! Thanks to your
love and support, we're bringing you your favorite show live from the Madison Square Garden arena. On tonight's episode, three contestants will share their stories—the hardships

they've been through and what's led them to
their breaking points. We've hand-selected
these contestants based on their generosity
and willingness to take their lives on live
television and in front of thousands in the
flesh tonight. You already know how it works!
The contestant with the most votes will give
their cash prize to their estate or charity of
their choice! Now, let's hear it for our martyrs!

**CROWD APPLAUDS. THE STADIUM SUDDENLY GOES
DARK, THE L.E.D. SCREENS IN THE CENTER AND
AROUND THE STADIUM REVEALING CONTESTANT #1—
TWINS CONJOINED AT THE WAIST—IN AN INTIMATE,
DIMLY-LIT STUDIO ROOM.**

DOROTHY: Can you start by telling us a bit
about yourselves?

CONTESTANT #1 (twin-left): I'm Scarlett. I'm
29.

CONTESTANT #1 (twin-right): I'm Jane, also 29.
We're conjoined twins, attached at the pelvis.

CONTESTANT #1 (twin-left): Life is… tough… for
reasons you'd imagine. We—

CONTESTANT #1 (twin-right): We share everything.

CONTESTANT #1 (twin-left): I was about to say that. Don't cut me off when I'm talking. You always cut me off when I'm talking.

CONTESTANT #1 (twin-right rolling her eyes): We share everything. From our stomach to the men we sleep with. As you could assume, it gets pretty complicated.

CONTESTANT #1 (twin-left): It gets *really* complicated.

DOROTHY: I can only imagine. I'm sure the challenges you face are unfathomable to most people you encounter daily. Have you sought "solutions" to these problems you face?

CONTESTANT #1 (twin-right): If you're referring to surgery, the answer is yes. We've talked to surgeons all around the world. A handful of those surgeons even offered to do the procedure for free—well, they offer to do it so that they can say they operated on conjoined twins.

DOROTHY: And what's kept you from doing the procedure?

CONTESTANT #1 [TWINS] GLANCE AT EACH OTHER.

CONTESTANT #1 (twin-left): Every surgeon says the same thing.

DOROTHY: And what's that?

CONTESTANT #1 (twin-right): Since we're split almost right down the middle, they can only save one of us, and it's up to us to choose which should be saved and which should die.

DOROTHY: How could they make you choose who lives and who dies? That is just terrible.

CONTESTANT #1 (twin-left): We won't choose. We can't choose. It's both of us…

CONTESTANT #1 (twin-right): Or none.

DOROTHY: And that's why you're here today?

CONTESTANT #1 [TWINS] NOD, THEIR GAZES DIS-HEARTENED.

DOROTHY: What do you plan to do with the winnings?

CONTESTANT #1 (twin-right): If we win, we want the money donated to our parents. They have been nothing but supportive. They spent all the money they had on our therapists and treatments. They've flown us to just about every surgeon so that they could find a way to help us justify this life—*our* life. And so, we're done… and we want them to be rewarded for the effort they put into raising us because—

CONTESTANT #1 (twin-left): Because us living is harder on them than it is for us.

DOROTHY: Wow. Just wow. Your story is truly inspiring, and I hope you know that the sacrifice you're making for your family requires obscene amounts of courage.

L.E.D. SCREENS FADE TO BLACK. A SPOTLIGHT REVEALS CONTESTANT #1 [TWINS] RISING FROM THE PLATFORM BELOW AS THEY SIT IN A PLUSH ORANGE CHAIR. THE CROWD APPLAUDS AND WHISPERS AMONG EACH OTHER FROM THEIR SEATS. CONTESTANT #1 [TWINS] WAVE FROM THEIR CHAIR.

NORA (standing behind CONTESTANT #1 [TWINS] with hands on their backs): We feel for you both, Scarlett and Jane. We commend you for your bravery and willingness to take your own life for a good greater than yourself.

NORA (to camera): And now, let's meet our second contestant.

THE L.E.D. SCREENS IN THE CENTER AND AROUND THE STADIUM REVEAL CONTESTANT #2 IN AN INTIMATE, DIMLY-LIT STUDIO ROOM.

DOROTHY: Can you start by telling us a bit about yourself?

CONTESTANT #2 (holding down button on throat device): I'm—Dwayne. I—have—laryngeal—cancer. The—cancer—led—me—to—rely—on—this—device—to—communicate.

DOROTHY: We're so sorry to hear that, Dwayne. Does it hurt to speak?

CONTESTANT #2: It's—hard—to—speak. But—it—doesn't—hurt.

DOROTHY: Was your laryngeal cancer caused by something specific?

CONTESTANT #2: I—smoked—cigarettes—since—I—was—15. After—22—years—of—smoking—a—pack—a—day—I—found—out—about—my—condition.

DOROTHY: Smoking truly is a nasty habit, isn't it?

CONTESTANT #2 CLOSES EYES AND NODS.

DOROTHY: What inspired you to apply for Greater Good?

CONTESTANT #2 (teary-eyed): My—wife—left—me.
Finding—someone—new—with—this—condition—is—
nearly—impossible.

DOROTHY: How tragic. What do you intend to do
with the cash prize if you win?

CONTESTANT #2: I—want—the—money—donated—to—
lung—cancer—research.

CONTESTANT #2 LOOKS DIRECTLY AT THE CAMERA.

CONTESTANT #2: If—you—can—stop—smoking—then—
stop. Don't—lose—everything—like—me.

**THE L.E.D. SCREENS FADE TO BLACK. A SPOTLIGHT
REVEALS CONTESTANT #2 RISING FROM THE PLATFORM
BELOW AS HE SITS IN A PLUSH ORANGE CHAIR. THE
CROWD APPLAUDS FROM THEIR SEATS. CONTESTANT #2
WAVES FROM HIS CHAIR, WHICH FACES OPPOSITE OF
CONTESTANT #1 [TWINS].**

NORA (standing behind CONTESTANT #2 with hand
on his back): We feel for you, Dwayne. Hopefully, people will keep from smoking because
it truly is a nasty habit. We commend you for
your bravery and willingness to take your own
life for a good greater than yourself.

NORA (smirking at camera): And now, let's meet
our third and final contestant.

THE L.E.D. SCREENS IN THE CENTER AND AROUND THE STADIUM REVEAL CONTESTANT #3 IN AN INTI-MATE, DIMLY-LIT STUDIO ROOM.

DOROTHY: Can you start by telling us a bit about yourself?

CONTESTANT #3: My name is Nicky Williams…

CHAPTER FIFTEEN

JOSEPH

I caress the bouquet of flowers in my quivering hands. The bouquet weighs more the closer I get to her. I keep my head down, not knowing what to say or where to begin. A cool breeze rustles the branches of the naked trees around me, and I wish there were more noises filling the silence, anything to keep me from the guilt banging on the back door of my conscience.

After all these years, my wife hasn't moved. Despite the highs, lows, and everything in between. Even though I never took a second to visit her, she still never left. She's the greatest wife I could have ever asked for.

"I brought you flowers," I mutter without looking in her direction. "I, uh… I know you're probably upset with me. You know, for cutting you out of the picture after the accident."

The bouquet shakes in my hands, my breath becoming less stable. I'm starting to think it was too soon to come here. In reality, it's probably too late. How could I go about my daily life avoiding my first love? How could I act as though the mother of my child isn't worth a second of my time? I'll tell you how… I ran from reality. I distracted myself with other people's problems. I made up make-believe stories. I picked up stupid little magic tricks. I helped others so that I would be too busy to help myself.

I inhale, blinking toward the sky to keep from crying. It's now dusk, the sky painted in hues of orange and pink gently embracing the fading sun just over the horizon. Faint stars twinkle a few light-years away. Eventually, I can't hold my breath any longer. My eyes land on the tombstone that reads, *"Elizabeth Verita, Loving Mother & Wife."*

"I haven't been ignoring you." I lower the flowers to my side. "I've been busy, I… I guess I've been trying to be busy, I…" *I'm rambling.*

I want to apologize, but I've already apologized. For years, I've apologized through my actions. From adopting responsibility for the people around me to cutting out my vices, my way of life is a result of how fucking sorry I am for that night. The cold, hard truth is that an apology won't bring Elizabeth back. An apology won't rewrite the part of the story where I lost the love of my life and ruined my son's life on a single ride home. So, I won't apologize. Instead, I'll try to make her proud.

"I'm becoming the man you always wanted me to be," I state, gripping the bouquet tighter. "You used to tell me I was too hard on myself, that one day I would change the world. I didn't believe you then, but Elizabeth, if…" My voice cuts out. I clear my throat, pushing through my own disbelief. "If you could see me now, I think you'd be so damn proud. The people… they see me as this symbol of hope, which is something I've lacked for so long. Since I lost you, there was this shadow that covered my world. But since I started this movement, there's this light. I catch glimpses of it, like when Stevie looks at me. I see it when people acknowledge me on the streets. I read it in their comments and messages. And I'm starting to see it in my own reflection."

I let out a laugh, tears now trickling down my cheeks. "I made a friend. That's right. I became friends with the guy renting our guest house. Get this… my first impression of the guy was him holding me at gunpoint at a gas station," I chuckle. "His name is Nicky. I like to think that you sent him to be my friend because the way we met is something you would've found funny. Anyway, Nicky is gonna be a dad and he's real nervous about it, the same way I was before we had Stevie. It's a shame, the way he clings to his past and all the mistakes he made. I try to get him out of that headspace, but you know how it goes. There is never a perfect time to have a kid, but that's the beauty of it. Nicky will realize that. I'll make sure of it."

My smile flattens. "Stevie has had it pretty rough at school since the accident. I mean, he has his ups and downs. I can't begin to tell you how difficult it is for me to watch him struggle without being able to do anything about it. You would know how to handle it, though. You always knew how to handle tough situations."

I tap the bouquet against my thigh, sifting through my thoughts. "I tell him stories, Elizabeth. I make them up as I go every night and he loves it. Well, he loves it now, but I'm sure he'll grow out of it. I still bring him Kit Kats. You'd be upset to know that I let him eat them before bed."

My eyes drop to the bouquet. The colors remind me of the dress Ava wore the night we went to dinner, and it suddenly dawns on me why I came to see Elizabeth after all this time. It's not to catch up, and it's not to make her proud.

Before the words even leave my lips, the trickling of tears becomes a flood. "I met somebody," I somehow manage to say. "I never planned this, you know? Everything, from the car accident to hiring Ava to having these feelings for her. A part of me is dying, knowing that I have feelings for a woman who isn't you, but that woman is also giving me life. It was always you, Elizabeth. And I will spend the rest of my life knowing that I let Death take you from me, but I didn't have a choice. Just know, if you're up there somewhere… if you're listening… I will always love you, even while I love somebody else."

I take a knee and set the bouquet at the base of the tomb-stone. As I rise to my feet, my fingers trace a path over the weathered stone slab, its surface cool against my rugged hands. This could be the most difficult conversation I have ever had, but it's necessary. It took me years to get to the point where I could speak the way I've just spoken, and I know that it's not by my power alone that I was able to. The power belongs to whatever has been working in me since the movement began, and I thank God for it.

When I get to my car, I notice a blue light illuminating the steering wheel. My phone is lying face-up on the seat, the screen flooded with missed calls and texts. I quickly open the door to see six missed calls from Kit. I call him back, and with-in seconds, his panicked tone fills my ear. "Joseph?! Joseph! Where the fuck have you been I've tryna I've been tryna get ahold of you man you gotta do something you gotta stop him before–"

"Kit!" I shout into the phone. "Calm down. What's going on?"

"It's Nicky! They got him."

"Got him? Who's got him?"

"Greater Good! Nicky's on the show right now!" Kit wheezes. "He's the third contestant."

◆ ◆ ◆

I've never driven this fast. My hands grip the steering wheel, my knuckles white against the leather. I swerve through traffic, from left to right to left again. Each twist and turn is a pulse of urgency, every screech and honk a desperate plea for God to bend time and space in my favor. The road stretches out like a tapestry of possibilities, each intersection a crossroad of fate I need to conquer.

Remnants of my phone call with Kit linger in my mind,

forcing me to fight the world from blurring before my very own eyes. How did Nicky get on Greater Good? *Why* did Nicky get on Greater Good?

Before our conversation ended, I gathered from Kit that the show is being broadcast from Madison Square Garden. There's still time to make it, to save my only friend from making a grave mistake. I imagine how frightened Tanya must be, her palm firm against the curve of her belly where Nicky's child rests.

With one hand on the wheel, I call Ava with the other.

"Joseph," she answers, as if waiting by the phone.

"Ava, Nicky is–"

"I know. Kit came here looking for you. He's here with Stevie."

My eyes widen. "You have to turn off the T.V. Don't let them watch a second of this."

"It's unplugged," she assures me. "What are you going to do?"

"I don't know yet. I'm headed to the arena now."

"Be careful, Joseph," Ava warns. "It could be a trap. Mendax could be setting you up because they know how close you and Nicky are."

"I'll deal with the consequences when the time comes. Is Tanya there?"

"She's not in the guest house and isn't picking up her phone. How did Nicky even manage to get on the show?"

"I don't know. Out of all the people who apply, too…"

I pick up speed, seizing gaps between moving cars with the arena now in my sights. To my demise, I'm forced to stop at a red light. My gaze lands on the steering wheel, and my mind jumps to the last time I was in this car with Nicky. It was the day we drove to Stevie's school, the same day Nora gave me the Golden Guest Pass. My heart plummets in my chest when I realize exactly how Nicky managed to get on the show.

I remember him subtly slipping the pass into his pocket

after he took it from me. I didn't think much of it then. I didn't think about it at all. Did Nicky take the pass to save me or because he wanted it for himself? We won his case. He has a kid on the way. How could I have missed any indication that my only friend would be willing to end his own life?

When the light turns green, I floor it. "I need to go. I'm pulling up to the arena."

"Be careful," Ava warns.

"I will."

Upon parking, I throw the car door open and sprint toward the shimmering stadium. I'm a whole block away and it still towers so high, it scrapes the heavens. My shoes pound against the pavement. The distant roar of the crowd reverberates through the air like a battle cry, propelling me forward with a surge of determination.

My breaths come in ragged bursts, my lungs burning as I weave through a crowd gathered outside the arena. The closer I get, the thicker the crowd appears to be. My weaving between bodies turns into shoves. Every step now comes with a deliberate push, the whispers and scoffs creating a whirlwind around me. I keep my eyes on the entrance doors that are barricaded by a wall of security guards, the next obstacle I intend to face head-on.

I shove somebody aside, and they drop their phone. As it lands on the ground, I read Nicky's name written out on the screen, listed among two other names. *They're voting.*

"No! Stop!" I shout. "Stop voting! Don't vote!"

I do a full spin, my eyes panning over the various faces illuminated by the eerie glow of their phone screens. The air is heavy with an unsettling silence, broken only by the soft tapping of fingertips on screens. The crowd remains captivated by the fate of three contestants in their palms. One by one, their faces look up at the stadium wall. An orange hue casts itself over their vacant gazes.

I look up over my shoulder, my jaw dropping at the sight

of a colossal L.E.D. screen depicting Nora. She flashes a chilling smile, her eyes locked on me as she says, "And the votes are in."

No. God, please no.

I stand still, the bottoms of my feet becoming one with the earth. The single screen is divided into three, each third showing a live stream of the contestants in their plush orange chairs. Unable to look away, I take one step toward the screen, then another. The yellow numbers and orange bars appear next to each contestant, prepared to display the number of votes each contestant received. My legs shake as I continue toward the screen, fixated on the rising bars. The numbers rapidly increase, the bars rising roughly around the same height.

I begin to sweat as Nicky takes the lead. Contestant #2 takes the lead next. Nicky again, Contestant #2 again. My heart beats so vigorously I can hear it in my head. It nearly stops when Nicky takes the lead, this time by a long shot. The height of his bar grows taller with every passing second. The rising numbers begin to slow down, Nicky's bar now nearly twice the height of the other contestants' bars.

The camera cuts to Nora standing behind Nicky's chair. Her pale hands envelop his shoulders. Though he's significantly larger, her presence on-screen overpowers him. "And it looks like we have our winner!" she announces with a cunning grin. "Let's hear it for Contestant #3, Nicky Williams!"

The screen cuts to a close-up shot of Nicky as he stands. As he's escorted to a second platform, it's evident that his eyes are filled with sorrow and regret. He looks down at the wooden chair that rises from below the stage. A spotlight highlights the freshly-glossed seat, metal cuffs drilled into each armrest.

While crew members cuff Nicky's wrists to the armrests, Nora looks into the camera, saying, "Now, Nicky will commit an act out of sheer bravery, courage, and generosity. I've just been informed that the voter donation amount we've received tonight is the most we've ever received in a single episode!"

The crowd roars, shaking the walls of the stadium. The sea of people cheer behind me, the sound crashing against me like a tsunami. Nora raises her hands. "And now, Nicky will die for the greater good of his soon-to-be-newborn!"

A line shows between Nicky's brows, his jaw clenched as his platform is lifted into the air. A close-up camera angle picks up the sweat dripping down the side of his face, the droplets becoming one with his own tears. He closes his eyes, grinding his teeth as he wrestles with regret.

The platform stops rising halfway between the stage and the top of the arena. A gentle mist is sprayed from above the chair Nicky is cuffed to, a thin layer coating his head, neck, and arms.

"Why are they spraying him with water?" someone near me asks.

The wooden chair under Nicky suddenly catches fire.

"That ain't water they're sprayin'," someone else answers. "That's gasoline!"

The crowd around me cheers, hollering for the fire to catch Nicky. As if on command, the fire consumes Nicky's entire lower body.

My eyes drop to the wall of security standing in front of me. Every muscle in my body tenses, coiled with the energy of a raging storm, ready to be unleashed on this vile world. I scream at the top of my lungs, throwing my full weight into the nearest security guard. I fling my arms in every direction, my fists making contact with faces I can't even see. I need to get inside of the venue. I need to ruin Nora for ruining the minds of these people–for ruining Nicky's life. I'm focused on wrath and intend to wage war on Mendax and everyone behind this morbid monstrosity.

WAM!

I receive a blow to the head, and it sends me into a second guard. Before I can retaliate, I notice a man charge the guard next to us. The guard holding me lets go to help the other, and

I fall to the ground. The crowd behind me remains fixated on the screen above us, the fire consuming Nicky reflected in their darkened eyes. Within seconds, a third guard beats me with a baton.

My right eye begins to swell, but I'm able to see that among the brainwashed viewers, people sprint from the crowd, emerging like lions from the embrace of the wilderness. My eye continues to swell shut, my head now throbbing. I watch as the people rush toward me with violence written across their faces, and I prepare for my final moments, trampled by a mob I only sought to help.

I let out what may be my final breath, unable to stand to my feet. The first wave of people gets closer and closer until… they're gone. They continue right past me, colliding with the guards who were beating me. One after another, these people emerge from the crowd of viewers to charge at the arena doors.

I lie the back of my head against the pavement, looking at the black sky above. A face appears, then another, and another. "Is he alright?" one of them asks the other.

"Doesn't matter," the other replies. "Get him to safety."

I'm pulled up by my coat lapels. A man and woman wrap their shoulders with each of my arms. People continue appearing from the crowd, fending off security guards as I'm escorted back through the sea of people. "Another way," I say. "The crowd is too dangerous."

"As long as that screen is on, these people aren't going to look away," the woman on my left replies. "See for yourself."

I stumble forward with the help of the two strangers. As we split the crowd, my eyes pan around to see the people fixated on the screen that's now behind us. They smile. They clap. They cheer. They watch my friend burn before their very own eyes. And they can't look away.

"Who are you?" I ask the strangers helping me.

"We're a part of your movement," the man on my right states, facing forward. "BizKit posted about you coming here to save Nicky. He said you might need our help. We got here as quick as we could."

We make it out of the crowd, their screaming and cheering now a distant hum. The throbbing in my head lessens as I'm escorted into the back seat of an S.U.V.

"Take him home," the woman says to the driver.

She shuts my door, pats it twice, then turns back toward the crowd.

"What address?" the driver asks.

"No, they could follow us. They can't know where I live," I reply. I think through the safest places I could be on a night like this. Now bruised from head to toe, processing the tragic and televised death of my only friend, plus having a target on my back, I find myself at the mercy of the force greater than myself–greater than *Death*. I've gotten myself wrapped up in a spiritual war, and at this point, there is no better place to be than the one place that's had its doors open to me since the very beginning. "Take me to the church," I say. "The one off Fordham Road and 3rd Ave. The Bronx."

CHAPTER SIXTEEN

NORA

"You'll go down in history for that performance," Samuel declares as security escorts us through the stadium tunnel and into our Escalade. The praise from fans is muffled from inside the car as we leave the arena. Samuel undoes the button on his blazer, then leans back in the seat facing mine. His stained teeth reveal themselves between his thin lips. "Not only were you captivating, but casting Joseph's friend as a contestant… Nora, that was brilliant."

"I can't believe it." I struggle to contain my giddiness, feeling the adrenaline propel me into euphoria. "Did you see how many people were out there? Did you hear them?"

"I could feel them." Samuel tightens his fist, pride swirling in his abyssal gaze. "Before you created Greater Good, we had fans. We had shows with viewers. But tonight I witnessed a form of worship." He leans forward. "With the number of eyes on us, with their interest, with their willingness to surrender their attention to such a wicked display, there is no telling how much deeper we can drown them in their own morbid curiosity."

His eyes flick right, and the passing city lights cast a glow upon the side of his face. "With the crowd pouring their time and energy into Greater Good, their minds are ours. The world is in the palm of your hands, Nora. All you need to do is take it."

The world is in the palm of my hands.

My eyes are fixed on Samuel, and I see the future of Greater Good unravel between us. I see world tours. I see merchandise and spin-off shows produced in different countries. I see our morbid displays revolutionizing morosity itself. And when it's all said and done, I will be immortalized in history for having successfully done Death's bidding. I'll never need to worry about my name being forgotten.

Samuel pours two glasses of celebratory champagne. He hands me a glass, then clinks his against it. "Here's to living forever."

I lift my glass to my lips, hiding my grin. Samuel downs half his glass and then pulls out his phone. As his attention shifts to the screen, I feel like I'm left alone in the back of the Escalade. I consider pulling out my phone, too. I want to text somebody, asking what they thought of tonight. I want to call somebody, asking if they want to celebrate this win with me.

I finally give in, scrolling through recent messages. There is a long list of incoming messages from celebrities I've become acquainted with over the past month. Most of the messages are trivial questions about the show's after-party tonight, not a single text rooted in a genuine connection. Amid the thread of self-centered chatter, my thumb stops over my conversation with Ryan. An ache manifests in my core when I see the preview of the last texts he sent me. I open the last conversation...

RYAN: Are we still meeting for dinner?
RYAN: Not sure if you ended up working tonight.
      Regardless, I'm at the restaurant so let me
      know

As I put my phone down, I'm left with a heavy heart. It becomes painfully clear that Ryan always saw the light in me long before I sold myself to the dark. Glorifying Death granted me a world of opportunity. Hell, glorifying Death gave me the world, but it stripped me of my connection with the world. It robbed me of the only light in my life. My obsession with fame and my fascination with Death cost me true love. Is it possible to have both the world and true love? Maybe that's a question I should've asked myself before I chose the world.

"Nora." Samuel's thunderous voice fills the back of the car. "I've said your name three times," he adds. He tilts his head, reading my mind before his eyes drop to my phone. "Is it important?"

"Is what important?" I ask, picking up my glass.

He frowns. "Whatever you're looking at on your phone."

I shake my head, then finish my champagne. Before Samuel says another word, I extend my empty glass in his direction. He narrows his eyes, knowing I'm avoiding his question. Despite his suspicion, he refills my glass anyway. "We'll be at the after-party any second. I suggest you get your thoughts in order before you get out of this car."

"You suggest I get my thoughts in order? Or *your* thoughts in order?" My words feel sharp against my tongue, but I can hardly regret speaking them. They came from a heart I forgot I had until Ryan's texts reminded me.

Every muscle in Samuel's face remains still except for the corners of his lips, which curl into a crooked smile. The car comes to a slow halt, and I don't let him hold my gaze for another moment. I chug my champagne and step out onto the sidewalk.

Cameras flash from both sides of the walkway leading into the hotel. Celebrities are gathered in front of the branded step-and-repeat walls, posing for photos with "MENDAX" and "GREATER GOOD" printed repeatedly behind them. With my eyes fixed on the hotel entrance, I don't look back for Samuel.

I know he'll be using a private entrance like every time before, leaving me to be his puppet for the press.

Eyes, chin, shoulders. I straighten my posture, but not for photo ops or interviews. I ignore the microphones and cameras trying to keep me from the entrance. The doormen open the doors for me, and I feel the eyes of partygoers and hotel guests watching me enter the luxurious lobby. I scoop a cocktail from a waiter's drink tray and finish it before I'm in the elevator.

My buzz grows heavier with every floor I ascend past. By the time I reach the top floor, trying to stand straight becomes a fun little game I play with myself. I stumble out of the elevator into a narrow hall, which opens to a rooftop terrace where celebrities and public figures are gathered, all flaunting their success and stature.

As I reach the terrace, I'm welcomed by a chilling breeze. I embrace it with my eyes closed and arms spread wide. "Cocktail, Nora?" a waitress asks, offering me her tray of elegant drinks.

I flash the waitress a smile, wiggling my fingers over the various glasses. I lift one to her lips. "Take a sip," I urge lightheartedly. She giggles nervously, surveying her surroundings like she is being tested. Little does she know she *is* being tested.

If there's one thing I've learned from the success of Greater Good, it's that there is a tolerance for what you can get away with. Through piloting test episodes, twisting a narrative, and casting pretty people, it became clear that we underestimated the tolerance of our viewers. Getting people to off themselves on live television shouldn't be easily tolerated by the crowd. But then again, Mendax and the media have been testing the crowd since long before I came into the picture. And now I'm a part of that test.

So, now that I've seen what Mendax can get away with… *what can Nora Fictus get away with?* Can I get anything I want from the people at this party? Can I completely unhinge myself–reveal all my secrets–and still be accepted by this crooked community?

"Go on. Drink some," I urge the waitress again.

She sucks in a quick breath, then sips the cocktail. When she hands it back, I smirk. Her eyes widen when I finish the glass in a few gulps and grab another. I turn my back to her and continue deeper into the party.

Strings of twinkling lights adorn the edges of the rooftop, casting a warm glow over society's elites. Now that I've reached a level of fame and power higher than anyone here, I find myself unamused. Life is less fun without boundaries to push, less fun without something to chase.

My mental clarity is fleeting with each sip I take. Attendees relax in plush sofas and velvet cushions. They express their superficial looks of admiration, fighting for the chance to have me look their way, to breathe the same air.

For once, I refuse to entertain these people. Instead, I entertain myself by testing the next person I lock eyes with. I smile sadistically at a man wearing a silver wedding band around his ring finger. I pull his attention from his group by simply walking in his direction. I lick the rim of my glass without breaking eye contact and a smirk plays on his lips, affirming his interest in me. He opens his stance, dragging his eyes down my body until I pivot in the opposite direction of him.

I convinced a waitress to drink on the job.

I convinced a married man to unwittingly engage in a flirtatious exchange.

It's possible that with my newfound stature and spiritual allure, I will always get what I want. I will always win, so now I'm on a mission to lose because I've learned that always winning isn't as fun as I thought it would be. Tonight, the most valuable win will be to walk away having lost.

The drinks flow through me at a dangerous rate. I start finding it difficult to gauge risk, blurting out thoughts and ideas before I think them through. How far can Nora go? The most handsome men open their stances to me when I get close. The most influential women offer their full attention when I speak.

This is influence.

This is power.

A hand gropes my ass.

This is interesting.

"I didn't know you got down like this." I turn to see Danny Davis standing over me, wearing a cocky grin. "Is tonight the night I see the side of you cameras don't?"

I narrow my eyes on him. It's been a while since he interviewed me on his talk show, yet the way he holds me suggests we've been together ever since. His otherworldly aura of stardom radiates, his thick strands of hair falling loosely over his sharp cheekbones. A layer of sweat coats the sides of his face, his pupils dilated.

Danny's lips meet my ear. "You were astounding tonight," he breathes into me. "I probably shouldn't be telling you this, but my publicity team thinks we would stir up real press by hooking up."

The alcohol makes it easier for me to look him in the eyes. "Is this your way of asking me to dinner?"

Danny lets out a laugh. "Let's skip dinner." Despite his sleaziness, he's somehow still charming. But also trouble. Mostly trouble. I know this because he reminds me a bit of myself. "I can have my driver take us to my place within the hour. Second thought, he can take us now."

"If you knew what I do, you wouldn't go anywhere near me," I slur.

"You entertain." Danny shrugs. "This is a Mendax party. We all entertain."

"I entertain?" I laugh, then bring myself centimeters from his lips. "I do Death's bidding." He blinks at me, confused at my remark. "That's right." My voice grows louder. "*You* entertain, Danny." I turn, pointing to the people around me. "You entertain! You entertain! I don't fucking 'entertain!'"

Nearby conversations fade, giving me the silence I need to expose myself once and for all. My eyes land on Dorothy, who is shaking her head for me to stop, but it's too late. *How far can Nora go?*

"I'm not like you!" I shout. "I'm not like any of you, which is why I don't expect you to understand what I actually do here!" My tone is raspy, my own words fighting me from sharing them. "I was given a gift! Death came to me with Greater Good as a way for me to do its bidding! That's right, I created a machine that murders people… I manipulate innocent, broken people on live television, and you all praise me for it! The world thanks me for it! And my viewers worship me for it!"

My heart is beating out of my chest as I stand at the center of the terrace. Everybody keeps their distance as I raise my glass. I fixate on Samuel standing in an elevated section above me. "So, here is to making deals with deceivers…" My eyes meet Danny's. "Here is to being beautiful, but only on the outside…" My eyes pan over the eyes of everyone else. "And here is to death being the only constant. You can distract yourselves with fame, drugs, sex, and money, but Death is coming for us all the same. And I sure as hell hope that whoever Death introduces us to shows us mercy for all we've done on this broken planet."

The rooftop terrace is filled with frightened expressions, all but one. A malevolent grin spreads across Samuel's deranged face. He's the only one raising his glass with me. I lift my chin, finish my glass, and then spike it into the ground. I watch him laugh before I storm back into the building. I'm nearly sober, boiling blood replacing the alcohol in my body.

It's taken me a month to realize that I've been Mendax's pawn, a mere cog in a machine that serves to push its narrative. These aren't my people. This isn't my world. I'm not who they want me to be. I'm not even who I want to be. Everything I earned on the outside was at the expense of who I am on the inside.

The elevator doors open to the lobby, and I feel Death's presence pulling at me like never before. I have no desire to go home. I have no desire to be anywhere at all.

As I approach the lobby doors, it dawns on me that the only place I can go to escape Death's hold on me is the only place Death has the least influence. The place I decide to go to frightens Death, and I feel it trying to steer my attention away.

Death tries to pull my attention to the lobby bar. *Get another drink.*

Death tries to pull my attention to my phone. *Go home with Danny.*

Death tries to pull my attention anywhere but where I've decided to go.

It's been years since I've last been there, and truth be told, I don't even think I'm welcome anymore. But I don't have a choice. I made a deal with darkness, and this is my last chance to find the light.

◆ ◆ ◆

I shut the taxi door behind me, now staring up at the weathered church. It's been years since I went to my last support group meeting here before my pursuit of fame blinded me from my pursuit of peace. Not much has changed, though the paint has faded and the steps are severely worn. I can't help but think it mirrors my deteriorating soul over the time passed since I've last been here.

A hesitant sigh escapes my lips. The weight of my poor decisions appears to be lighter the closer I get to the front doors. With cautious steps, I push them open, their creak echoing throughout the silent sanctuary. Wooden benches stretch from the middle aisle to either side of the church. A massive cross stands under a spotlight directly ahead. It reaches for the ceiling, propped against the wall behind the stage.

Forget focusing my eyes, forget lifting my chin, forget cocking my shoulders back. I slouch forward, finally giving in to my exhaustion. After taking a few steps, I undo one of my heels. After a few hops, I undo the other and keep moving. My bare feet are cool against the smooth floor.

I stop in the middle of the aisle a few rows from the front. A wave of humility washes over me when I realize it's the middle of the night and the cross is still illuminated by the spotlight. In every production I've ever been a part of, the spotlight eventually turns off. The show eventually comes to an end. But why is it that, in the middle of the night in a battered old church in the Bronx, the cross is illuminated on center-stage?

In the few support group meetings I attended here, I failed to accept that I was broken like the world and the people in it. I developed this mantra that my image is everything, when in reality, image is merely what you see, which doesn't necessarily make it real. The image I created of Greater Good is a lie. The image I created of myself is a lie. The only truth we hold is that we don't know the truth.

A sniffle echoes from my right, and I turn to see a man sitting in the third row. The spotlight from the stage just barely reveals half the man's face, a scar etched along the left side.

Joseph.

Joseph says nothing while staring at me with an exhausted expression. I return the stare with the same intensity, which is little, if any at all. Here sits my enemy, the man who threatened to destroy my only chance at leaving a legacy. All I ever wanted was to be somebody worth remembering. It was never my intent to corrupt the world in the process.

After a few silent beats, Joseph moves his coat from his left side to his right, an invitation for me to join him. The silence between us is deafening as I stare at the empty spot beside him. He faces the cross.

I cautiously accept his invitation, slowly side-stepping between the benches until I sit to his left. The two of us stare directly ahead, fixated on the cross. A shimmer in his lap catches my eye, and I notice him weaving a gold coin between his fingers. It glides in, out, and around his hand without him even looking at it. In the blink of an eye, the coin disappears. My eyes flick up to see him staring at me.

"You know why I learned magic?"

I'm caught off guard by his question. It's so random, so trivial. We've waged war with each other over the past month... we're finally face to face... and he asks if I know why he learned magic? We have every right to strangle each other right now. I threatened his family, he threatened my career. I persuaded his friend to end his own life, he persuaded the crowd to protest Greater Good.

I aimed to crush Joseph's spirit so he would stop telling people their lives are worth living. *Fuck, maybe I* am *some kind of witch*. It makes sense for him to wring my neck or bash my head repeatedly against the bench until I'm no longer recognizable. Instead of doing either, he reaches around my shoulder and pulls the coin out from behind my ear.

"I learned magic to steer somebody's attention anywhere I wanted," he says. My eyes are locked on the coin until he holds up my phone.

My jaw drops. "How did you—"

"I had you focused on the coin," Joseph explains, handing me my phone. "Whenever I wanted to avoid tough conversations, I used little tricks like that to change the subject."

"Why are you telling me this?"

He looks over his shoulder and I notice the fresh bruise swelling over his right eye. He looks forward again and winces at a pain in his side. "I use magic to hide the pain in my life. What kind of pain are you hiding behind Greater Good?"

I face the stage, chin raised. The closest I ever came to opening up was with Ryan. I've never considered myself strong enough to voice or think about it. The reason behind why I seek to leave a legacy through my name and not through children is something I've kept locked away in the abyss of my mind. But given my current situation, I no longer see the use in hiding it.

"I'm barren," I confess, lowering my head. "I'll never be able to have kids." When I face the cross again, my vision is blurred by tears I refuse to let fall. "When I die, there will be nothing left of me. It's why I've become so obsessed with Greater Good. If I can get it big enough, the world will know my name. Then I won't need to worry about it being forgotten. It's the legacy I'll leave behind."

Joseph pulls a handkerchief from his pocket and hands it to me. It's baffling how two enemies can show such respect for each other in heated times like these. The paradox unfolds before my eyes, revealing how even the fiercest opponents can pause to acknowledge the brokenness that binds humanity.

"I should be happy to hear that you struggle. And I should hate you for everything you've done," he exhales. "But you only did it because you're broken, just like everyone else in this fucked up world."

I can't shake the notion that Joseph carries a light similar to the one I saw in Ryan. But there's also this intangible weight–a spirit–that accompanies him. Like my relationship with Death, the spirit's presence lingers near Joseph like an echo, and it offers me peace. This form of peace is different from any I have ever experienced, and I can't help but come clean.

I suck in a quick breath. "This is going to sound crazy, but I know Death." A line shows between Joseph's brows. "I've always had this morbid curiosity, and one day, Death gave me this idea. I was to do Death's bidding in exchange for the success of Greater Good. I knew it would be my legacy, and everything would fall into place as long as I performed. I thought that if I could sell myself to Death by doing its bidding, it would help me leave a legacy that would live on after I die."

Joseph's gaze penetrates into the depths of me. I can feel his empathy as if the two of us feel the exact same. "I know

Death, too," he finally says. "I watched Death take my wife from me, and since that night, I heard it in the silence. It would call to me in a whisper, especially when I watched your show."

I squint at him. "Y-you… you hear it, too? The whisper?"

He nods. "I will say, I haven't heard it since I started Look Away."

"Why do you think that is?"

He fixates on the cross. "I think it's because I picked another path. I chose to find the beauty in life instead of fearing death. Ever since I started wholeheartedly choosing life each day, Death lost its hold on me."

"I can't help but think that we're a part of something so much greater than this world–that we're just pawns on the chessboard, soldiers in battle, but not just any battle. It's a spiritual battle. One between good and evil, God and the devil, life and death."

Joseph smirks, his eyes still on the illuminated cross before us. "I think we *are* pawns, for sure. Easily disposable. Some pieces are stronger than others, but it doesn't matter because, in the end, we're just pieces in a larger game."

"You have no idea," I mutter. "I sat in a room with people who basically run the world. And the world will never know their names or what they look like. If you think Greater Good is the end goal, you're wrong. It's just a distraction to keep people from discovering the real end goal."

"What's the real end goal?"

"No clue." I shrug. "Knowing Mendax's narrative must be above my pay grade. My only job is to keep the crowd distracted so the people above me can do whatever they want." My eyes meet Joseph's. "Are you afraid of dying?"

Joseph puts serious thought into my random question. I guess it's a pretty loaded question, especially for a guy who knows Death personally. Or, maybe it isn't. Maybe it's a simple question that requires a simple answer.

"I used to be afraid. But now? I'm too focused on living

to worry about dying," he says softly. He grabs his coat and stands. "I have a son to get home to," he exhales before passing me toward the aisle. "Listen, Nora. No matter how the war between us pans out, I think it's safe to say there is a bit of good in you. I didn't think that before, but after this conversation, I think it's there. You just have to find it. The path is yours to pick. You'll realize that even though you know Death personally, you were born to live."

Joseph turns, jams his hands into his pockets, and walks up the aisle. My eyes fall to the handkerchief he left in my lap. It's the remnant of a simple gesture that serves as so much more. I was so focused on being remembered after I die, I forgot to live. And in the process, I created a monster that's wreaking havoc on the human spirit.

I could petition to shut down Greater Good, but Mendax will ruin me before I gain momentum. On the other hand, if I join Joseph's movement, I'll lose Mendax's trust, which would ruin my chance of taking down Greater Good from the inside. I'm pinned. But then again, the world's eyes are on me. With Greater Good's viewership at an all-time high, I've never been more famous or influential. I have a chance to use the platform Death gave me in order to give my life meaning. Knowing what I know about Samuel and Mendax, they will never let me out of this business alive. But I'm okay with that.

Because the greater good I'm willing to die for…
is greater than Greater Good itself.

I pull out my phone.

"Nora?" Dorothy answers my call, her charisma radiating through the phone. "Are you okay? I saw what you did at the party, and I thought–"

"I know, I know," I cut her off. "I fucked up. I'm sure everyone thinks I'm crazy."

"Let me finish," she says sternly. "I was going to say that I thought what you did was brave. Some would also say brilliant, if they weren't too scared to say anything at all."

I nearly blush. "If you think that was brave, you're sure as hell gonna get a kick out of what I'm about to propose."

"I'm listening…"

"After the scene I made tonight, there is no chance Samuel will let me host again. I have a feeling he's going to ask you to host, and I need you to do something for me. I need you to announce me as a contestant." I pause, waiting for Dorothy to respond. Silence. I clear my throat, then continue. "Everyone loves you, Dorothy, and rightfully so. Our fans have idolized you from the start, myself included."

I pause again, refusing to continue until Dorothy proves she's still on the line. I hear a sniffle. My eyes narrow at the stage before me as I process the fact that Dorothy genuinely cares about me… of all people, the person I once considered a threat–the person I once envied the most…

"You can't," her voice cracks. "Nora, this is a mistake. You're making a mistake if you go through with this."

I shake my head, gripping the phone with my now-quivering hand. "I made a bad deal," I admit. "And I know too much about what goes on inside of Mendax. If they know I want out, they'll come after me. The irony is… they'll make it look like a suicide, just in my own apartment." A laugh escapes me. "If Death is planning to take me, I would rather it be on center-stage."

"And if I don't call you to the stage?" Dorothy retorts hesitantly. "What if I don't want you to end your life?"

"My life ended when Ryan's did."

A few silent beats pass between the two of us. It's evident that neither of us know what to say. It's also evident that we both know this needs to happen.

Dorothy sighs. "Nora–"

"Dorothy," I cut her off, my voice now concrete. "I know you can win over the crew members and security. I know you can get the prize handlers to distribute my cash prize. And I know Samuel will ask you to host. All I ask is that you call me on stage when we go live and hand me the microphone. The last thing our viewers want is a Greater Good finale, which is exactly why we're going to give them one."

CHAPTER SEVENTEEN

JOSEPH

The taxi's engine fades in the distance, leaving me standing on the curb. The night wraps around me like a soothing embrace, a stark contrast to the rollercoaster the past month has been. The chaos of the city has dimmed since I ended up at the church tonight. After what might be the longest night of my life, I'm left in peace and silence standing outside my home.

The cool night air fills my lungs with every deep breath. There's no trace of Death, no whisper. Just the serene hush that settles over the neighborhood. I used to complain about this neighborhood, my house, and everything in it. Looking up at it now, I couldn't be happier to call it home. The hallway light is on, which means Ava is still up. The sound of my fatigued footsteps echoes throughout my unkempt front yard.

I'm sifting through my keys at the front door when it suddenly opens. Ava's eyes widen, her hand on the edge of the door. "I've been trying to get a hold of you. I've been watching the news and checking the front porch every 10 minutes. I saw what happened to Nicky and then they showed footage of you charging the police and getting beaten and I didn't know where you–"

I caress the sides of her face and mold my lips to hers. The distance between us dissolves, my exhaustion replaced by my yearning for Ava's touch. A moan escapes her as we force each other through the entryway and into the hall. For once, I do the opposite of what I've always done.

I don't shy away from her touch. *I embrace it.*

I don't reject her love. *I receive it.*

Her back meets the orange-plaid wallpaper, and I pull back, but I don't look away. I couldn't look away from her if I tried. With my hands still on her cheeks, my eyes flick between hers. I want–no–I *need* to take her beauty in. She pulls me to her by my coat lapels, and we move deeper into the hall. We keep silent, our hearts beating mercilessly against each other. She nearly tears off my coat before introducing it to the floor. I nearly rip her shirt, adding it to the trail of clothing that leads to the living room.

I lift her from the ground. My tongue sweeps hers, and I pour my willingness to love her into every part of me that meets every part of her. As I carry her to the couch, she drags her palm against the wall until it flicks the light switch. In an instant, the room goes dark. The moonlight seeps through the back window, and I see the light in her eyes–a beacon that has guided me from the darkness I willingly let into my life for so long.

I lay her down on the couch and unbutton my shirt. Not as fast as I would like to, so the bottom few buttons fall to the ground as I tear open the rest. Ava exhales into me as I lay over her, her gaze appreciating every inch of my scarred face like I was intentionally created this way by God. The once-prevalent thought of not deserving her love is naught. I don't care whether or not I deserve this woman. She just needs to know that I cherish her for giving me a reason to keep living. And all I care to do is prove it here and now.

A breath escapes her. "At one point, I didn't think you would ever feel this way about me."

"I was afraid to," I admit. "But fear itself couldn't keep me from you."

I bury my lips in her neck, my tongue discovering the smoothness of her skin. Her aroma gives me new life... a life free of struggle, pain, and doubt. Her breath gives me new hope... a hope for a future, family, and purpose. My right hand curls behind her neck, heat flowing under my skin until it settles at my waist.

Ava's eager eyes drop slowly from my eyes to the length of me. She gently separates the trim of her thong from her hips, and I smile, pulling it off and dropping it to the floor where it belongs. I rub my tip against her, watching her eyes roll back before I'm even inside of her. She grabs the hair on the back of my head, the anticipation gnawing at our desire for one another.

It's been five years since I've slept with a woman and over a decade since I've slept with a woman who wasn't my wife. But Ava is not just any woman and Ava is not my wife. So, I choose to make love to her with the same thrill that comes with embracing a new way of life. I chose life over death, and I'll choose Ava every day that she'll let me.

Her grip grows tighter around my curls the deeper I am inside of her. Her jaw drops, pleasure swirling about in her gaze before her eyes roll back. With every thrust, I accept realities that were once harsh. Our bodies become one. Our hearts become one. Our lives become one, and I invite each reality with open arms.

Loving this woman was never planned–never part of some script. It's real. You love some people because of how they treat you or what they say to you. I love Ava for one reason, and it's that–throughout my hardships, pain, and doubt–*she was there*. She never gave up on me, she never left. She's the angel who gave me the grace I needed to fight my demons.

◆ ◆ ◆

"You're a hero, you know." Ava's tone is so calming it could put me to sleep. "They can say whatever they want about you on T.V. The message you're preaching is saving lives."

As we lie on the couch, she twiddles my gold chain between her fingertips. Her cheek is warm against my shoulder, and I savor her touch now as much as I have the past few hours. I feel like a new man, set free from the cell I locked myself in all these years. While I'm ashamed to have waited this long to feel for somebody, I'm happy to finally feel for Ava.

"Ava, you've done so much for me when I refused to do anything for myself." I prop myself up on my elbow, looking her dead in the eyes. "*You* saved *me*. Without you, there's no telling whether or not I would have put myself on that stage the way Nicky did. I will spend the rest of my life loving you for giving me a reason to keep living."

Ava's fingertip delicately traces my cheek. In the depths of her gaze, I see a tapestry of emotions too profound to be turned into mere words. She already knows that the reason I'm breathing here and now is because she gave me air when I was suffocating.

THUD!

A sudden noise shatters the calm. Ava and I are sent into a panic, and it takes me a moment to realize the sound came from the backyard. After a quick glance at the kitchen clock, I see it's just past five in the morning. The sun is starting to rise, casting faint orange hues in thin strips across the room.

"Stay here," I whisper. My heart races as I hop across the living room, slipping my pants on. With my bare shoulder pressed against the wall, my fingers separate the blinds. I see Tanya outside, picking up her belongings, which fell out the bottom of her distressed luggage. I open the back door and make my way down the stone steps. "Tanya? What are you doing? Is everything alright?"

Tanya frantically continues picking up clothes and jewelry, stuffing it back into the ruined bag. "I'm fine! I'm alright," she assures me without looking up. Her hands tremble, betraying the calm facade she struggles to maintain. I reach her in a few steps, kneeling beside her to help. "Joseph, please just–"

"I can help," I say, gathering a handful of clothes. Tanya nervously glances over my shoulder and down the alleyway. I turn to see a taxi in front of the house. "Are you coming back from somewhere?"

I look down at the random items littering the ground between us, then fixate on the white envelope with Mendax's address printed on the top left. Tanya's face is stained with guilt and it suddenly dawns on me that she's not coming back. She's running away.

"What did they send you?" I ask, my voice sharp.

She stares at the envelope lying between us. Without answering, she lunges toward it, but I swipe it before she can. "Joseph! That's not for you!" I turn my back to her, absorbing her slaps. "Give it to me!" she screams.

I tear open the envelope, walking halfway down the alley before I see that it's a check. My heart drops at the sight of the eight-digit number. The check is made out to Tanya from Mendax. The memo reads, *"Granted to the estate of Nicky Williams, his greater good."*

With one hand holding the check above my head, I fend off Tanya with the other. "You're taking the fucking money and running?!" I snarl. "Nicky hasn't even been dead a full day, and you're just gonna up and leave! What about his cousin, Kit? Have you considered that some of this belongs to him?!"

"That's *my* money! Nicky left it for me and my baby; now give it back!" She whacks the side of my face, but her words are what catch me by surprise. "What do you mean, '*My baby*?' You mean, '*Your and Nicky's baby*!'"

Tanya lays off for a moment. The ferocity in her eyes becomes a sheepish retreat.

Ava steps out from the back door, her eyes flicking between Tanya and me. "Is everything okay?"

"Say the baby belongs to you and Nicky," I demand Tanya, pacing side to side. She places her hand over her stomach. "Tanya, he took his life for that baby. Tell me that baby is his." Her bottom lip quivers. "Say it, dammit!" I scream.

"I can't."

A defeated breath escapes me. It's not even Nicky's kid. He robbed that gas station, carried the stress of becoming a father, and took his own life for a lie. "You let him go on that show," I whisper. "You knew why he was doing it. And you just... watched? You watched my friend burn alive for a lie. Did you even love him?"

"How dare you!" Tanya shouts. "How dare you question whether or not I loved Nicky..."

"Did Nicky know the baby isn't his?" Ava interjects.

Tanya turns to Ava. Eyes now pools of sorrow, she lowers her head in dismay. "He didn't know."

My jaw tightens. "Nicky didn't end his life for nothing." I lift the check toward Tanya, and there's a gleam of hope in her eyes as she reaches for it. Before she can grab it, I rip it down the middle. I rip it again, and again, and again, until all that's left are paper shreds I let fall to the floor. "Get the fuck out," I state.

Tanya collapses to her knees, cursing, crying, and screaming until her voice gives way. With a heavy heart, I ascend the steps and go back inside with Ava. I know, deep down, Nicky didn't end his life for nothing. Despite Nicky's decision and the questions that gnaw at my mind, I cling to the belief that Nicky's sacrifice holds a deeper meaning.

As Tanya's cries echo in the background, it becomes clear that Nicky's legacy is more profound than any material possession. It's a reminder that life is intricate, often veering away from the paths we can see. And though this world is designed to mislead, I will do my best to ensure that Nicky's story is far from over. The echoes of his presence will continue to be heard, shaping Look Away in ways we can't yet fathom.

CHAPTER EIGHTEEN

NORA

"Nora, what are you doing here?" a crew member asks as I enter the studio. "Aren't you supposed to be getting ready in the green room?"

I continue past the crew member toward center-stage. At one point, this was the only place in the world I'd rather be, on set with the cameras and lights creating the illusion of reality. The air is thick with the hum of energy and activity as crew members move with passion and determination–a determination to tell a story–to put on a show.

Since I began my journey in entertainment, being on set felt like being in on a secret. I'm one of the few who see what happens behind the scenes, but I've learned that certain secrets we could live without discovering. I've seen the imperfections and flaws that viewers are blind to, and I see the lies that fuel what the world perceives as truth. There's an alluring sense of power that comes with knowing what others shouldn't know, and no human is ready for that power. It has put me above the masses. It has separated me from the crowd. And now, I question whether or not it was worth the chase.

Standing in the middle of the studio, I take in my surroundings. The freshly glossed, wide-paneled wood flooring makes up center-stage. The now-classic three orange chairs are evenly spaced on the stage, each facing the stadium seats rising behind me. The back wall behind the stage is made up of one massive screen reading, "GREATER GOOD," in vibrant, retro-style orange letters. But it doesn't feel the same as it once did. In a month, Samuel and I were able to turn Greater Good into the world's most-watched show. I sacrificed late nights working through a concept that later sacrificed innocent people. We used our platform to prowl on the weak-willed, and I lost my sanity and my ability to love in the process.

"Dim the main lights," I whisper into my pretend ear-piece. I spread my arms, inhaling the sweet aroma of a perfect set prepped for a perfect show. When I turn, my eyes meet Samuel's.

"Admiring your work?" he asks, his voice now lacking its ethereal allure.

Admiring? Yes. But I'm ready to watch it burn.

He steps beside me, analyzing my expression. "You seem off. I notice you've kept your distance from me since your little display at the after-party last week."

"I'm fine," I lie. "I was drunk that night, and I'm sure everyone knows it. I'll be alright to host tonight."

"I'm sorry, but the decision has already been made for you to no longer host. It was made the moment you decided to announce what you really do to all those people."

"Did I lie?" I clench a fist. "You said it yourself. I was called. I answered. I accepted. Why should it be a secret?"

Samuel shakes his head, whispering, "You couldn't live with the secrets kept within the walls of Mendax. I know more than you. I've seen more than you. As a result, I *am* more than you. And still, I don't know everything."

"Will we ever know?"

"We're not the ones making the calls, Nora. We answer the calls, and we do what we're told." Samuel's eyes hover

over the studio set. "You learned that firsthand."

I'm dissatisfied with Samuel's answer, but I guess that's the point. As humans, we are limited. We are confined by our five senses, some of us by six. But even with a sixth sense, we cannot fathom our existence wholly, and that's partially what makes us mortal. We are called by forces, both good and evil. Sometimes we accept, sometimes we reject. But in the end, Death will take us when it is our time, which is what makes life so precious.

Samuel looks back over his shoulder. With a slight tilt of his chin, he gestures for someone to join us. "Dorothy will host moving forward. I can't afford another outbreak from you. You've worked too hard for this. I won't watch you tear down what we've built."

The two of us turn to face Dorothy. She's wearing an orange blouse and high-waisted orange slacks. The expression on her face lacks emotion, making it difficult to judge whether or not she's happy about being rehired for the job I stole from her. "Nora," she greets dryly.

"You're replacing me after one episode," I accuse Samuel. "So, that's it? I'm no longer the host of my own show? The same show that put Mendax back on top? I saved your network. I brought the crowd to your doorstep and this is how you repay me?!" Frustration fuels the conviction in my voice. "I was just a pawn in your game, easily disposable. Just a small loss in the big picture."

"Nora, don't you see?" he asks softly. "Getting rid of you is for the greater good of Mendax."

"Don't use my own script against me," I growl. Samuel takes a step back, signaling for security to take me away. I step toward Samuel, but I'm stopped by a heavy hand. It pulls me into the firm embrace of two security guards. "Let go!"

The surrounding crew members turn their heads at the sound of my shouts. A few habitually step up, ready to defend me, until Samuel raises his arms to calm the room. "This is exactly what I mean. How do you expect to be on camera in front of millions when you can hardly control your emotions behind the scenes?" In one swift, silent step, he closes the distance between us. The hairs on the back of my neck stand when he whispers, "You wasted the gift you were given."

He's right. My relationship with Death hasn't been the same since the night I spoke with Joseph at the church. If there's anything I've felt, it's detached from Mendax, Greater Good, and the world around me. I no longer see a future within the walls of Mendax. I no longer see a future for myself at all.

"Let her watch," Dorothy mutters toward the ground before looking up. "It's the least Mendax can do. She created all of this, didn't she?" She shrugs. "Before you get rid of her, I think she deserves to watch a final episode live."

"*Before you get rid of her.*" She speaks the words as if they don't suggest they're going to kill me off the way screenwriters kill off their characters. My time of shining is coming to an end, the light dimming within me. I've let myself learn too much about what goes on within the walls of Mendax, and as a result, they won't let me out of this building alive. Once you sell your soul, you don't get to buy it back. Death held up its end of the bargain and I didn't hold up mine.

Death's presence seeps into the room, attaching itself to me in a way like never before. It's calm, peaceful, friendly. As Samuel ponders whether or not to let me watch, he follows Death's aura while it envelops me in a warm embrace. It has claimed me for its own, making it obvious to the two of us that tonight will be my last. Samuel's black eyes meet mine, neither of us saying a word. We both receive the same message from Death, knowing it's here to take me when this episode ends.

Samuel nods. "I'll allow it. You can watch from the control room with me." He checks his watch before pointing at security. "Escort her up there now. We're on the air in twenty minutes."

I'm pushed toward the staircase separating the audience

section. I look over my shoulder between security to see Dorothy watching me head up the stairs. With a cautious nod, I catch a glimpse of her sympathy toward me. I would warn her not to make the same mistake I made, but she already knows.

Dorothy Meadows doesn't have my gift...

Which means she won't be cursed the way I've been cursed.

As I stand in the corner of the control room, my gaze hovers over the wall of screens. It saddens me to realize that the once-magnetic allure these screens held no longer exists. I once marveled at the power I possessed, dictating which angle was being broadcast to the public. I blended both art and science into a narrative I once found entertaining and, in some ways, enlightening.

I want to hate myself for tainting the art I set out to create. I want to wallow in my loneliness as a punishment for pushing Ryan away. I want to escape my own mind–the same mind that poisoned millions of others. But Death comforts me. *Soon, none of it will matter anyway.*

Samuel sits comfortably in his chair, entertained by the fact that I've been deprived of what was supposed to be my legacy. His yellow-toothed grin spreads across his wrinkled face. He knows that, at one point, I would have killed to make a name for myself. I wonder if he realizes that I actually did kill to make a name for myself. And I wonder if he realizes that I'm not finished killing. After all, every impactful show must be brought to an impactful close, a finale that will leave its audience rising to their feet.

So, as I stand here watching the show play out, I reflect on my performance and the lives it's impacted for the better and worse. I'm forced to consider that fame truly is temporary. As generations come to pass, the narratives told through entertainment will twist and turn. They will embody truth, they will embody lies. Above all, they will distract the crowd from the harsh realities of the world, but only for a short time. Eventually, the crowd will look away. And they will eventually forget what they once found entertaining.

I watch Dorothy deliver her lines with such grace, you wouldn't believe she's reading a prompter. Her charisma radiates through the screens, her essence and aura captured by the cameras. It's everything I always wanted for myself, and I will say that I enjoyed it for the short time I experienced it.

"And now, let's meet our first and only contestant." Dorothy delivers the line with poise and an undertone of reluctance. "Please welcome *Nora Fictus* to the stage."

Samuel's grin dissolves as he frantically looks around the room. "N-no! Absolutely not! I will not let you make a martyr of yourself." The crew members lower their heads and security releases me, all aware of the episode Dorothy and I scripted behind Samuel's back.

"You don't have a choice," I say softly. "This might be your network, but I run this show."

The security guards grab Samuel by the arms and force him back into his chair. "Get the fuck off me! You work for me, not her!"

Samuel's shouts fade as I step out of the control room. I see myself appear on the screen lining the wall behind the stage. With all cameras now pointed toward me, I slowly walk down the staircase and to the stage.

Eyes, chin, shoulders.

Dorothy turns away, subtly wiping tears from her cheeks. The crowd is silent until a pair of hands claps. Another joins, then another, and another. The claps become an applause, and by the time I'm halfway down the staircase, the applause becomes a standing ovation. As I near the stage, Death prepares to invite me into its comforting embrace.

With Dorothy's hand muting her microphone, she whispers, "Are you sure about this?"

I smile.

Her lip quivers as she slips her hand into mine and holds it up. "Nora Fictus, the creator of Greater Good!"

The crowd's roar engulfs me, a surge of energy manifesting under the spotlights pointed in my direction. White and orange lights dance over the entire set–my set. I catch glimpses of faces in the crowd, individual souls lost in the narrative I breathed life into. The crowd settles as I'm handed a microphone. With the subtle raise of my hand, the praise comes to a close.

It's showtime.

"The floor is all yours," Dorothy says.

"Thank you." I inhale one last deep breath, then speak the truth in its entirety. "I want to start by saying… you praise me when you should hate me. What you see is controlled, manipulated. It's anything but real. Greater Good wasn't created to better the lives of others. It was created to distract you from the truth. And the truth is…" My eyes lock on the control room window behind the top row of the audience. If Samuel's watching from up there, I'm sure he sees me looking at him when I say, "The truth is that Mendax is manipulating you into believing your lives aren't worth living. Because if you don't value your life or your mind, you become easier for them to control. And if they can control you, they can inject you with whatever narrative they want you to believe."

I narrow my eyes at the nearest camera, the cameraman nodding for me to continue. "Inside of your brain is a survival instinct. I refer to it as, 'morbid curiosity.' Mendax is taking advantage of this instinct. Once the morbid curiosity takes over, Mendax desensitizes you to death so that you can be tricked into devaluing your own life."

I exhale. "I gave Death this platform. You watch my show when you should look away. The powerful people who work with Mendax behind the scenes will come after me before I leave this building, but I refuse to let Mendax take my life. I will die with the legacy I created. I will die with the broken, misled souls who died on this stage before me."

When I raise my hands, the crowd erupts in applause. From crew members to the audience section, people cheer and shout my name. Their applause is deafening, bringing tears to my eyes. As the tears run down my cheeks, I smile and blow kisses in their direction.

Here I come, Ryan.

I set out for praise.

I set out to befriend Death.

And here I am, having achieved both.

It is not the way I intended, but it is finished.

And this is my finale.

CHAPTER NINETEEN

JOSEPH

KNOCK! KNOCK!

Ava perks her head up at the sound from the front door. "I'll get it," she says, standing up from behind the camera. "Keep practicing."

I read over part of our script, making sure the words naturally flow from my lips… "*Your reality is a reflection of your state of mind. The true horror is realizing you can be betrayed by your own mind, so ask yourself, 'At this point in time, is my mind my best friend or my worst enemy?' Make it your best friend. Respect it. Purify it. Control it yourself before the wrong person controls it for you.*"

It's become easier for me to see the camera for what it truly is: the bridge connecting me to my viewers. Motivating the masses comes naturally now, and after losing Nicky, I'm more determined than ever to convince anybody that their life is worth living.

My eyes glide over the next section of the page until Ava walks back into the room. I raise my brows upon seeing her flustered expression. "It's for you," she whispers hesitantly. "It's somebody from Mendax."

In one swift motion, I get up and pull Ava from the hall-way. "They know where I live," I whisper in a panic. "Did they threaten you? Who is it? Is it Nora?"

She shakes her head. "It's a lady. She doesn't seem threat-ening at all."

I cautiously press my back against the wall, then peek around the corner. At the end of the hall, a woman stands straight as an arrow. Her thick, tight curls hang over the sides of her round face. With a sweet smile, she quietly studies the entryway.

"I have a gun," I lie, observing her from behind the wall with one eye.

The woman's smile is equally as sweet as it was before I threatened her. She raises both hands, one of them gripping a white envelope. She speaks her next words in a silky tone. "Don't shoot the messenger."

I cautiously step into the hall. "What's the message?"

The pinstripe suit she wears has been tailored to accen-tuate her frame. No bulging pockets or bags that could hide any sort of weapon. The street behind her is empty, besides a blacked-out Mercedes Benz parked curbside. Even her car win-dows are all rolled down, an indication of her visiting alone. She wants it to be known that she comes in peace.

My shoulders loosen as I approach the door. "You're from Mendax?"

"Yes!" She nods, still smiling. "My name is Rana. May I come in?"

"No chance," I snap.

My rudeness doesn't faze her. With the utmost respect, she replies, "I understand your position, Joseph, but you and Mendax are no longer threats to each other. The proof is in this envelope, which–believe me–neither of us would want the public to see you receive."

I turn to Ava for a response. With her lips pursed, she nods. "I think you should let her in."

I open my stance, and Rana glides into the room, each step more graceful than the last. "Shall we meet in the kitchen?" she asks without turning back.

"I-I guess that's fine," I stutter.

Rana seems considerate, judging by how she waits for Ava and I to sit at the kitchen table before her. She raises a palm over the seat closest to her. "May I?"

I glance at Ava, who responds, "You may." She forces a smile under her confused gaze. "Can I get you something to drink?"

Rana courteously declines while setting the envelope on the table between us. "I won't be here for very long." She laces her fingers in her lap, her plump cheeks rising as she beams at us. Her tone is rehearsed as she states, "I am one of the Prize Handlers for Mendax's T.V. show, Greater Good, the show for the morbidly curious."

I struggle not to express that I know who Mendax is and they know who I am. While I want to speak up and tell Rana to quit whatever charade this is, I muster up the patience to let her proceed.

"Organizations, charities, and loved ones related to our winning contestants have benefited tremendously from our philanthropic efforts since the first episode aired. Having raised a generous amount of over one hundred million dollars during the show's first season, our goal is to ensure that our winners' cash prizes are delivered to whoever they chose as their beneficiaries."

Ava and I lean forward as Rana gently slides the envelope toward us. "The winning contestant of the Greater Good 'Season One Finale' is none other than the show's brilliant creator, Nora Fictus, who took her life for a good greater than herself."

"Nora?!" My jaw drops.

It was a little over a week ago that I last saw her. I remember sitting next to her at the church, the two of us opening up to each other. It was a moment of mutual vulnerability, a moment of mutual respect. Since the beginning of my war with Nora, I saw her as my enemy, but I meant what I said when I told her I think there's good in her despite the evil she let consume her.

Not once did I think Nora would fall victim to her own morbid curiosity the way her crowd had. Ava wraps her hand around mine under the table. My eyes meet hers, tears blurring my line of sight. I would be a hypocrite to think that Nora doesn't deserve to live while preaching that message to everyone else.

Rana places a sympathetic hand over her heart. "I am extremely sorry for your loss." Her words are a blend of sincere sentiments and practiced phrases. I find it unsettling how, even as she offers her condolences, it's only because it's the job Mendax gave her. "But even in loss, there is much to gain," she adds softly. "I think you will be happy to know that Nora Fictus did not die in vain." She taps her finger against the envelope in the middle of the table. "Inside this envelope is the cash prize, a check for $11,340,285.41. It's been written out to Joseph Verita on behalf of Mendax Productions."

My stomach tightens as my eyes fall on the envelope. It takes on the form of a paradox, mocking me while promising a better future. How could I scold Tanya for accepting Nicky's cash prize and then accept Nora's? How could I convince people to look away and not look away myself? I should rip up this check in front of Rana, sending a direct message to Mendax… *I can't be bought.*

Rana flattens her palms over the table. "If you don't have any questions or concerns, then I believe it's best that I get going."

Ava opens her mouth to speak, but nothing comes out. I don't blame her. What more is there to say?

Rana stands, respectfully nods, then makes her way to the front door. Ava's chair skids out from under her as she walks Rana out. I lift my eyes from the envelope and slowly follow them through the hall. My thoughts are heavy, their weight threatening to pull me away from the present moment. I stand beside Ava as Rana steps onto the porch.

Rana faces us. "I'd like to speak off the record for a moment." Her once-scripted demeanor dissolves as she locks eyes with me. "I have children of my own–children I have to provide for. I need to conform because I have bills to pay, Mr. Verita. While people like me work for a company like Mendax, it doesn't mean we support what Mendax stands for."

She slowly raises her right palm, covers the side of her face, and looks away.

Ava and I stand still, shocked by Rana's motion. *She's a part of the movement.*

I'm not alone. In fact, I'm far from it. The truth of the matter is that I was never alone. We're all broken, looking for the right fix in the wrong places. For years, I let myself become consumed by my brokenness and the pain that comes with it. I let my reality become infected by my own illusions, closing myself off from truth and light. Now, it's my responsibility to spread both the truth and the light.

I didn't take down Greater Good by myself. I contributed to its downfall, shedding light on the darkness that worked through it. Many were lost by its corrupted influence, Nicky and Nora included. Regardless, the spiritual war between good and evil will always wage. Soldiers will rise and fall from both sides. Truth and lies will be weaponized. We will become victims and victimize others. We will prosper at times and we will break. But regardless, we will do what we feel is right or be misled by wrong.

As I step back into the kitchen, my eyes fixate on the envelope lying on the table. I stood against Nora, but I can't blame her for becoming a vessel for Death. I can only sympathize because spiritual forces are beyond our human comprehension. They will speak in whispers and sometimes shout. They will answer our prayers or they will cut deals with us.

And each day, we have a choice to make–a path to pick...

Will we choose good or evil?

Will we seek truth or fall for lies?

Will we find the will to live or surrender to Death?

"Life's Lifeline…" Ava wraps her hand in mine, now standing by my side. "What's our next move?"

"We *live*," I reply, smirking at the envelope.

ONE YEAR LATER

"You ready?" Ben gives me an encouraging pat on the back. "I've never seen the church this packed before."

I adjust my shirt collar, suppressing my nerves. "Ready."

It's been a year since Greater Good's finale. Since then, Nora's cash prize has worked wonders for Look Away. Ben, Ava, and I renovated the church, making it a safe space for any-one needing saving or support. Shortly after the finale, Positive Pathways went from being a basement-filled support group to an international organization we renamed, "THE WILLIAMS FOUNDATION," an organization that gives broken people around the world the tools they need to fix their lives. *Nicky would've loved it.*

The Look Away movement is thriving now more than ever across social media, run by Stevie and Kit. Our inboxes are overflowing with messages of gratitude, people sharing their stories of their lives changing for the better thanks to the impact we've made so far.

As I stand backstage with Ben, I run my thumb over the golden plaque that reads, "***The renovation and renewal of this building honor Nora Fictus's incredible legacy, and will help spread God's Word and prove that all were born to live.***"

I watch Ava standing center-stage, her voice filling the room as her grace radiates from the podium. Stevie listens to her speech from the front row and Kit records Ava from the seat next to him. The crowd cheers as Ava introduces me, and I take the stage, overwhelmed with emotion for the applause that nearly shakes the building. I kiss Ava, our eyes welling with tears of joy.

I face the crowd, gripping each side of the podium. As they continue clapping, I place a thankful hand over my heart. I find it hard to believe that I didn't think my life was worth living not too long ago. My heart aches at the mere thought of ending what turned out to be such a beautiful life. Therefore, I will do the best I can to convince others to pick life while making peace with death.

As I've learned more about life, I realize I was wrong about Death all along.

I ran and hid from Death, only because I didn't understand Death for what it truly is.

Death is not something that will introduce itself to us in a morbid display.

Death is not distant, and it's not a moment in time that marks the end of life.

Death is a process.

Death lives among us and it's nothing to fear.

We meet Death each day, for the time that passes us belongs to Death.

It's a matter of not fearing Death, which will give great value to life.

And it's life we have now and are gifted with each waking moment we live.

Though it's taken me a while, I have accepted that with the great evil in this world, there is also a good that is far greater. But that good is not of this broken world. That good comes from God and it lives within us. It's with this pure and moral good that we find the true meaning in living. So, I have picked my path. I will always pick the path that leads to life, for we were not born to die.

We were born to live.

MENDAX PRODUCTIONS PROMISES NEW TELEVISION SHOWS FOR YEARS TO COME

Tuesday, September 1st, 2020

Greater Good enthusiasts, prepare to be dazzled as Mendax Productions promises an electrifying array of new shows that will captivate and entertain in the upcoming season. The network has learned valuable lessons from the previous season's unfortunate cancellation last year, caused by Greater Good's Nora Fictus.

The autopsy report has been cleared for public release, revealing that Nora Fictus was severely under the influence when she took the stage the night of the final episode. By threatening the lives of Mendax employees behind the scenes, Fictus was able to manipulate her way onto the stage, where her mental breakdown took place before millions of viewers.

Samuel Roth, Owner and Founder of Mendax Productions, took to the press, recently stating, "Mendax was unaware of Nora's declining mental state. Had we known she was unfit to host, we would have offered her the help she needed and deserved. Though her death was unfortunate, we commend her for her bravery and willingness to take her own life for a good greater than herself... which is higher standards for all of Mendax's future productions."

Coming off the successful first season of Greater Good, which aired last year, Mendax is determined to release quality content for years to come. In the meantime, make sure to download the MENDAX+ app or tune in to MENDAX, Channel 6!

ACKNOWLEDGMENTS

To the ones who sometimes question whether or not life is worth living, this novel is for you. When I wrote the line, "You were born to live," I meant it. The world is a broken place, and it's up to us to fix it the best we can by shining light on the dark. Sometimes, simply living is an act of courage, and I'm thankful that you've picked the path that leads to life–others are thankful as well, some just don't voice it nearly enough. I promise that I will.

I want to thank Joseph and Nora for being my outlet. This year has been one of the most difficult for me, and these two characters embody both my triumphs and losses throughout the time I wrote this novel.

Mom and Dad, thank you for being there for me through this experience. You know the challenges I faced while writing this novel, and I am forever grateful for your support. You have taught me valuable lessons that I poured into my characters, and I'm confident my characters will pass those lessons on to my readers. Nikki and J.P., you two have always had my back. Thank you for listening when I would read you my drafts, and thank you for checking in on me from time to time.

A big thank you to Sammy, Austin, Taylor, Genesis, Jaycie, and Kyra for beta-reading my novel. It's your responses that either validated my vision or challenged it until it was perfect. I spend months in my own head while writing, so it is truly beneficial for me to have received such valuable feedback from you. Thank you.

To my readers, I am so incredibly grateful for you. If you have been on this journey with me since I wrote *Night After Night*, I think you will agree when I say that we have come a long way. And yet, we have ways to go. Thank you for continuing to give my characters heartbeats, and thank you for bringing my stories to life.

Above all, I want to thank God for this novel. Three years ago, I prayed for purpose, and God put a pen in my hand. I haven't stopped writing since. This journey has been full of some seriously impactful experiences, some of which I would not have gotten through without the grace of God. I am forever grateful and credit my success to Him, forever and always.

Thank you for reading this far.
I have big plans for my stories...
And I need you by my side every step of the way.
This is only the beginning.

ALSO WRITTEN BY JULIAN FONT

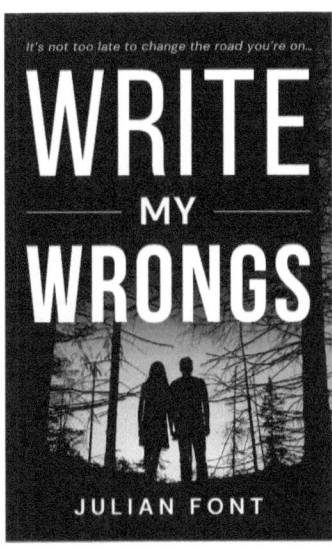

The dual POV, rockstar romance novel about two songwriters who fall in love through the songs they write together.

SCAN TO READ

The epic party novel about an up-and-coming nightclub promoter who is exposed to the dark side of the Hollywood party scene.

SCAN TO READ